The War in Sallie's Station

The War in Sallie's Station

Mignon Franklin Ballard

Five Star • Waterville, Maine

Five Star First Edition Women's Fiction Series.

Published in 2001 in conjunction with Laura Langlie Literary Agent.

Cover photos from the collection of Mignon F. Ballard.
Cover design by Carol A. Pringle.

Set in 11 pt. Plantin.

Printed in the United States on permanent paper.

Library of Congress Cataloging-in-Publication Data

Ballard, Mignon Franklin.
    The war in Sallie's Station / Mignon Franklin Ballard.
        p.   cm. — (Five Star first edition women's fiction series)
    ISBN 0-7862-3377-X (hc : alk. paper)
    1. World War, 1939-1945—Georgia—Fiction.
2. Women school principals—Fiction. 3. Reminiscing in old age—Fiction. 4. Georgia—Fiction. 5. Widows—Fiction. 6. Girls—Fiction. I. Title. II. Series.
PS3552.A466 W37 2001
813'.54—dc21   2001033194

This book is dedicated with love to the memory of my father and mother, Bernard and Mignon Harlan Franklin, and to their town and its people.

Acknowledgments

First of all, I want to express my gratitude to the courageous men and women who served our country, and to whom we owe yesterday, today and tomorrow.

Thanks to my pillar and agent, Laura Langlie, for her friendship and for believing; to my editor, Hazel Rumney, for loving my book (and crying in the sad parts!). Thanks, too, to my family for their confidence and support; to my friends, Tommye Lewis Johnston, and Jim Lay, for caring and remembering; to Ruth Moose, Dannye Romine Powell, Donald Maass, and Ellen Bache for their helpful editorial advice; and to my "other family," the Charlotte "Wednesday" Writers' Workshop, thank you and Amen!

— M.F.B. —

Chapter One

Franny Hughes knew right away the letter was from Hannah. Even if she hadn't recognized her blunt handwriting, nobody else called her Franny V.

Franny thought she was probably the only person in this whole world named for a tearoom. Her mother claimed she was named for a couple of long-diluted cousins—one on her side of the house, and one on her father's, but Franny never believed it. She was named for the Frances Virginia Tearoom that used to be on Peachtree Street in Atlanta. All the white-gloved ladies from Sallie's Station ate lunch there when they came to the city to shop, and they served things like frozen fruit salad with crumbly cheese straws and lemon chess pie that made you want to pucker up and kiss the cook that made it. Franny thought her mama must've had more than her share of it when she was pregnant with her.

The letter was written on dog-eared motel stationery, probably saved from some trip or other, and Franny eased her bag of groceries to the top step and sat on the splintery porch floor to read it.

So Hannah was really coming! Lately, Hannah had been on her mind. Each September when school began, Franny thought of her old friend, just as she thought of crisp gingham dresses, the pinch of new shoes, and that awful thing that happened with Miss Havergal.

Only this year she sensed a persistent warning, like a sore gum just before a tooth comes through, that all that long-ago business was about to work itself out. And it was going to hurt all over again.

Hannah Kelly, now Whitaker, and Franny Hughes had been best friends since they met at the corner on tricycles, but Franny hadn't seen her friend since Hannah's mother died about six years ago. Georgia is a big state, and she and Hannah wound up on opposite ends. Now she was coming back. A hurricane had hit the coast a couple of weeks before and dumped about a foot of water into their house. Besides, she had to make up her mind what to do about her family home here in Sallie's Station, the cranberry brick with the ski slope roof about a block and a half from Franny's. And she had something to tell her, Hannah said.

Hannah had been renting out the old family place for several years, but the present tenants were moving, she wrote, and she had to decide whether to rent it again, sell it—or what.

A teasing word, *what*. Did it mean she might move back to Sallie's Station? Or was Thomas Wolfe right when he wrote that bit about not being able to come home again? Well, what did Franny know? She'd never left.

And as far as she knew, Hannah hadn't outgrown her inclination to bait her just for the hell of it. Could be she just won the lottery or maybe she'd decided to shave her head, join a cult, and move to Katmandu. She would just have to wait and see.

What mattered was, Hannah was coming, and she wanted to stay with her if she still had that extra bed in Winnie's old room.

The pink chrysanthemums by the front steps were turning a rusty brown in the late September sun and Franny stooped to pinch off a few brittle heads. Death row. That's what her mama always called the would-be flower border in front of the house where Franny grew up. They could never get anything to grow there. Her sister Winnie claimed it was because when Franny was little, she used to squat behind the nandena bush when she couldn't make it to the bathroom.

Smiling, Franny picked up her paper sack and started inside to tell her mother the news. Marjorie Gordon still thought of Hannah as her third daughter and would probably start hauling out cookbooks, thumbing through favorite recipes.

"I just can't understand why that rascal Hannah hasn't been to see her mother in so long," she'd announced over her crossword puzzle just last week. "Why, she used to come and check on Alice at least once a month and was always so sweet to drop by and visit."

"Mama, Alice Kelly's dead," Franny said. "Been dead several years now."

Her mama rattled her newspaper. "Well, that's no excuse."

Franny found the TV silent when she went inside, and there was nothing burning in the kitchen. Obviously her mother wasn't home. Then she remembered she was playing bridge with the girls over on Alma Cranford's sun porch this afternoon. At eighty-three, her mother was the youngest of the group, and she claimed none of them could hear, half were blind, and they all cheated, but she wouldn't miss her bridge games for anything. Usually they ate so much junk food she didn't want any supper. Right now the four were on a Chinese kick since Alma discovered egg rolls.

It was close to five o'clock, about time for the ladies to wind things up for the day, and Franny almost expected the phone to ring when she pushed open the swinging door to the kitchen. What she didn't expect was to see a table covered with sandwich makings and a strange man rummaging through her cabinets.

The sun streamed in the western window so strong Franny could just make out a vague masculine back. Good. He didn't know she was there.

Her hand was inching toward the butcher knife when he turned around. Thank God she hadn't done anything foolish! Franny almost didn't recognize her own son.

"Hi, Mom, got any pickles?" He'd found a can of ripe olives and some marinated artichoke hearts that together cost more than his first pair of shoes.

"Gibson Hughes! Do you realize I was about one inch away from that knife? What are you doing here?"

Her son slammed the cabinet door and deposited his booty on the table and a glancing kiss on Franny. "Welcome home, Gib! It's so good to see you," he said, glopping mayonnaise over half a loaf of French bread.

"Of course I'm glad to see you, silly." She returned his kiss and rescued the olives and artichoke hearts. "But I'm saving these for the Hysterical Society's covered dish." That was their family's name for the Echota County Historical Society, and they had said it so often, Fanny had to be careful not to let it slip in front of certain people with no sense of humor—such as Neely Curtis, the organization's president.

She put the relishes back on the shelf and stood with her back to the sink facing her son. He busied himself slicing onions and lining them up like wheels on his ham sandwich. He wouldn't look at her.

"Why *are* you here, Gib?"

Something was wrong, she knew it. You don't mother an offspring for twenty-eight years and not sense when trouble's brewing. When they were little she felt it through walls, across city blocks like some kind of comic book freak. And when they telephoned from college, Franny could pinpoint their moods just from the way they said, "Mama . . ." Usually it fell into one of three categories: good, bad, or wants something.

Her only son hunkered down in his chair and bit into his sandwich. The reek of onions burned Franny's eyes all the way across the kitchen table. "I'd go easy on that. Wuzzy won't let you in the same room with dragon breath like that."

Gib had been married for almost two years to a girl with the perfectly normal name of Deborah, but she chose to call herself Wuzzy.

He swallowed loudly. "Won't let me near her anyhow. I've left her, Ma."

He sort of choked on that, and Franny didn't think it was the bread. She went over and put her arms around him, drew his head against her stomach, ruffling his straight, wheat-colored hair as she had when he was small. So, here it is, Franny thought. But isn't it usually the wife who comes home to her mother? Aloud she said, "Gib, I'm sorry. What happened?"

He pulled away from her and took another bite. Whatever it was hadn't affected his appetite. Franny waited until he'd washed it down with milk. "It just isn't working out like we thought. Wuzzy thinks—well, we both think we need some time apart." Gib wiped his mouth with a crumpled paper towel and propped his face in one hand. "Is it okay if I stay here awhile, Mom?"

"Of course, if you're sure this is what you want, but marriage isn't easy, you know. You have to work—"

He held up a hand. "I know, I know. You have to work at it. Easier said than done. Especially if your wife wants everything her way. Now."

Franny turned briefly away. She would really like to believe this problem was none of her son's doing, but she found out the Easter bunny was a myth when she was barely five. Gibson was her only son, a middle child, and Franny had raised him and his two sisters alone when their daddy died in an automobile accident when Gib was fourteen—just about the time his older sister, Faith, was starting college. The three of them had spoiled him, she guessed, trying to make up for the father he didn't have, and his Grandmother Gordon had made him king when they had to move back home. Franny Hughes took a deep breath. Her son was irresponsible, and she would accept her share of the blame.

But not all of it. "What about your job?" she asked. Gib and Wuzzy lived in Atlanta, or near enough to it so they could commute to their jobs in less than an hour. Wuzzy worked for an ad agency whose name Franny couldn't pronounce, and her son sold radio time. Last year he worked for an insurance company, and before that, he was assistant manager of a sporting goods store.

"Gib, you haven't quit?" She folded her arms. It was getting a little hard to breathe.

"No, but I'm gonna start looking around, see if I can't find something—"

"No," Franny said.

"What?"

"No. You have to help Wuzzy with the rent, and there's that enormous car note you took on. How do you plan to manage that?"

She was lecturing. Not the best time for lecturing, but when is?

He shoved back his chair and stood. His face was red, and Franny knew he wanted to tell her to go to hell. But well brought up children don't tell their parents to go to hell in Sallie's Station, Georgia. Not if they wanted to live.

"If you don't want me here, Mother, just say so. I'll find another place to stay."

"And what place would that be?" Franny asked. If she remembered correctly, they had chopped up the tree house for kindling.

Franny considered the bottle of Chardonnay in the wine rack and was tempted to pour herself a glass—about iced-tea size—but then she remembered that warning about alcoholics drinking under stress and put on the kettle instead. Tea wouldn't be as much fun, but at least it gave her something to do with her hands. Hands that tingled to shake Gibson Hughes until he spewed common sense.

He looked so forlorn she wanted to hold him. "Gib, this is your home. You're always welcome here, you know that. You'll just have to get up earlier to get to work on time—that is, until you and Wuzzy can work things out."

"Thanks, Ma." He smiled and turned to get his things from the car, she supposed, leaving the mishmash from his afternoon meal.

"Put your things in Granddaddy's study for now," Franny said. "I'll get some sheets for the day bed."

He frowned. "But there's no closet in there. What about my own room?"

"Hannah's coming next week for awhile. I'm putting her in there." She fished a tea bag from the canister. "Honey, I know you're upset, you need time to think, but I honestly don't believe you'll be here long." *Please God, give me a break!*

He just stood there with his arms dangling and shook his head, looking so much like his daddy her heart sang "Jesus Loves Me," and she felt all forgiving inside. For a minute. And then she remembered how his daddy had died because he'd had a few drinks too many before driving home from his Wednesday night poker game, and left her with three children to raise on a fourth-grade teacher's salary.

"After you've cleaned off the table," Franny said, "we'll sit down and decide what you can afford to pay for your board."

If the phone hadn't rung just then, Franny would have sworn he was about to keel over right there on the kitchen floor. "I've been ready to leave for almost half an hour," her mother said. "Are you coming to get me or not?"

Her son still stood in the doorway with his mouth open. "I'm going to get Gramolly," Franny said. "We'll talk when I get back."

Gib smiled when she mentioned her name. Grandma Molly: Gramolly, his champion, her mother. "Want me to pick her up?" he offered.

But she was already on her way. One down, one to go. Now she had her mother to contend with. Franny hurried across the front porch where brown leaves drifted, past the empty swing where her mama had entertained both her children and Franny's with tales of growing up at THE HOME PLACE, that hallowed estate a few blocks away that her family lost in the Depression. Whenever they passed there, her mother turned her face away. But she also made them laugh with stories about how her hot-natured Aunt Six wiggled out of her corset and put it in her pocketbook while sitting in the Fox Theatre in Atlanta, and of her brother Ben who jumped out the window at school when the teacher came after him with a peach tree switch.

The swing, thick with layers of paint, was her mama's favorite seat. In the afternoons she'd waited here, always with busy work in her hands, for Franny and her sister Winnie to come home from school.

Her mother was loyal almost to a fault, and brave enough—or crazy enough—to laugh at things that would cause a normal person to shudder. Several years ago, after a rash of neighborhood break-ins, her mama greeted the would-be burglar with a can of cooking spray and gave him a liberal scooting. By the time Franny came home from teaching, the police had already caught the man with oily sprinkles down his chest about three blocks away, and Molly Gordon bragged about having scared off a "slick one" and vowed as how he wouldn't have "sticky fingers" any more.

Franny smiled as she drove to Alma's remembering how Mama had coped with the stocking shortage during World War II by painting seams up the backs of her legs with an eyebrow pencil, and concocted a wonderful sugarless dessert of fruits, nuts and honey. Her mama called it "sweet revenge."

If it were possible, Franny thought, her mother would have tried to keep the awful facts of war from her children altogether. But even Mama couldn't do that. And after all the things that happened back then, she never did believe them about Miss Havergal.

It started with Mr. Gregory, their school principal, going off to war and that horrible woman coming to take his place. Or maybe it began with what happened to Franny's great aunt Six and Mr. Rittenhouse. For awhile, things just started to topple, one after another, like dominoes in a line, and nobody seemed to be able to stop it or change it. Franny felt as if someone took a great big rubber band and stretched it from her toes to her head, pulled it tighter and tighter until she thought it would break . . . and then they let go. Sometimes it still hurt.

Chapter Two

Franny Gordon could hardly remember before Miss Havergal. The pre-war years when Mr. Gregory was principal of Sallie's Station Grammar School were almost like a fairy tale—the happily-ever-after part—and she couldn't wish them back no matter how hard she tried.

It was freezing that December afternoon in the smokehouse storage room in Betty Joyce Whitfield's backyard, and the stifling smells of dust and mildew would bring it forever to her mind.

"We've got a problem," Wesley had told them, "and it's not going to go away. It's time we did something about it. If anybody wants to back out, now's your chance."

The five of them stood in that frigid little room and nobody said a word. Franny felt like an electric child, the way she did when they played scary games or told ghost stories.

"This is what we have to do," Wesley whispered. And Franny knew it wasn't a game anymore.

In the years to come, she would think of that time as the Havergal months, and they would always be colored in gray. At first she was merely an inconvenience, like the war that suddenly threatened their childhood. The new principal's term would soon be done with, they thought, and she would go away. Only it wasn't, and she didn't, and no one would listen. Not even the oldest and wisest.

September 13, 1943

"Mama, if I wrote a letter to Hitler, you reckon he'd get it?" Franny flipped through her fifth-grade speller (condition good) and stacked it on top of a broken-back copy of *Adventures in Arithmetic*. It was September, and a new notebook filled with crisp Blue Horse paper waited, blameless and full of promise.

"Why, Frances Virginia Gordon, why in the world would you want to write that dreadful man?" Her mother sat in the porch swing stringing the last of the snap beans from the victory garden. Nothing was left but a few wormy green tomatoes and Franny was glad. Canning made her mother tired and cross.

Her mother's friend Mr. Rittenhouse sat beside her, his cane across his long, bony knees. Mr. Rittenhouse was older, skinnier, and smarter, Franny thought, than anybody in Sallie's Station. Now her mother gave him one of those little "bear with me" smiles and snapped a bean in two. "Well, we'll just let the military take care of him," she said.

But what if they don't?

Franny knew she couldn't let her mother know how much she worried about Hitler. Like the boogey-man or Gunny Sack Sam who carried off bad children in his burlap bag, he dwelled in that dark, swampy place where nightmares lived. With her friends she yelled and booed at him in newsreels at the picture show, but his evil face haunted her: the thumbsize mustache that looked as if somebody had colored it in with a black crayon, straight dark hair falling over his forehead. It was like looking at the devil himself.

Franny leaned against the porch column and closed her eyes, letting the comfortable noises wash over her. The creaking of the swing, words, low and rhythmic, interspersed by the thudding of beans in the pan, and now and then her mother's even laughter that somehow kept her world on course.

They had forgotten she was there. Franny's mama and her friends acted downright peculiar when they talked about the war. If they noticed she was listening, they whispered or changed the subject, as if what was happening had nothing to do with her. Kind of like the way her mother had reacted when Franny asked how come Mavis Shoemaker got her baby so soon after she married.

Now, Franny's father, rejected by the army because of his age, wore his scratchy tan uniform every Monday night, as captain of the Georgia Home Guard, to drill his men at the armory behind the high school. And whenever a siren shrilled after dark, he patrolled his assigned section of town to be sure no lights were showing. As an air raid warden, her daddy was supposed to wear a helmet and an arm band, but he never did. He said everybody knew he was an air raid warden.

Although her father was disappointed at being turned down for active duty, Franny liked knowing he would be safe at his hardware store across from the courthouse, and could walk home every day for dinner like always.

Now she eased the wrapper from her Blue Horse paper to add to her collection. If she saved enough of them, she could get a prize. Why, Travis Kimbrough claimed his cousin in Cedartown had almost enough for a bicycle! Franny wrote her name carefully at the top of the paper. Since the war, the synthetic rubber erasers made ugly black marks on the paper.

"Well, those Italians have finally thrown out that awful Mussolini!" Her mother set the pan of beans on the floor with a metallic thump. "And now that the Allies have landed over there, maybe it won't be so long." She sighed. "If we can defeat Italy . . . well, who knows? After all, how long can this war go on?"

Mr. Rittenhouse folded gnarled hands over his cane. "As long as necessary, I suppose. I'm afraid this is just the beginning."

Franny felt his words settle on her like a dark cloak and knew he was speaking the truth. Mr. Rittenhouse had been all over the world and his house was filled with curious relics: heather from Scotland, ivory beads from Egypt, tiny wooden statues from Africa. He had planted the big oaks on Salacoa Street when he first came to Sallie's Station before the beginning of the century. Every stone wall, bench, fountain and statue pedestal in Echota County was built by Mr. Rittenhouse during what Franny's daddy called his "Stone Age." Now, reddish-purple skin stretched tightly over his skull, making shadows where his cheeks should be, and his great nose and chin jutted out as if they were trying their best to meet.

"Frances Virginia?" Her mother's voice had a mildly putout inflection. "Have you been sitting there all this time? I thought you were doing your homework. Come and say hello to Mr. Rittenhouse then."

Franny had grime on her hands, her sash was untied, and R. W. Duggan had torn her pocket playing chase at recess. She wiped her hand on her skirt and offered it. The old man accepted it gravely. That was one of the things she liked about him. Mama said Mr. Rittenhouse could sit down with King George or with Cephus Carmichael, the town drunk, and make them feel equally at ease.

"We have a new principal," she said. "Name's Miss Havergal. You seen 'er yet?"

Just saying that awful name made Franny feel as though she'd swallowed something rotten, but if Mr. Rittenhouse sensed this, he didn't let on.

"No, I don't believe I've met that lady," he said.

"I don't like her. Nobody does." Franny stared at the spot beneath the swing where she and her sister had worn away the paint. "She's here to take Mr. Gregory's place. He's in the army now. Daddy says he's a ninety-day wonder." She said it with pride. A ninety-day wonder sounded almost as exciting as Superman or Captain Marvel.

"God didn't make but one Matthew Gregory," her mother said. "I'm afraid Franny and her friends expect too much from this poor woman. After all, she's scarcely been here two weeks."

But it had taken Franny less than a day to realize something wasn't right about Miss Havergal, and it wasn't just that she was replacing Mr. Gregory. Nobody could replace Mr. Gregory. Hadn't he taught her the multiplication tables by bouncing a rubber ball on the playground at recess rather than let her fail at math? And he could imitate Red Skelton so well you almost believed the red-haired comedian himself was right there on the stage at assembly.

"It's the math, Franny." Her mother might as well have said, *It's the black plague, Franny*. "Miss Havergal teaches math, and we all know that's not your best subject." She stripped beans from a leathery pod and tossed them into the pan. "Give the woman time to adjust."

Mr. Rittenhouse nodded. "Why not make do for a time and see?" he said. "Give this Miss Havergal a try . . . after all, we should be used to making do. We've all had our share of it lately."

"Yes sir." Franny ran a bare toe around the dusty porch floor. She had taken off her shoes as soon as she got home. They were a symbol of oppression. Mr. Rittenhouse's brown shoes were as glossy as a beetle, but his black socks, she noticed, had a tiny run. She really hadn't expected him to understand, but there *was* something wrong with this new principal. She knew it; her classmates knew it. Franny just hoped the war wouldn't last too long so that Mr. Gregory could hurry back. If something went wrong at school, Mr. Gregory put it right. And if something was wrong with the world, she was certain he would take care of that too.

Franny climbed onto the banisters and leaned against the porch column, seeking the slim shade. Through the ragged fronds of her mother's Boston fern she watched fat Mrs. Littlejohn and Travis Kimbrough raking crab apples across the street. Mrs. Littlejohn raked them; Travis picked them up, one at a time, and tossed them into a bucket a few feet away. Now and then Mrs. Littlejohn leaned heavily on her rake and yelled at Travis. Then he started to throw the crab apples two at a time.

At the funeral home on the corner, Damascus Jones, the undertaker, stood sentry in the sun with at least one eye out for business. Hands clamped behind him, head thrust forward, he smiled sadly at people passing by, watched them out of sight. Franny's best friend, Hannah Kelly, said he had a glass eye. Franny was always careful while roller skating past Damascus Jones. If she were to fall and hit her head, she was sure he would swoop upon her in his buzzard-black suit and whisk her inside. Death and Damascus Jones were one and the same to her.

A truck rumbled past, and next door a mocking bird scolded the Willinghams' cat. Franny's mother asked her friend if he knew what those new people were planting on the south lawn of THE HOME PLACE where that big lilac used to be, and he said it looked like day lilies to him.

Franny spit on a finger and washed a pale circle on her knee. "Mr. Rittenhouse? What do you think—about the war, I mean? Do you really think it's gonna last a long time?"

Her mama rose and crushed the newspaper into a wad, scattering curly green strings to the floor, but Mr. Rittenhouse held up a blue-veined hand. "I wish I knew, Franny. But I'm afraid this war is going to continue for a good while—much longer than we expected."

"Do you think we're going to win?"

His old voice was surprisingly firm. "We'll win," he said, "because we have to."

After her mother went inside, the two of them sat in the dying afternoon and talked of war and shortages. Franny didn't like doing without dessert every day, she admitted, and she'd almost forgotten how bubble gum tasted.

Mr. Rittenhouse missed being able to travel when and where he liked, he said. "But do you know what I'd really like to see? Balloons! Great, colored balloons. There's something so festive about them. They're such happy things, balloons are." The swing see-sawed as he leaned forward on his long, puppet-like frame. "I especially like the blue ones," he whispered. "It would be nice, I think, to have just one more."

Franny sprawled in the swing after Mr. Rittenhouse left and listened to the courthouse clock bong five times. What a curious man he was, she thought, and when he talked about the balloons, his smile had been sad.

Franny had a hurtful feeling she had to do more than buy savings stamps and collect paper and scrap metal to "Slap the Japs with Scrap" or something awful would happen. Something too terrifying to think about, even in daylight.

And when the lights went out, the threat of it haunted her dreams, curling, lurking in dark corners like a poisonous vapor. And Damascus Jones was there. Waiting.

Or was it Miss Havergal?

The next day Frances Virginia Gordon wrote a letter to Adolf Hitler.

Dear Mr. Hitler,

Well, you have really made a mess of things! Why do you want to start wars and kill people? You are going to be sorry. We will win and you will die. I think you are the ugliest man I ever saw and I hate you.

A loyal American,
Frances Virginia Gordon

Chapter Three

"Could I speak with Hannah, please?" Vance Whitaker spoke with the polished assurance of one who is accustomed to giving orders: courteous, but only to a point. Franny knew it was Hannah's husband on the phone because she recognized his no-nonsense voice, and because Hannah was backing away from her shaking her head and silently mouthing words she couldn't understand. Franny got the message.

"I'm sorry, Hannah's in the shower right now," she said.

"This is Vance. Ask her to give me a call if you will." Not a 'howdy-do' or a 'kiss my foot' or anything. How had Hannah put up with that man all these years?

"What was that all about? He knows you're here. I'm not playing this game, Hannah." Franny backed her into the living room where her mother slept through a Braves game on television, and onto the front porch. Hannah dislodged their cat Sylvester and flopped into a rocking chair, drawing jean-clad knees to her chin.

From a distance, Hannah looked much the same as she had in high school: wiry and tan with a cute little chipmunk face and Hershey colored eyes, but the straight bobbed hair was more salt than pepper now and her eyes had lost some of that "dare me" look.

"He'll just want to know when I'm coming home. Why, I don't

know." Hannah picked at a speck on her jeans with a blunt fingernail. "Life at our house hasn't been a bucket of fun lately, and it's not all because of the hurricane." She sighed and stretched ninety-eight percent fat-free legs, crossing her feet on the porch railing. "He knows, Franny. Vance knows."

"Knows what?" Franny watched Susan Sizemore, the little girl who lived up the street, amble home from her weekly piano lesson, much as Hannah had done at that age. Only Hannah never ambled. Life was a race.

Even now she couldn't sit still, although she'd only arrived about an hour ago. Her small hands kept time on the arms of the chair as she rocked. "The *baby!* Vance found out about the baby." Hannah stopped rocking to look at Franny, and her smile was sweeter than any bride's. "I've seen her, Franny. She's beautiful. And can you believe this? Her name is Alice, like Mama's. Even looks a little like her."

"You mean Vance *didn't know?* All this time . . . well, I guess I just assumed . . . How? When?" Franny was sputtering.

Hannah leaned back in her chair. "She called me earlier in the summer. I never looked for her, you know. Didn't want to intrude. I gave her up, and that was that. I thought. Of course I never forgot her for a minute, always wondered how she was, where she was. If she was happy."

Franny scooted her chair closer to the railing and waved at Betty Joyce Frix as she drove by and blew her horn. Betty Joyce had graduated a year ahead of Franny and Hannah, and even though she lived next door, Franny didn't see her neighbor much now that her husband Hubert had retired. Betty Joyce spent so much time running things over at the Baptist Church, Franny wouldn't have been surprised to hear she'd taken up preaching. Her mama said if Betty Joyce were Catholic, she'd give the Pope some competition. Still, Franny thought, I really ought to have her over while Hannah's here.

Maybe for lunch or something.

"Anyway," Hannah said, "when they relaxed the rules for adopted children looking for their natural parents, I put my name in the pot." She shrugged. "Didn't want to mess up her life after forty years, but I did want to be available in case she tried to find me."

"And she did." Franny plucked a brown frond from the hanging fern. "But why on earth didn't you tell Vance? We're past the days of *The Scarlet Letter*, Hannah. You must've known this might happen."

"Yeah, well, I meant to. Just kept putting it off. Remember, this is *Vance* we're talking about, Franny V., not Phil Donahue. If I want warm and fuzzy, I wear bunny slippers. After all that, it was about three years before my daughter got in touch with me. Didn't even start looking until after her mother died."

Hannah laced her fingers together, made a steeple. "Her *mother*. Well, she was, wasn't she? And she did a fantastic job. 'Course she had quality material to begin with." She grinned. "She's so pretty, Franny! Guess I told you that, didn't I? Small framed like me, only taller, and looks about half her age. Allie. Calls herself Allie. Teaches history at Georgia State. A college professor! And I'm a grandmother too. She has two sons, twelve and fifteen, both smart and good-looking. We went rafting together back in August."

Franny prepared herself for a drum roll. Hannah reminded her of a little old nut brown jumping bean—all shiny and bright—sitting right here on her porch. She was probably the only one of her contemporaries who didn't have grandchildren, Franny thought, although Faith was finally expecting after seven years of disappointments, and she hadn't yet heard of one grandchild who turned out to be stupid or ugly.

This Allie must be close to perfect. "Have I missed the Second Coming?" Franny asked.

Hannah's explosion of laughter startled the cat who had leapt into her bony lap to resume his nap. "What can I say? She's even more wonderful than I expected. All those years of carrying around that hurtful empty place—you just don't know, Franny V. And to finally get to know my daughter after all this time, makes me feel like nesting again—at my age!" Her hand rested briefly on Franny's arm. "And I have pictures. Wait'll you see."

"What does Martin think about all this? Has he met her?" Martin is Hannah's son. Writes for a newspaper in West Virginia and looks enough like Vance to be his clone. Thank goodness he has his mother's sense of humor.

"It was a blow, naturally, but he's coming around. We plan to get together Thanksgiving. It's Vance I'm worried about." Hannah stroked Sylvester's glossy back. "Guess I've handled this all wrong."

Poor Vance. Franny was almost beginning to feel sorry for him. He had no part in this, and that wouldn't suit. That wouldn't suit at all.

She and Allie had communicated by phone at first, Hannah said. Her daughter lived in Atlanta, about two hundred miles away, and not too far from the town where she was raised. When they first met, it was such a private time, such an emotional time, Hannah explained, she couldn't bring herself to share it. Consequently, her husband found out about it a few weeks after the two women met when Allie left a message on their answering machine.

Hannah, it's me—Allie—your long-lost offspring. Give me a call, will you?

Vance thought it was a joke until Hannah told him the truth. This was in July.

"I've confessed, cajoled, even cried. Not to mention the thousand times I said, 'I'm sorry.' " Hannah flapped away a fly. "No dice. He won't even come halfway. I'm being punished for something I did before I even knew him."

"You'll work it out," Franny told her, and knew at the time it was a trite thing to say. How did she know they would work it out? Or even if Hannah wanted them to.

To hell with Vance Whitaker, Franny thought. But it was a

thought she meant to keep to herself. She didn't actually dislike Hannah's husband, but if she were going to host a dinner party for ten, he'd be about number 107 on the guest list. Franny never understood why Hannah had married him. Except for a love of sports, the two seemed to have little in common. And maybe that was enough, but from what she could tell, Vance was all take and very little give. Couldn't the fool see how lucky he was?

In his younger days, before he became a successful car dealer, Vance had been a semi-professional golfer traveling the country with Hannah in tow. And later, with Martin in school and the dealership thriving, she went to work for her husband keeping accounts. When Martin graduated from college, Hannah graduated into playing tennis and volunteer work. She was like a windmill with no wind. Until now.

Out of the corner of her eye Franny saw a tall, buxom woman with hair the color of a new penny waltzing up the street with a peculiar halting gait. The smoke from her cigarette trailed like a wisp of veil behind her.

"Shh!" She put out a warning hand to Hannah. This was not the best time to deal with Hollywood Dot. They slunk down in their chairs until the passerby was out of range.

"Oh, lord, Franny V., that's poor little Dottie, isn't it?" Hannah stood to watch the woman out of sight. "Wouldn't Miss Addie Grace just fold up and die if she could see her baby now? Remember how she used to dress her like Shirley Temple?"

How could she forget? How could any of them? Franny nodded and turned away. "I can't bear to look at her. Hannah, I wish there was something we could do."

"Like what? A little late for that, isn't it? How old is she now? Must be over sixty. I know she wasn't more than three or four years behind us in school." Hannah scraped at a chip of paint on the porch railing, then thought better of it and patted it back in place. "I guess she still thinks she's some kind of movie star?"

"From back in the fifties. Remember when everybody smoked? Goes with the image, I guess. She lives with her brother's family, and they try to keep matches away from her. She's not supposed to light those things."

You didn't have to be around Dottie Crenshaw long to realize something wasn't right. The same year Franny married Will Hughes, Dottie dropped out of high school and took off for Hollywood and the good life. She managed to get on as an extra in a couple of grade B movies and came home after a year with a paper napkin signed by Tab Hunter and some sort of infection that required a whole lot of penicillin. Since then her tales of love and stardom would make Cinderella pale. According to Dottie Crenshaw, she heard regularly from Clark Gable, and Cary Grant phoned faithfully.

"Bless her heart, she always was different," Hannah said. "You know she was, Franny V. I'm just glad her mama can't see her now."

Addie Grace Crenshaw, Dottie's mother, had been their Sunday School teacher way back when. A misguided woman, but Franny knew she meant well. "I don't suppose you know about bad things like that in heaven," she said, "or else it wouldn't be heaven, would it?" Franny thought Dottie's mama had more than enough to contend with while on earth. Burdens were for the living.

She watched her son's bright red car, one of those things with an X in the name, turn the corner into Salacoa Street and got up to make a tossed salad for supper and turn the crock pot on low. Gib was a meat and potatoes man; her mama liked what he liked—only about a fourth as much—and Hannah ate almost anything as long as it didn't have mayonnaise in it. Tonight they were having beef stew, and Franny could smell it as soon as she walked in the door.

The ball game was over, but her mother still snoozed in front of the television. Franny kissed her forehead to wake her and brought a sweater from her room. "Why don't you keep Hannah company on the porch?" she said. "I think she needs you right now."

Marjorie Gordon smiled, patted her daughter's hand, and

scooted out the door in no time flat. Franny heard Hannah say, "Good golly, Miss Molly, I thought you were gonna sleep all day! Come over here and sit by me. Wanna cat?"

She and Hannah had been friends long enough for Franny to know her mother could help her more than she could, and Hannah was more likely to accept advice from Franny's mother than from her. They had always been close, and when Hannah became pregnant at eighteen, Franny was surprised—yet pleased—at how her mother, with her Victorian standards, stuck by her. She had since wondered if her mother would have reacted the same if it had happened to her, Franny.

Franny was peeling a cucumber for the salad when Gib came through the kitchen door with his shirts from the cleaners over one arm and a couple of winter sports coats on the other. A bad sign. It rarely got cold enough there for those wool jackets until at least December. Did he plan to stay that long?

One look at her son's face told her he had not spoken with Wuzzy that day or if he had, the exchange didn't have the desired effect. He gave her a grim little smile and went to hang his clothes in the big oak wardrobe in the upstairs hall. Franny knew it would be just a matter of waiting it out to see how long it would take before Gib started ironing his own shirts again. The cleaning bill must be contributing to the Black Hole in his budget, along with those booger-bears, rent and car note, and Franny didn't like to iron any more than Gib did. Before she married, her mama gave her one major piece of advice: *Never iron shirts*. So far, she'd had absolutely no problem following it.

A quick peek through the living room window showed two rocking chairs in perfect cadence, with Hannah's whirligig hand resting now and then on Molly's sweatered arm. How much was she telling her? Franny knew her mother would do more listening than advising, just as she had all those years ago when Hannah Kelly had cried into the Wonderfluff Strawberry Swirl Cake.

That Friday afternoon in April the two friends were stirring up a fancy dessert for the bake sale their high school drama club planned for the next day. Hannah had ripped the recipe from the latest issue of her mother's *Ladies' Home Journal* and sat across the kitchen table methodically mashing strawberries into a syrupy red mess.

"Hey, you're spattering your dress," Franny said. "Want me to get you an apron?"

"No." Hannah jabbed at the pulp with a potato masher and sloshed pureed fruit into the bowl of batter. She wore a yellow print dress her mother had ordered from Davison's Department Store only a couple of weeks before, and now a blob of crimson oozed a trail down the front.

Franny snatched a dish towel and quickly wet it. "Here, hurry and wipe it before it stains." Hannah's mama would kill her.

"I don't care." Hannah gripped the towel in both hands and pressed it against her face, held it there silently.

"Hannah, what's wrong? You sick?" Sometimes she got these headaches.

She shook her head. The towel covered her face, dripped water onto her thin chest. It took something awful to make Hannah Kelly cry, but she was crying now, and Franny didn't know what to do.

And then there was Mama standing in the doorway with a face so sad it hurt to look at it and a voice soft as sponge cake. "Hannah?"

"Oh, Miss Molly! Miss Molly, I'm going to have a baby. What am I going to do?" Hannah sobbed. And Franny's mother knelt beside her and held her in her arms for a long, long time.

And Franny knew her mother would comfort Hannah now with the quiet strength of her presence. But when Vance Whitaker phoned again, and he would, Hannah was going to be responsible for her own lies. As irritating as the man was, Franny couldn't believe he was angry with Hannah for having a child out of wedlock as much as he resented the fact that she hadn't confided in him. Franny couldn't blame him for that.

She set the round maple table in the breakfast room with a yellow cloth and her new daisy-splashed dishes and put the pot of bright pansies Hannah had brought in the center. Four settings for three of her favorite people. Why couldn't they all be happy?

Hannah wandered into the kitchen as Franny dished up the stew. "Brr—getting cold out there!" She rubbed her hands together. "Smells great. What can I do?"

"The French bread should be hot enough by now." Franny snatched it from the oven. "Here's a basket for it, and you can fix the tea."

They worked together in silence pouring iced tea, putting food on the table. Franny heard her mother in the bathroom getting ready for supper. Primping probably. She would wear her amethyst peacock pin Franny's daddy gave her for their fortieth anniversary. Upstairs Gib changed into his "slouchy" clothes.

Hannah put the old green glass pitcher back in the refrigerator and leaned against the door watching her light the candles. "Well, how is he? Have you seen him? I heard he was back in town."

Franny had wondered how long it would be before she asked about her baby's father.

Chapter Four

September 20, 1943

"I'll bet I know something you don't know!" Travis Kimbrough balanced precariously on the stone drinking fountain in the school yard, one arm around the stern bronze Indian who stood permanent guard at the top. The fountain, with its four marble bowls (only one ever worked), was one of Mr. Rittenhouse's earlier contributions. The Indian statue was supposed to represent Sequoyah, the inventor of the Cherokee alphabet, but he didn't look anything like him.

Travis swung a scuffed brown shoe into nothingness and edged behind the figure's metallic leggings. "Somebody was home on leave last weekend," he chanted. "Somebody took Miss O'Donnell out to dinner!" His round, freckled face grinned from beneath the Indian's raised bow arm. "Don't sit under the apple tree with anyone else but me," he sang, swinging his foot in time. "Anyone else but me, anyone else but me . . ."

"Who? Mr. Gregory? You saw Mr. Gregory? You come down right this minute, Travis Kimbrough, or I'm gonna climb up there and push you down!" Hannah scrambled for a toe hold in the rocks.

Travis watched her climb halfway before his red head disappeared over the other side, and he dropped to the ground laughing.

31

"Be still a minute, will you, Travis? Where did you see him? When? You'd better not be lying!" Franny grabbed a fistful of green-striped shirt and dragged him, kicking and squirming, to a bench at the edge of the school yard.

"Damn it all, Frances *Virginia!* You're gonna tear my shirt." He jerked away and wiped the dust from his face with a dirty arm. "Miss O'Donnell had a *date*. With you-know-who. I'll bet they're gonna get married."

"With Mr. Gregory?" Franny rubbed her shin where he had kicked her. "Was he really here last weekend?"

"Had a twenty-four hour pass," Travis said with a swagger. "Could be he proposed."

"And could be he didn't," Hannah said. "They've been dating for over a year."

"Yeah, but he'll be going overseas soon. I'll bet they get married before he leaves—or at least engaged." Travis snickered. "She's crazy about him. I saw them kissing once backstage in the auditorium. *On the mouth.*"

Hannah sniffed. "Miss O'Donnell has lots of boyfriends. There's that navy guy from Atlanta, and there's—"

"Damascus Jones." Franny made a face.

"Aw, there's nothing between her and Damascus Jones," Travis said with a shrug. "They just play bridge together and stuff like that."

Franny hoped he was right. She had been promoting the romance between Mr. Gregory and Miss O'Donnell since the young woman first came to Sallie's Station to teach "expression" and moved into Miss Opal's boarding house across from the school. They were like a couple out of the movies: Greer Garson and Walter Pidgeon, or Jane Wyman and Lew Ayres. He was tall and straight with corn husk hair and dark-blue eyes, and she had hair that shone like the polished wood of her mama's mahogany drop leaf table, and eyes the color of Still-Whisper Pond. Her name itself was a song, Franny thought. Eileen O'Donnell. She prayed for them to marry and have three children: a boy and two girls. They would move into a house nearby, a small house with a fence around it, and invite her to supper—using their best china and silver, of course. And Franny would bring flowers for the table and play with the babies.

"Mama says the war will probably be over before too long," Hannah said. "Maybe Mr. Gregory won't even have to go overseas."

"Mr. Rittenhouse thinks it's gonna last a whole lot longer," Franny said. "He told me so just the other day."

Hannah screwed up her face. "So? What does old Double-A know? What makes you think he's so smart?"

"Well, because . . . because he *is* smart, that's why. Mr. Rittenhouse has been everywhere—all over the world. He knows a lot of stuff." Sometimes Franny just wanted to slap Hannah Kelly.

A lot of people in Sallie's Station were sort of awed by Mr. Rittenhouse, Franny's mother had said, because he was different—set apart from the rest. Even his name was curious. Everybody called him Double-A because his first two names began with that letter, but nobody knew what they stood for.

Double-A Rittenhouse never married, lived alone, and wore long-sleeved white shirts with black string ties even in hot weather. Erma Jean Leslie, whose daddy ran the Home Store Grocery, said that Mr. Rittenhouse was so modest he wouldn't even ask for toilet paper, but wrote what he wanted on a scrap of paper and gave it to the clerk. And he didn't go to the same church as anyone in town. Mr. Rittenhouse belonged to the Lutheran Church, and since there wasn't one in Sallie's Station, he had to go all the way to Dalton on the bus every Sunday.

Franny wasn't sure what Lutherans did. Hannah thought they were kind of like Holy Rollers because Mr. Luther Gutherie who worked down at the Pure Oil station was a Holy Roller and she reckoned they named the Dalton branch after him. But Franny couldn't imagine Mr. Rittenhouse hollering and shouting and getting his clean white shirt messed up rolling around on a dirty floor.

Now she shoved her face into Hannah's so her friend had to sit abruptly on the bench to keep from falling. "This war could go on for a year or more, Miss Smarty! H. V. Kaltenborn said so on the radio." She swallowed, and it felt like she had a rock in her throat. "Why, we could all be in high school before Mr. Gregory comes back."

"I don't think that old Havergal woman's gonna let me live that long," Travis said.

"Me neither." Hannah grabbed her throat and made choking noises. The new principal had whacked Hannah's palm the first day of school because she'd forgotten her sevens table, and their relationship hadn't improved. "I'll be lucky to make it till Christmas," she said.

Travis picked at a scab on his knee. It bled. "We gotta do something —about Miss Havergal, I mean. Hateful old witch threw my secret code ring in the trash can, and I had to save ten box tops to get it."

It was the war. Everything was because of the war, Franny thought. It was like when a relative came to stay—somebody you just couldn't stand—and you had to give up all the things you liked and tiptoe around all the time. She kicked a crab apple that had fallen from the tree behind the bench, kicked it all the way into the street. "Maybe we will do something," she said. "At least we can try."

Hannah sighed. "We do try. We collect paper and metal, don't we? Save grease and tin foil; we buy Savings Stamps and don't waste paper—at least *I* don't. And we write to the servicemen. Why, I wrote Singleton just the other day, drew him a picture of Miss Havergal, the old snake! He can use it for target practice."

Singleton was Hannah's older brother. Tall and lanky with dark hair that wouldn't stay put, and laughter that wouldn't stay inside, he had either teased or ignored Franny for years, but he became her instant hero when he joined the army at eighteen. She even forgave him for the time he shut Hannah and her in the chicken yard with the meanest rooster in the world. Suddenly Singleton looked older, handsome, sort of mysterious in his crisp khaki uniform. And although she'd rather die than admit it to Hannah, Franny thought she might marry Singleton Kelly some day if he would just wait a few years until she grew up.

Now she nudged Travis aside and sat on the warm cement bench. "Wouldn't it be great if we could be spies? Steal secrets and battle plans—stuff like that. Nobody would ever suspect us."

"You reckon there really are spies around here?" Hannah asked.

"My daddy says they're everywhere," Travis said, smearing the blood on his knee. "People you wouldn't even suspect. Haven't you ever seen that sign in the bus station? *Enemy agents are always near. If you don't talk, they won't hear.*"

"Why would anybody want to spy in Sallie's Station? We don't have any secrets." Franny jumped up to dodge Travis's bloody finger. "Get away from me, Travis. Mama just washed this dress."

He wiped his hand on his shirt. "Don't be too sure. We're real close to the Bell Bomber Plant at Marietta, and they have all kinds of secrets."

"I'll bet old Miss Havergal's a spy," Hannah said. "Doesn't she talk funny to you? She's so mean, she's probably kin to Hitler himself. She even has a mustache! I'll bet she's his cousin."

Franny turned to face them. A kind of delicious terror bubbled inside her. "Then let's spy on her. Let's spy on Miss Havergal!"

"I don't know, Franny . . ." Travis dug a hole in the dust with the toe of his shoe.

"Or maybe I could write another letter to Hitler." She watched his face, waiting. When Franny had told Travis about her letter, he had slept under his bed for a week because she'd put her return address on the envelope, and he was afraid the Germans would bomb their street.

"Aw, Franny, I wish you wouldn't do that!" Did his face turn a little pale? It was hard to tell under all the freckles and grime.

"Oh, leave him alone, he's chicken. We don't need him anyway," Hannah said.

"Am not! Heck, me and Wesley will both spy if you'll gimme that arrowhead, Franny," Travis said. "Please? I need it for my collection." He followed along behind her as she gathered up her books. "Whatdaya say, huh? You don't care nothing about arrowheads anyway."

"Well, I care about this one, and you're not going to get it." Franny had found the arrowhead the summer before up on Crooked Oak Hill. It was the only one she had, and Travis had been after her about it ever since. She shoved him away. "Go find your own arrowhead!"

Travis made a face at her as the last bell rang, then raced up to butt into Wesley from behind. *Adventures in Arithmetic* and Wesley's neat homework slipped to the ground.

Travis Kimbrough and Wesley Fuller had been best friends since the first grade and everybody wondered why. Wesley was quick where Travis was slow, lean where he was husky, dark where he was fair. Wesley was a good student—far better in math than his classmates. Travis rarely bothered to bring in his homework. Wesley liked chess, sports, practically anything written by Alexander Dumas, and brewing smelly bubbling potions with his Lionel Chemistry set. Travis read comic books, collected arrowheads, sent off box tops for secret codes, and called storekeepers on the phone to ask if they had Prince Albert in a can.

They built treehouses together, picked on girls, and camped out overnight in Mr. Fuller's pasture. Back in the fourth grade—or maybe it was the third—both Franny and Hannah had wasted most of an afternoon trying to kiss their elbows so they could turn into boys and join them.

The classroom was already hot and smelled of floor polish, musty raincoats, and banana sandwiches. Franny rolled her eyes at Hannah as she shuffled past her to her desk. Across the aisle, Shirley Puckett wrote love notes to R. W. Duggan who ignored them. Her mousy brown hair was pulled tightly back from her forehead with a pink, plastic barrette. She turned her flat, rag-doll face to Franny and stuck out a purple tongue with a LifeSaver on it. Franny pretended she wasn't there.

She wished it were true. Shirley Puckett was the hatefullest girl in school, and the bossiest. She was also the best softball player, which was why she always got to be captain and choose her own team. She usually picked Franny last.

Franny hated Shirley Puckett almost as much as she hated playing softball, which Miss Havergal insisted they do every day. Now she dreaded recess as much as she dreaded arithmetic, which the principal taught.

This morning Mrs. Hightower, Franny's homeroom teacher, sipped from a cup of tea as she called the roll. She smelled like Yardley's Old English Lavender and wore her graying hair in a bun where she tucked an extra pencil. On the wall over her shoulder a quote she had done in needlework as a girl hung in a modest frame: *Whatsoever a man soweth, that shall he also reap.* Mrs. Hightower said that applied to women as well, and that they should pay attention to it. Every morning since school began, Mrs. Hightower brought a fresh rose from her garden. Today it was pink. "All right, class, it's quiet time," she said, putting the roll book aside. "Neely Louise? You may begin."

Bowing her head, Franny scanned the spelling words while Neely Louise Warren read the Fifteenth Psalm in her shrill, roller coaster voice: "Lord, who shall abide in thy tabernacle? Who shall dwell in thy holy hill?"

It was Neely's week to lead devotionals, and all her best friends took part. Now, Shirley Puckett crunched the last of her LifeSaver and marched forward to lead the class in the Lord's Prayer.

They stood for the Pledge of Allegiance and the singing of the National Anthem. Billy Ben Maxwell got them started on the right note—not because he was a special friend of Neely's, but because he was the only one who could sing it. Feet apart, head thrown back, his clear soprano soared upward with "the rockets' red glare" while everybody else dropped an octave.

Back at her desk, Shirley Puckett waved her hand in the air and bounced in her seat like she was about to wet her pants. "Miz Hightower! Miz Hightower! Franny was studying the whole time I was leading the prayer."

The teacher leaned on her desk. "How do you know she was studying, Shirley?"

"Well, she didn't have her eyes closed. I saw her."

"You say you *saw* her?" Mrs. Hightower smiled at her in a funny way and Shirley twisted in her seat and scowled while the whole class laughed.

Later, sweating in the outfield at recess, Franny smiled just thinking of it.

"What are you grinning at, stupid?" Shirley glared at her from the pitcher's mound. "You'd better watch what you're doing, and if a ball comes your way, try—just try this once not to drop it."

Franny turned her back. If she shaded her eyes she could see the tall roof of the house where her mother grew up on the other side of the block, and the top of the oak tree the child Molly had climbed with her brother Ben. One of these days, her daddy said, when his ship came in, he would buy THE HOME PLACE back, and Franny would have her own room.

"Play ball!" Miss Havergal stood in the shade of the building, square and stocky in her tailored gray skirt and brown oxfords. She had removed her jacket, and Carol Delaney, who had a sprained wrist and couldn't play, held it: rooted to the spot, her arm out like a coat tree with the jacket folded over it. Poor Carol! How awful to have to stand there like that while something that had touched Miss Havergal's skin touched yours.

Wesley's team was up to bat. Miss Havergal liked Wesley because he was good in math, so he usually got to be a captain. Neely Louise stood behind him, confidently waiting her turn. Wesley always chose

Neely first because she was pretty and had a bosom—or the beginnings of one.

The first pitch went wild and Wesley lowered his dark brows at Shirley and tapped his bat on home plate. "Hey, I'm over here, remember?"

Shirley remembered, and the next ball was a beaut. Wesley sent it soaring over Shirley's head toward Billy Ben Maxwell in center field.

"Catch it, Billy Ben, catch it!" Shirley jumped up and down, losing the pink barrette in her frenzy.

Billy Ben reached a skinny white arm into the air and winced as the ball bent back his fingers.

"Butterfingers!" Shirley slapped her knees and made a face that made her look a lot like the scarecrow in *The Wizard of Oz*. "Throw it to first—hurry!"

Billy Ben groped for the rolling ball with his good hand and pitched it jerkily to first. But it was too late. Wesley was well on his way to second base.

"Way to go, Billy Ben," Shirley simpered. "If you hadn't been so clumsy he would've been out." She gave an exaggerated shrug in Miss Havergal's direction. The corners of the principal's mouth turned up in a smile so quick it was barely there at all. The sun glinted off her gold-rimmed glasses. She spread her feet apart and bellowed, "Batter up!"

Billy Ben held his injured fingers under his left arm and shuffled back into center field. His face was red and Franny knew he must be hurting something awful, but Billy Ben couldn't risk complaining. The others would call him a sissy. He wasn't good at sports, and to make matters worse, he could sing and play the piano. But he seemed determined to play out the game.

When it was her team's time to bat, Franny hurried toward the cool shadow of the building to wait out the inning. Billy Ben sank quietly into a patch of shade; beads of sweat stood out on his forehead. His stomach felt funny, he said.

"Billy Ben, let me see your hand." She squatted beside him and gently lifted his fingers. They were swollen and turning blue.

Franny walked over to Miss Havergal who was correcting Shirley's batting stance. If it had been anybody but Shirley, Franny would've felt sorry for her. Caged by the principal's white-sleeved arms, Shirley's face was inches away from Miss Havergal's face; the woman's hands covered hers on the bat.

"Miss Havergal, Billy Ben's not feeling so good. His fingers are all—"

"Frances, for heaven's sake, get out of the way. Do you want to get hit by the bat?"

"No ma'am, but Billy Ben's really—"

"I don't believe in coddling." Miss Havergal rested large, tan hands on her hips. Tiny golden hairs stood up on her wrists. "The boy must learn to take part in activities. Perhaps the game will make a man of him."

"But he's—"

"Franny, will you *please* get out of the way so I can bat?" Shirley, released at last, stomped her foot.

Just then the bell rang and the classes lined up to march inside: boys on the left, girls on the right. Franny fell in behind Hannah and tied her friend's sash in a double knot.

Hunching over, Billy Ben edged out of line, and like an old man, inched forward a few steps at a time. "Miss Havergal, may I please be excused?"

"You've had twenty minutes to use the restroom, Billy Ben. Stand up straight and get back in line."

But Billy Ben, usually submissive, moved to the foot of the steps, still clutching his stomach. "Miss Havergal . . . I think I'm going to be sick."

And he was.

Chapter Five

In Franny's dream, her mama burned leaves in the backyard while she, her sister Winnie, and Hannah chased one another through trails of smoke. A baby cried, and Faith, wearing a sheer purple romper, toddled toward the embers. Franny ran to snatch her up before she reached the fire, but it wasn't Faith anymore, it was Gib. He squirmed away from her and was gone, lost in the thick gray swirls. His screams grew louder, but Franny couldn't find him. She called to the others to help, but Winnie, Hannah and Mama had all disappeared. Franny was alone.

The ringing of the doorbell jarred her awake so fast Franny catapulted out of bed. She sniffed. Smoke. Definitely. The cold floor shocked her bare feet and she shivered in cotton pajamas, but didn't stop for robe and slippers as she raced to the door. My God, was the house on fire? Why else would somebody be leaning on their doorbell at this time of night? But other than the vague, woodsy essence, she couldn't detect evidence of smoke or flames. In fact the house felt decidedly chilly.

Franny glanced at the porcelain clock on the living room mantel. It wasn't quite eleven. She had been asleep less than an hour after a tiresome day of cleaning and baking. The whole family would be there for Thanksgiving and she wanted to do as much as possible ahead of time.

Betty Joyce from next door, looking like a disagreeable ghost from Dickens' Christmas classic, stood on the front porch wrapped head to toe in the ugliest brown chenille robe Franny had ever seen. "The Home Place is burning!" she said through chattering teeth.

The smell of smoke was much stronger now and Franny saw the glow like a flaming sunset against a black sky where THE HOME PLACE should be. *The Home Place*, that hallowed acre that made her mother all choked up and weepy. When Franny was small, she'd halfway believed that God Himself lived there. She had grown up less than two blocks away from that house, yet she'd never been inside. Why did she feel as though someone close to her had died?

"Sorry to wake you like this," her neighbor said, "but I kept getting a busy signal. Phone must be off the hook. Miss Molly—is she all right? You know how she has trouble getting to sleep . . . I was afraid she'd be awake and see it . . . and, well, who knows what she might do."

Mama. How was she going to handle this? There was no way she could keep her from finding out. Franny pulled Betty Joyce inside and closed the door behind her.

"This will just about kill your mama," her neighbor said, seeking the nearest floor register. "Nudge that thermostat up a smidgen, will you, Franny? It's freezing in here."

Franny did, but nothing happened. Not even a click. She checked on her mother and found her sleeping, a slight ridge under a mound of covers. She spread an afghan across her feet and tiptoed out. Upstairs water ran in the shower and a remote voice of the TV weatherman predicted cold. No kidding.

Betty Joyce moved to the fireplace where she stared gloomily at week-old ashes. "Is it just me or is it like the North Pole in here?" She glanced in the direction of Franny's mother's room. "She asleep?"

Franny nodded. "Something's wrong with the furnace. I'm afraid it's finally given up the ghost. Let's go in the kitchen, I'll turn on the oven."

She left Betty Joyce huddled in front of the stove while she went upstairs to warn Gib. The bathroom was now empty and warm with steam. Franny paused to savor it, then followed the theme music from *The David Letterman Show* down the hall. Her son sat on the bed, naked, with his wet towel on the floor and his head in his hands. His eyes were red, and Franny didn't think it was the shampoo. Wuzzy. Now she knew why their neighbor had gotten a busy signal.

"You'd better put on some clothes," she said. "The furnace is out."

Gib flushed and grabbed a pillow, hugging it in front of him. "My god, Mom! Have you ever heard of knocking?"

"Have you ever heard of closing a door?" Franny scooped up the damp towel with her foot and turned away while he scrambled into pants. "THE HOME PLACE is on fire," she said.

"What?" He ran barefoot to the window and opened the blinds. Against the orange blaze, dark figures dashed about. Franny could see two fire trucks and heard the wailing of a third.

"What happened? How did it start? Does Gramolly know?"

"She's still asleep, thank goodness. I'm hoping she won't find out until morning." Franny stood behind him watching the sparks eddy in a dragon-belch of smoke. "It's a little warmer in the kit—"

"Oh, Mama . . ." Her son turned and threw his arms around her. Cold droplets from his wet hair sprinkled her face, and his skin felt cool and damp. Another part of his safe little world was crumbling, and she held him until he pulled abruptly away.

"Betty Joyce is downstairs," Franny said. "It's not as cold in the kitchen. Why don't you come down and I'll make us something hot?"

He snatched a sweatshirt from a pile on the chair and pulled it over his head. Mumbling, he headed for the door.

"What?" Franny still stood with the wet towel in her hand.

"Gotta get outa here," he said, grabbing a jacket on his way. A few seconds later she heard the front door shut.

All was quiet downstairs. Thank heavens Mama still slept. Betty Joyce had boiled water and sat waiting for tea to steep in the old blue pot with yellow daisies. What was it about the calming qualities of tea, Franny wondered. It always helped to ease her, to give her sagging spirits a boost. Maybe it was the English in her, or all those cozy illustrations in children's books. And she was glad her neighbor was there to share a cup. Hannah was in Atlanta to hear her grandson in a piano recital, and if her mama were to wake, Franny didn't want to have to face her alone. *Oh Will, why did you leave me? I miss you—damn it!*

"Wonder how it started," Betty Joyce said, stirring sweetener into her cup. "Could've been some kids making out. That's a popular place for romance, I'm told."

"And for smoking pot. I just hope no one was hurt." Franny warmed her hands around her cup. "First the old school and now this. A lot has happened since then."

Betty Joyce nodded, sighing.

"Every year about this time I can't help but think about Miss Havergal," Franny said, watching her neighbor's face. "Regular as Halloween. Reckon there's a connection?"

Betty Joyce studied the bottom of her cup. "That was a long time ago, Franny."

"But doesn't it ever bother you?"

"We were children. I try not to think about it." Betty Joyce wiggled sock-clad feet in front of the oven. "I'm afraid there'll be heck to pay in the morning," she said with a nod toward Molly Gordon's room. End of that conversation.

"I know, but she's strong, and the old house has been empty so long." Franny wished Hannah were there. Hannah could get her mama to smile over almost anything.

"Having Gib home should help." Betty Joyce smiled. She must

44

not have heard him leaving earlier. "You're lucky to have two of your children close by."

Her neighbor's only child, a son, lived in Colorado, but he had a good job and had been married to the same person almost twelve years.

"Uh-huh," Franny said, and took a big swallow of tea.

Betty Joyce squirmed into her shoes. "Are you going to be all right over here with no heat? We have extra beds, you know."

"Thanks, but I'd rather not wake her. I have an electric blanket somewhere. I know they're supposed to be bad for you, but one night shouldn't hurt."

"Better than freezing," her neighbor said, rinsing her cup in the sink.

After Betty Joyce left, Franny spread the electric blanket on top of the covers and climbed in beside her mother. "Furnace is out," she explained when her mother opened her eyes. The repairman had told her it might not last when she had had him out the month before, but she had put off buying a new one. The thing was so out of date, she could probably donate it to the Smithsonian and claim a tax deduction, Franny thought.

Her mama sat up and sniffed. "Are you sure it's not on fire? Smells like smoke in here."

"Burned out motor." Franny pulled the covers to her chin. "Go on back to sleep."

The worst part of it was, her mother didn't cry, but sat for two days in her room with her back to the window and wouldn't eat a thing but chicken noodle soup and oyster crackers. Wouldn't even come to the table.

Franny phoned her old classmate, R. W. Duggan, who had taken care of her mother since he finished his residency at Emory, and he came out and looked her over. That's when she learned about Dottie Crenshaw.

"I hate like the devil to be the one to tell you this, Franny," he said, "but I'm afraid poor old Dottie's done it this time for sure." She had gone to THE HOME PLACE the night of the fire, he told her, supposedly for a rendevous with a phantom lover. A childhood "crush" had once lived there, and she still thought of the house as it was when she was young.

Arson investigators believed she'd either fallen or gone to sleep in a pile of leaves and rotting debris in what used to be the dining room, and that her cigarette had started the fire. Dottie was rushed to a burn center in Atlanta with serious burns over a major portion of her body. Bandages covered her face.

Oh please, not Dottie, not this too! Franny wanted to curl in a corner and hide. What a rotten thing to happen! She and R.W. had been drinking coffee in her barely-warm kitchen, and now the brew churned in her stomach, rose in her throat. "Do they think she's going to live?" she asked.

"I hope to God she doesn't," he said. "But I'll deny I ever said it. Dottie's mind hasn't been right since—well, since most of us can remember, I guess, but her face was smooth as a girl's. I hope she never knows what happened."

Franny shuddered. "This is going to kill Mama."

R.W. touched her shoulder as he stood. "There's no way you can keep it from her. Your mother's a strong woman. She'll handle it, you'll see."

Franny hoped she could do the same.

"At least Mama's eating again," she told Hannah. "But she seems to keep to herself a lot and avoids that side of the house." Her mother hadn't said a word when she told her about Dottie, but she looked so distressed, Franny found herself pretending it hadn't happened. If only that would make it so. Now she waited for the dam to burst.

Hannah had accepted the news silently. "I can't bear to think about it," she said at last, "so I won't. At least not right now. What good would it do little Dottie? Besides, autumn's too brilliant for brooding."

Franny had told her friend about Dottie Crenshaw as they walked to the drugstore to pick up her mother's prescription.

Now Hannah stopped in the middle of the sidewalk and stared across the street. "Franny V.! They're tearing down the school. Why?"

"Meant to tell you. They've built a new one out on the highway near where the stone arch used to be. They're naming it for Mr. Gregory. And remember Precious Bailey—used to work for Aunt Six? Had a daughter named Daisy . . . well, her granddaughter's principal there."

"*Daisy's granddaughter?* Come on, it can't have been that long!"

"Think about it," Franny said. "Daisy was a grown woman back when we were in grammar school. Went up to Detroit to study nursing, remember?"

Franny started on down the street thinking Hannah was just behind her. When her friend didn't answer, she looked back to find her sitting on the wall in front of the house where Betty Joyce Whitfield used to live. The Whitfields' magnolia now took up one side of the yard and made the old house look dark and sad.

And so did Hannah. "It just looks so bare over there with the main building gone . . . and the belfry. Franny V., where's the bell? What happened to the bell?"

So much for not brooding, Franny thought. "Don't worry," she said. "The 'Hysterical' Society saved it. They're going to build a tower with an appropriate plaque and put it in the park." She kicked aside a discarded hamburger wrapper and sat beside Hannah, who seemed to be about two sniffs and a swallow away from crying.

"And Sequoyah? The statue of Sequoyah. What'd they do with that?"

"Fear not. They have him too. As soon as they build a pedestal, he'll go in front of the courthouse." Franny thought about Mr.

47

Rittenhouse. Nobody did that kind of stone work any more. "But they'll have to replace his bow. It got lost somehow in the transition, or somebody stole it.

"I'm sorry. I know it's a shock," Franny said. "The first time I saw it, it sort of did me in too, but then I knew it was coming." The thing that bothered her now about the school being demolished was that her mother could sit on their porch and see that dark ruin that had been her home. Even before it burned, THE HOME PLACE had been in disrepair for several years, and when the last tenants moved out, it must have been too far gone to save. But Mama never forgot what it used to be.

Hannah took out a tissue and blew her nose. "Why'd they have to go and tear down the school? That old place had character. What was wrong with it?" Her voice sounded like a little girl's.

"Character's about all it had," Franny said. "They've been patching up patches for years. Remember the fifth grade room? When Gib was there he said the roof leaked something awful. It just didn't meet the building codes, been vacant for a couple of years now. The Baptists are putting a big new church there. Betty Joyce is head of the building committee. You ought to get her to show you the plans."

"Show offs." Hannah, who was a Methodist like Franny, sniffed and dug out another tissue. "They *are* leaving the trees, aren't they?"

"Most of them." The huge red oaks had been old even when they'd played among their twisted roots and left secret messages in the crevices. Franny had hidden behind that big tree by the wall to cry that long ago October day, when Miss O'Donnell found her there.

The rough wall in front of the Whitfields' old home etched into Franny's thighs and she stood and dusted off her rear, scattering acorns on the walk. "I remember when we would've gladly torn that old place apart brick by brick," she said, hoping for a smile from Hannah.

She didn't get one. "It wasn't the building I wanted to destroy." Hannah looked up at her. "Do you ever think about what we did, Franny V.? About Miss Havergal, I mean?"

"I try not to, but it doesn't do any good. We were *children*. We shouldn't be held responsible, I tell myself. But just when I think I can live with that, this other thing happens." At least she wasn't like Betty Joyce who pretended it never took place at all. Funny, Franny thought, how people edit their lives.

Hannah walked a couple of feet along the low stone wall before jumping to the ground, matching Franny's long-legged stride without so much as an extra breath. "But don't you ever wonder . . ."

"Wonder what?"

"You know. Why?"

Franny shook her head. "I don't think I want to know."

They walked past the rambling white house on the corner where most of the teachers used to board. The Sandersons who lived there now had an offspring in just about every other grade in school, and a child's playhouse now stood where Miss Opal grew her Victory garden. A baby cried from its swing on the porch.

"Funny, I haven't thought about that woman in ages," Hannah said. "I guess it was seeing the school—or what's left of it, and then that awful thing with Dottie." She stopped and pressed a hand to her mouth as if to hold the bad memories inside. "She wasn't normal, you know—Miss Havergal. Something bad wrong there."

Franny knew. "Remember Wanda Culpepper, used to be in our class?"

"Yeah. Didn't she marry real early? Dropped out in about the tenth grade?"

"Big mistake," Franny said. "The jerk left her with two babies. Don't you remember? She went to live with Mrs. Hightower for a while, helped her take care of her invalid husband."

Hannah shook her head. "I heard he had MS and she couldn't leave him alone, but that must've been during that time

49

when—well—after I left."

"I think Wanda worked for a while in the high school cafeteria," Franny said. "Then somebody told me they'd moved."

"That woman was a pit viper," Hannah said, and Franny knew she was talking about Miss Havergal again. "I'll never forget how she treated that poor girl."

They crossed the narrow street at the corner, and Franny paused on the other side, but Hannah kept on walking, her face all scrunched in a frown, eyes on the pavement in front of her. "Somebody had to do something," she said. "But it shouldn't have been us, Franny V."

"You're right," Franny said. "It shouldn't."

All those years the phantom of that woman had hovered in the background. Now her shadow crept over their lives again, and the coldness made Franny shiver. It was all Miss Havergal's fault. Would her wretchedness never end?

Chapter Six

October 7, 1943

The war in Europe and the Pacific was nearing the end of its second year, but the battle with Miss Havergal had hardly begun. It was warm for October, and the sweater Franny had worn to school felt scratchy and hot by mid-afternoon as she threaded her way through drooping cockscomb and zinnias to where her mother sat rocking on her aunt's porch, groceries at her feet. Aunt Six sprawled in the swing across from her fanning with her apron, her ruddy face more flushed than usual. She had been making chow-chow from the last of the green tomatoes, she said, and Franny smelled the spicy vinegar all the way out on the porch.

Aunt Six was tall and large boned and dyed her hair blue. Franny had never heard her called anything but "Six," a nickname her aunt had earned as a child when her little brother had trouble pronouncing sister. Franny's daddy had let it slip once that his aunt had been christened Eddie-Ella after her grandparents, but Franny pretended she didn't know.

Aunt Six had a black cat named Hellcat she said was her familiar, and sometimes threatened to put a hex on Franny. Franny's daddy said that if Great Aunt Six had lived back in Old Salem, they would have made a bonfire of her.

Now she mopped her face with a red bandana and sighed. "Precious isn't speaking today," she said.

Precious Bailey was her aunt's cook, housekeeper, and confidant. It seemed to Franny the two of them couldn't get through a week without having some sort of argument.

"I don't know why you and Precious have to fuss all the time," Franny said. "Looks like you'd be able to get along by now."

"You mind your tongue, Franny Gordon," her mother said. "But she's right, Aunt Six. Why, Violet Price has worked for Caroline Greer almost thirty years, and never a cross word between them."

"How boring," Aunt Six said.

"I think Her Royal Highness has some molasses cookies out in the kitchen," she told Franny, flapping that old apron again. "Maybe you'd better just taste one first in case she's laced them with turpentine."

She found Precious huddled over the kitchen table, bony hand cupped to one ear, listening to *The Young Widow Brown* on the radio. Franny knew better than to interrupt. She grabbed a handful of cookies and took them to the porch. They tasted fine to her. "Aunt Six," Franny said, plopping in the swing beside her, "I sure wish you'd teach me how to put a hex on people. There's somebody I want to get rid of real bad."

"Why, Frances Virginia!" Her mama stopped rocking so suddenly she almost went head first onto the floor. "You know your aunt's just joking. I don't like to hear you talk like that."

"Who did you have in mind?" Aunt Six looked interested.

"That new principal, Miss Havergal. She gets meaner every day. Can't none of us hardly stand her."

"*Any* of us," her mama said. "The woman obviously doesn't understand; after all, she's only been here a few weeks." She shook her head at Aunt Six. "Honestly, I wouldn't be in that poor soul's shoes for a million dollars. Imagine having to take Mr. Gregory's place."

Franny told them what the principal had done to Billy Ben. "And she makes Junior Massingill read word problems too—out loud —every day. She just does it because he stutters. Everybody knows Junior gets all upset when he has to read out loud. Mrs. Hightower always hears him read after school when everybody's gone." Franny offered Hellcat a cookie crumb and he arched his back and spat at her.

"Get away from here, you devil!" Aunt Six shoved him aside with her foot. "I never have liked that cat." Then she smiled a crooked little smile and slapped Franny on the knee. "I'll think about it," she said.

Franny was only ten, but she knew when she was being appeased. The last bite of cookie went down kind of dry.

"Honey Sue is after me again," Aunt Six said to Franny's mother, and her voice lost some of its strength.

"About living alone?" Molly Gordon frowned.

"Says I'm too old and frail. Do I look frail to you?" Her aunt waved her apron at a fly. "Besides, Precious comes in three days a week—more if I need her. I can't ask her to stay at night, she has her own family."

Honey Sue, Aunt Six and Uncle Carlisle's only child, was pale, fortyish, and popeyed. She complained of about a thousand allergies, hives, and numerous stomach disorders, and had a grown son named Elroy who looked and acted just like her. He had so far avoided the draft. That worried Aunt Six. She said Uncle Carlisle would turn over in his grave if he knew about Elroy. (Uncle Carlisle fought in the Spanish-American War and came home with typhoid fever.)

Nobody could figure out how Uncle Carlisle and Aunt Six managed to have a daughter like Honey Sue and a grandson like Elroy. Honey Sue had been after her mother for years to come and live with her in Macon. Aunt Six said she'd rather die. She didn't know anybody in Macon, and Honey Sue was allergic to cats. Besides, she was married to a lawyer and Aunt Six didn't like lawyers—never had, especially Honey Sue's lawyer whose name was Leon, and who always looked like he smelled something bad. Aunt Six said that having a lawyer for a son-in-law was bad enough, but having one named Leon was almost more than she could abide.

"Now she's wanting me to get an apartment down there," Aunt Six spurted, "so she can look after me. Now I ask you, can you see me living in one of those hot little boxes? Why, I couldn't even get my bed in there the ceilings are so low."

Aunt Six was proud of her big Victorian bed. It was walnut with clusters of grapes carved on the headboard. "I was born in that bed," she said. "And so was Honey Sue. I don't know how she could even ask me to give it up."

"I'll write to her," Franny's mama said, gathering her groceries. "Honey Sue never did realize how independent you are."

"Don't you dare go without taking some of this chow-chow," their aunt said as they were about to leave. "Just let me get a couple of jars, I'll only be a minute."

Franny followed her inside to grab another handful of cookies and heard Precious laying into her aunt before she got halfway down the back hall.

"If you hadn't went and made all that chow-chow, you wouldn't be sittin' out there like some floppy-legged doll with a face as red as that dish towel there. It's hotter than the backside of Hades in this old kitchen." A pan clattered on the stove and somebody slammed a cabinet door. Hard.

"Bossy. Good Lord, you're bossy! They oughta turn you loose over there in Europe—let you run the army. Why, I'll bet that Hitler would throw his mean self plumb off a cliff just to get away from you." Aunt Six snatched two jars of still-warm relish and poked them at Franny.

Precious slammed another cabinet door and ignored her. They both ignored Franny. She helped herself to the cookies and walked out.

"Honey Sue can't really make her mama move to Macon, can she?" Franny asked as they started home. Sallie's Station without Aunt Six was more than she could bear on top of everything else.

"Oh, Honey Sue's not happy unless she's making a fuss about something," her mother said. "Don't you worry about your aunt Six."

But Franny did worry. She worried now as she walked sideways to keep from stepping on a crack. It was a serious responsibility.

Step on a crack, break your mama's back;
Step on a line, break your mama's spine.

She tiptoed through mud in the Richardsons' front yard to avoid a segment of chipped pavement and teetered on the low wall past the Llewellyns', but her mother seemed unconcerned with her struggles on her behalf. Franny hopped down and joined her. Imagine having such alarming power in the tips of your toes! Imagine having any power at all.

The air had a golden-blue October smell and Franny took a deep gulp of it. A dog barked from inside the Llewellyns' house and Franny looked up to see Miss Willie Llewellyn waving from her upstairs window. Her dog, Joker, a collie mix with one black eye, stood with his paws on the sill like royalty surveying his subjects. As far as Miss Willie was concerned, he was royalty. All her dogs were, but especially Joker who had slept at her feet for at least ten years. The rest of her menagerie consisted of a small terrier of dubious lineage, a boxer who seemed bored with it all, and a honey-colored cocker that wet the floor.

Miss Willie was almost as old as Mr. Rittenhouse, but not nearly as spry. It was hard for her to get around since she broke her hip, and she spent much of her time in a chair by the window. Sometimes she tossed Franny a dime to bring her an ice cream from the drug store or a bag of popcorn from the picture show. Of course Franny always got one too. And sometimes Miss Willie just wanted to talk.

Today as Franny and her mother passed the Llewellyns', a white curtain twitched as the old woman fluttered pale fingers, motioning for her to come in the back way.

Franny waved good bye to her mother, then pushed open the rusty old gate and rode it in. It creaked and sagged on its hinges.

Miss Emmalee Llewellyn, Miss Willie's sister, glanced up from shelling peas on the back porch but didn't speak. She sat stiff-backed with the pan in her lap, her little black pointy-toed shoes planted side by side, as if her feet were locked together. Franny's daddy said Miss Emmalee was so ugly her face would curdle spring water.

The three unmarried Llewellyn sisters lived down the street from the Gordons in a big Victorian house, but it seemed to Franny the oldest one, Miss Willie, was the only one who ever laughed. The other two liked to fuss about how hard they worked and how they couldn't get anybody to help them. One time after a big storm, Franny's mother made her pick up all those little sticks in their yard, and they didn't even give her a cookie or anything.

She found Miss Willie upstairs drying her hair by the window, brushing it with an ivory brush, and pinning it behind her droopy, biscuit-dough ears with curved tortoise shell combs. Miss Willie's hair was yellow-white like the pages in old books, and her face reminded Franny of the maps in her geography book with little ridges and valleys, and tiny blue-veined rivers meandering beneath her skin. Her room smelled of stale peppermints and talcum. And dogs.

The old woman smiled at Franny and held out her hand for the worn change purse on the dresser, and when Franny gave it to her, dug around until she found a dime. "Well, tell me," Miss Willie said finally. "Is she as horrid as they say?"

Franny couldn't understand how anybody who lived mostly in one room knew so much about what was going on. It wasn't just that she was nosy, it was more than that. Miss Willie Llewellyn seemed to sense things.

Franny sat on the needlepoint stool at her feet and drew Joker's sleek head into her lap. "She's worse," she said, and told her how Miss Havergal had mortified her shy classmates. "Everybody keeps telling us she'll get better, but she won't. She likes being mean."

Miss Willie nodded. "I had a teacher like that once. Miss Sparrow—Gwendolyn Sparrow." She laughed her paper thin laugh. "We called her 'Buzzard' to her back. She called peanuts *ground peas*. 'Class,' she'd say, 'has anyone in this room been eating ground peas?' And of course we all denied it because what we were eating was peanuts!"

"What happened to her?" Franny asked.

"She left as soon as the term was up. I suppose we made her as miserable as she made us." Miss Willie put the dime in her hand. "Just bide your time, Franny. Try to grit your teeth and make the best of it.

"Now, how about running by the picture show? See if they'll sell us a bag of fresh popcorn. I've been working up a taste for some all day."

Grownups sure were good at handing out advice when they didn't have to follow it, Franny thought as she started back toward town.

Chapter Seven

Across the street, the spire of the Methodist Church poked through the brassy treetops, and Hannah stood, hands in her pockets, as if seeing it for the first time. "Is that the new fellowship hall they've added to the building back there?"

"Greer Annex," Franny said.

"Say what?"

"They call it the Greer Annex. Remember old Mrs. Greer down the street? Lived to be older than God, only twice as rich? Well, her family gave a wad of money for the building. It has a new kitchen, parlor, the works. We can go inside if it's not locked."

"Sure, I'd kinda like to see it—and anything else that would delay getting back to the house. Vance said he'd call later."

"You can't avoid him forever," Franny said, waving to Willadeen Hicks as she backed out of her driveway. "What is it with you two anyway?"

Hannah linked her arm in Franny's, pulled her across the street. "That's what we have to decide . . . and I haven't exactly been avoiding him. Matter of fact, I talked with Vance this morning."

"And?"

"He wants to come for the weekend. Told him I'd let him know tonight."

"He's welcome to stay with us," Franny lied.

"Thanks, but I made reservations at Hilltop." Hannah slowed as they rustled through drifts of yellow maple leaves before climbing the worn steps to the church, whose red bricks had darkened over the years. "We need some time together, but I still don't know what I'm going to say. Vance wants me to come home, I know that, but I can't right now. I just can't."

"There are all those workmen at your house here. Guess you can't very well go off and leave them." Hannah was adding a sunroom to the back of her old home and tearing down a wall between the living and dining rooms, but if she had made a decision about what she planned to do with the property, she hadn't mentioned it.

The door to the fellowship hall was unlocked, and through the window Franny saw somebody moving about. She pushed open the door a few inches, then closed it quickly and, she hoped, silently when she recognized Shirley Peabody—or was it Dilworth now? Franny couldn't keep up with all Shirley's marriages, but she thought she was on husband number three. "Move it! Let's go," she said to Hannah, almost pushing her down the steps.

But it was too late. "Frances, is that you?" Shirley stuck her lacquered head outside. "What are you standing out here for? And God bless—if it isn't Hannah Kelly!" She shoved her clownish face even closer. Her eyeliner reached almost to her ears. "What are you doing here?" she said.

"I used to live here, remember? Joined the church the same time you did, in fact. And it's good to see you too, Shirley," Hannah said.

Shirley snatched her inside. "Hey, I didn't mean it like that. Have you seen the new addition? We're having a wedding reception here next month—Loretta—my baby." She squinted at Franny. "I think she was a couple of years behind your Lucy, Franny.

"Hey, I reckon ya'll heard about poor ole Hollywood Dot. Lord, her elevator doesn't go all the way to the top! Never did, that I remember, but still . . . that's a god-awful thing to happen to anybody."

"I don't suppose you've heard of any change?" Franny asked. As receptionist at the local clinic, Shirley was in a position to learn first-hand of patients' medical updates.

"Still in a coma, last I heard." She sighed and shook her head, earrings waggling.

The two of them trailed after her, trying to leave a clear path to the door, but Shirley stuck like bubble gum to a hot sidewalk. "Say, where's Lucy now?" she asked Franny. "Find a job yet? Not ready to settle down, I reckon?"

"Guess not." Franny tried to edge past her into the kitchen. "She's doing what she likes, though. Got a part in an off-Broadway play last summer and has a couple of auditions this week." She didn't tell her just how far off Broadway her daughter's show was: Connecticut, or that she earned most of her living cleaning houses.

But Shirley had other details on her mind. She waved her arms about, bracelets clanking. "We'll put the punch bowl over here for the reception . . . Aunt Mae Ellen's letting us use that big old silver monstrosity—looks like a bath tub! And I guess we can squeeze the string quartet in the corner." She made a face. "Bore everybody to death, I reckon, but Loretta insisted. Likes that kind of thing, you know."

Franny didn't know Loretta liked much of anything except driving at breakneck speed down Salacoa Street, drinking beer, and hanging out with men who wear those little ball caps backwards, but she was glad she was more selective about music than her sister. Sallie's Station still hadn't recovered from seeing an Elvis look-alike, complete with white suit and rhinestones, shake out *Love Me Tender* at the altar when Sylvia Peabody married the Williams boy. Had to have the ceremony at some little church out in the country because their minister just flat-out refused.

"Pinch me, will you, Franny V.?" Later, red-faced and panting, Hannah leaned against the utility pole at the end of the street. "I want to be sure I'm still not back in the sixth grade. What is it about that woman? Every time I see her it's like stepping into a time warp. Reckon she still draws on her arm with purple ink?" She wiped her eyes with the back of her hand. "Shirley's still working over at the clinic, I guess."

"Working is not exactly how I'd describe it. Shirley Dilworth *rules* that place. And if you want to get in to see one of the doctors without an appointment, you'd better stay on her good side. Louise Logan didn't invite Shirley and her current to her Christmas party, and she says her son graduated from high school, earned a PhD, and married while she was waiting for her flu shot."

The two giggled all the way into town. What was it about walking those old broken sidewalks with Hannah that swept the years away? They had taken that same route nearly every day of their lives while growing up together, and Franny could almost pretend she had roller skates strapped to her feet and a sweaty nickel in her pocket instead of a prescription for her mama's blood pressure medicine. And if they hadn't been on a well-traveled street, she would have shinnied up that big sycamore that crowded the sidewalk and dangled by her knees over Mamie Lineberger's pansy bed.

From a few blocks away Franny could see the spire of the courthouse above the town. Aunt Six had said the walls were held together with dirt and tobacco juice, but the building's hybrid architecture of arches, turrets and towers spoke to Franny in classic tones. Aside from the courthouse, the old three story bank building—now home to the Historical Society and the Chamber of Commerce—was the tallest structure in Sallie's Station.

Behind the business district, the wooded hills circled the river-fed valley in a patchwork of russet and gold. Aunt Six had called this the *teacup town* because of the way it fit snugly into the lap of the north Georgia foothills. And whenever Franny came back after being away, the town said, "Hey, where've you been? Don't you know you belong to me?"

Franny still didn't like to look at the new credit union they built on the downtown lot where her aunt used to live. Gone was the quaint yellow house, the flower-jammed yard, the hemlock that shaded the tiny back lawn. The new building, sleek and glossy, intruded on her world. To get even, Franny invested her $3.98 in the Bank of Sallie's Station.

The courthouse clock, if she could trust it, said a quarter till five, and the main street through town was already jammed with traffic. The two women hurried to beat the light at the corner and stepped into the dim interior of Maxwell's Drug Store. The long narrow room with its pressed tin ceiling still smelled faintly of chili dogs with onions, although the soda fountain had been gone for years, and strongly of Kimbrell Maxwell's pipe tobacco. (His wife Tessie wouldn't let him smoke at home.) The store was barely hanging on in competition with the big chains at the mall, but Kimbrell, who had taken over the business from his father, still delivered, would open the store if necessary at three in the morning, and special-ordered that expensive brand of face cream Franny's mother thought she couldn't live without.

Hannah looked out the window over a dusty display of greeting cards while Kimbrell filled the prescription. "I see the picture show's closed," she said.

"They opened a new one at the mall. Shows seven movies at a time." Franny thumbed through the birthday cards and picked a nondescript one for Wuzzy, who would be twenty-seven next week. She didn't know the guidelines for communicating with an estranged daughter-in-law, but wanted her to know the lines were open as far as she was concerned. Franny knew Gib had spoken with his wife the night before because he'd shut himself in the back hall with the telephone and emerged a few minutes later looking like he'd been assigned a term paper in abstract expressionism.

"Lord, how many pictures you reckon we sat through in there?" Hannah shook her head and sighed. "What are they gonna do with the building?"

"The Arts Council wants to buy it if they can scrape up the money," Franny said. "They can't tear it down. It's cemented together with about sixty years' accumulation of chewing gum and Ju-Ju-Bs."

Franny couldn't be as objective about her home town as a stranger might. There was a time when she might have traveled, ventured somewhere else, but Will Hughes wasn't the venturing kind. Then there were the children and her mama. She had watched the changes through the years, good and bad: the huge recreation center, grand new homes in the hills above town. Yet every time a downtown store went out of business, an old landmark deteriorated in neglect, Franny felt diminished by it.

She put the birthday card on the counter, along with a bottle of vitamin C and a tube of toothpaste. Maxwell's was more expensive than the chain stores, but Franny didn't have time to go running around all over town. She had spent most of the morning taking her mother to the eye doctor in Rome, and they'd had lunch at Ivy's Bake Shop. A compromise. Every time the two of them went to Rome, Molly Gordon wanted to lunch at the General Forrest Hotel. The old place had been gone for years, but to her it was still standing right there on the corner of Broad and Fifth. "Franny, let's do stop at the General Forrest," she'd say. "You know, I think their banana pudding's almost as good as mine."

It was kind of nice to have nothing to do as she waited for the prescription, Franny thought. Somehow, before the Christmas season descended, she had to find time to have that back tooth crowned, make an appointment for her mammogram, and get her wild mop cut.

Melvin Haselden, who coached at the high school, came in sneezing and groaning the way men do, then closed in to tell them all about it. Franny tried not to smile as Hannah's eyes met hers. The two of them were practically doing a rain dance to keep their distance from him without seeming obvious.

63

The phone rang as Kimbrell added up her purchases, and he looked so serious as he answered, Franny thought for sure that somebody had a terminal disease. He threw her things into a bag and shoved it at her. "That was your mother, Franny. Faith's been having some bleeding. I think you'd better get home right quick."

Thank goodness Hannah was there to calm her mother, Franny thought, or she would have two calamities on her hands. Molly Gordon was almost in hysterics when Coach Haselden dropped them off. Faith had phoned asking for Franny, and when her grandmother told her she was out, Faith started to cry. Franny knew her daughter didn't cry easily. Of all their children, Faith had always been the most level-headed. The other two leaned on her so much, it was a wonder she didn't walk with a tilt.

Since Faith's doctor ordered her to bed, Franny arranged to bring her home. Faith could sleep in her bed, and she'd get Gib to bring that old rollaway from the attic for her.

Her daughter's husband, Reilly, was ghost-white and scared to death. He would have agreed to anything, Franny thought, to save this baby. They wanted it so. Reilly would never be rich, but the family's nursery business brought in a passable living, and if Faith needed an organ transplant, Reilly would give her his heart. She guessed he already had. The two started dating in high school and married right out of college. Franny thought it was too early at the time. She was wrong. They were like two pieces of a puzzle just waiting to be complete. Faith did a right thing when she married Reilly Thomas.

"I hate being so much trouble, Mama." Her daughter's freckled face was pale against the pillows. Faith had curly brown hair and looked so much like a little girl lying there, it was hard to believe she would soon be thirty-two. "You've got enough to do without waiting on me," she said.

"I can't think of anybody I'd rather wait on," Franny said, kissing her. "Better lie back and enjoy it while you can, because when this baby comes, you'll have to look up *relax* in the dictionary."

Twin tears began a snail race to the pillow and Faith chewed her lip. "Maybe it's just not meant to be. This is the third time. *The third time!*" Faith began to cry. "Mama, I want this baby so bad!"

Franny sat beside her and stroked her hair. She wanted to shake her fist at Mother Nature and tell her not to mess with her child. "Stop that," she said. "You'll give Ruby Esmerelda negative vibes. Do you want her to be like my cousin Honey Sue?"

Her playful name for the baby never failed to evoke a smile, and today was no different. Faith mopped her eyes with the sheet and propped her pillows against the headboard. "Poor Honey Sue! Gramolly says her glass was always half empty."

Right now Gramolly was in the kitchen baking tea cakes for Faith and cutting them out with the same scalloped cookie cutter she'd used when her own children were small, and the sweet, golden smell filled the house. Hannah was in there with her in her official capacity as tea cake taster-tester. And to be sure Gramolly didn't set the kitchen on fire.

"Do you feel like reading?" Franny asked. "Betty Joyce brought over a collection of James Herriot." Faith and her neighbor shared a love of anything with four legs and a tail and had read several times over just about everything the English veterinarian wrote.

Red roses from Reilly sat on the dresser by Faith's bed, and the faculty from the primary school where she worked as secretary had sent a huge basket of fruit with a teddy bear in it.

Her daughter pleated the top of her sheet. "Mama, do you think this time there's a chance I'll keep it?"

"Dr. Winthrop seems to think so, if you can just get through the next few days. He told you so himself when we saw him yesterday. This is a scare, honey—a bad one, but we're going to get you through it—one day at a time." *Please God, don't make a liar of me.*

Faith had only experienced minor bleeding, and that was scary enough in itself, but it had eased off in the last few hours. A good sign.

Faith was still dozing after lunch when Wyndie Kimbrough, who taught first grade, came by with balloons and handmade cards from some of the classes at the primary school. Wyndie was married to Jimmy Kimbrough, whose daddy, Travis, had been in school with Franny and Hannah. Contrary to most of his teachers' predictions, Travis didn't end up in the pen and had done all right for himself in the insurance business. He even had his own agency in Marietta.

"Can't stay," Wyndie whispered, tying balloons to the back of a chair. She glanced at her watch and made a face. "Faculty meeting at three. Just tell Faith we're on her side and cheering." She frowned. "I hear she's not coming back to school. We'll miss her."

The baby was due the middle of February, and Faith and Reilly had decided that if she could make it through the next few days without any more scares, she would hand in her resignation at school.

"Oh, I almost forgot," Wyndie said on her way out. "Papa Travis said to tell you he wants to sit together at the dedication."

Papa Travis. Franny had to choke back a laugh every time she heard that. It sounded so grandfatherly and dignified—made her want to hoot—but of course she didn't. "What dedication?" she said.

"Why, the school. The new elementary school. It's named for your old principal, you know. Mr. Gregory—the one he's always talking about. Auditorium's supposed to be finished by Christmas, and they're planning the formal dedication for sometime in February. Papa thought it would be a good idea if you all sat in a group. Would you mind passing the word?"

"Sure, I'll be glad to." Franny wondered if there would be enough of them around to make a group. Four of their classmates had died, and a few moved so far away nobody knew where they were. But she and Hannah would be there. And Shirley Puckett-Rary-Peabody-Dilworth.

66

* * * * *

Her mother went to bed early that night, and Hannah took Gib to shop for after-the-baby lounge wear for Faith. Not a flannel robe, she whispered, taking Franny aside, but something filmy and flowing like you'd see in a lingerie ad. "I remember how pudgy I felt after Martin," she said. "This will give her an incentive to lose that extra weight around the middle."

As long as she didn't lose it too soon, Franny thought, but so far, so good. Faith had smiled more during supper and seemed stronger since her doctor's visit later that afternoon.

There was still no news of Dottie Crenshaw. Franny prayed for a miracle, just as she prayed for her own daughter, but she knew chances were against the woman ever living anything close to a normal life. The best they could hope for, R.W. said, was release from pain. But R. W. Duggan didn't know what they knew.

After Hannah and Gib left that night, Franny sat at her desk in the living room to give Faith and Reilly a little privacy and went through her stack of bills. She had retired a few years earlier than she'd planned in order to stay at home with her mother, which meant less income, and it scared her to death to let debts pile up. The premium was due on Lucy's health insurance and she couldn't put it off. Her daughter's house-cleaning job didn't provide benefits, and the acting roles were too spasmodic to depend on.

Franny got the checks ready for the next day's mail and rewarded herself with a mug of hot chocolate and a couple of her mama's tea cakes. No telling how many Hannah had eaten warm from the oven, along with a sample from Faith's box of chocolates, but she'd never gain an ounce. Despicable of her, but Franny couldn't bring herself to be jealous. She and her Will had been happy—at least most of the time—before he wrapped himself around a tree out on Logan's Mill Road. Franny wouldn't trade that for a lifetime with Vance Whitaker.

Hannah's husband was due the next day, and the two of them

would be staying at the local inn for the weekend. Franny knew Hannah was dreading his visit, and she hadn't again brought up the subject of Allie's father. If the two of them had been in touch, Franny didn't know about it. As far as she knew, he had never been told of Hannah's pregnancy. Still, whenever her friend spoke of him, there was a flicker of softness in her eyes—a glimpse of Hannah at seventeen.

Reilly left a few minutes later and Franny was rinsing her cup in the kitchen when the doorbell rang.

Vance Whitaker stood on the threshold looking like the greeter at Jones' Mortuary. "Hannah," he said.

"I'm sorry, Vance, Hannah's not here. I don't believe she was expecting you until tomorrow." Franny was going to step aside and ask him in, but he nudged past her into the living room, slinging his jacket over a chair.

"Well, where is she?" he asked a little louder than necessary. Franny stepped away from him. She would've liked to blame his bad manners on alcohol, but the man seemed as sober as an Episcopalian in a dry county.

"Hannah and my son went shopping," she said in a low voice. "And I'll have to ask you to keep your voice down, Vance. My daughter's not well, and Mother's asleep. Why don't we go in the kitchen? I'll make us some coffee?" *Coffee? Why was she offering this antsy man coffee?*

He didn't believe her. She didn't have to be Miss Marple to figure that out, but he followed her into the kitchen and sat on that old yellow stool. "Any idea when she'll be back?"

"Pretty soon, I'd think. The stores should be closing about now." Franny filled the percolater with water. "I think she's made reservations at Hilltop for tomorrow and Saturday." *In other words, you came a day early, you damn fool!*

He smiled—or tried to. "Thought I'd surprise her, get an early start on the weekend."

And see what she was up to, Franny thought. She put some of her mama's cookies on a plate. He picked up one, then put it down.

"This fellow . . . the father of her child . . . didn't she go with some football player in high school?"

Football player? "Well, yes, for a little while, but—"

"A little while is all it takes." He broke a cookie in two, studied it.

And there was that cute boy from Cedartown she'd met on the debating team, and the tall, skinny sophomore from Georgia Tech. "Look, Vance," Franny told him, "this is between you and Hannah." Damn her for doing this to me, she thought.

"She's seeing him again, isn't she? Hannah's not ever coming back . . .

"Oh, hell!" Vance Whitaker slammed his empty coffee mug on the countertop, put his face in his arms and cried.

Chapter Eight

October 9, 1943

The first of October the Allies liberated Naples from Germany, and a few days later, Travis Kimbrough's mother liberated Travis from his tobacco habit. He had taken to rolling his own until Doris Kimbrough discovered pungent brown crumbs in her son's shirt pocket and cigarette papers in his sock drawer. She wouldn't let him go anywhere except to school for a week, and he missed seeing Bob Hope and Bing Crosby in *Star Spangled Rhythm* at the picture show.

Now, having served his sentence, Travis skidded around the corner at the top of the hill and brought his bike to a rubber-scorching stop inches from the lemonade stand Franny and Hannah had set up for spying purposes across from Miss Opal's boarding house. "Seen anything yet?" he said.

"Not much," Franny said. "That little pest Dottie Crenshaw was hanging around for a while, but we told her to shove off or the Germans would come after her."

Travis giggled. "She believe you?"

"She's gone, isn't she?" Hannah said.

"Miss O'Donnell and that new third grade teacher left for town about an hour ago," Franny told him. "We haven't even seen Miss

70

Havergal." They had only been there an hour and she and Hannah had already eaten most of the ice. The chrysanthemums in Miss Opal's yard looked droopy and parched, and the only thing that moved was a line of black ants marching across the roots of the big oak that jutted out on the sidewalk. It was a rotten way to spend Saturday.

Travis plonked a sweaty nickel on Hannah's mama's folding table and gulped half a glass of hot lemonade before spewing the rest on the sidewalk. "Holy moly! What's in this stuff?"

"Just lemons, water and saccharin." Hannah dropped his nickel in the money jar.

"Saccharin! No wonder it tastes funny. I want my money back."

"Nothing doing. There's a war on you know." Hannah held the jar behind her. "Anything happen last night?"

"Naw! That's the boringest bunch I ever did see." Travis crunched an ice cube. "Damascus Jones came over about eight and he and Miss O'Donnell, Miss Opal, and that skinny new teacher—Miss Cochran—well, they sat out on the porch and played bridge until I got so tired I went to sleep behind the privet hedge. Something just about chewed me up under there." And Travis scratched in a place where he shouldn't have. "Never did see old Miss Havergal."

"I followed her to the dime store yesterday," Hannah said. "But all she bought was a bottle of Listerine, some Evening in Paris perfume, and Honey and Almond cream."

"My mama and daddy won't believe me when I tell them all the hateful things she does," Hannah said. "They think it's just because she took Mr. Gregory's place. I heard Daddy tell Mama we wouldn't be happy with God Himself."

"Mama says if I don't pull my grades up, I can't go to the tent show to see Ernest Tubb and Pee Wee King when the Grand Ole Opry comes to town," Travis said.

Franny couldn't wait to see Minnie Pearl wear the price tag on her hat and hear her say, "Howdy!" The Grand Ole Opry had never been to Sallie's Station before and just about everybody in town was going, but she had passed only two quizzes in math since the beginning of school, and she wasn't getting any better.

"Uh-oh, there she is!" Travis rolled his eyes in the direction of the boarding house.

Wearing khaki slacks and a white shirt, the principal walked out on Miss Opal's porch and sat in the swing with yarn and knitting needles. Even from as far away as across the street, the sight of her made Franny want to hide. And she couldn't imagine what the principal was knitting.

"Socks," Miss O'Donnell told them when she and Miss Cochran stopped by for lemonade a few minutes later. "They're for the servicemen," she said.

Miss O'Donnell wore a simple blue cotton skirt with a ruffle at the bottom and a white peasant blouse, but she looked like a princess to Franny. Miss Cochran was small and dark and laughed a lot. They didn't look a bit older than Cynthia Swanson who had just left for Agnes Scott College, she thought.

"Is that what she does all the time?" Travis rode his bike in a circle. "Just knit."

"What a funny question, Travis." Miss O'Donnell frowned. "Of course she doesn't knit all the time." She reached into her skirt pocket and drew out a packet of seeds. "This afternoon we're all going to plant greens in our victory garden. You can help if you like."

"No thanks," Travis said. "I don't want to get any closer to greens than I have to."

"What he means is, he doesn't want to get any closer to work than he has to," Hannah said. "But Franny and I will help."

After dinner, which they had at noon, Franny piled the flattened cans her family had been saving into her wagon to take to the collection center. They saved empty toothpaste tubes too—anything with metal in it—and took them to the cotton gin where they were picked up for recycling.

Franny watched her short, choppy shadow as she dragged the wagon over bumpy pavement on the way to town. The courthouse clock whirred just before it struck three and the big hand jumped to twelve. A couple of little kids hung around in the skimpy shade of the movie marquee reading the posters for coming attractions. *Heaven Can Wait* with Don Ameche and Gene Tierney would be playing in two weeks.

A yellowed sign in the window of Franny's father's store still urged customers to: "Buy canning supplies for your victory garden at Gordon's Hardware!"

Next door, Sam's Dry Cleaning offered a dollar for a hundred coat hangers. The Gordons were down to draping clothes in layers, so Franny knew her mother wasn't about to give up any more of hers. Travis had over fifty at last count. No telling where he got them. Franny didn't want to know.

Miss O'Donnell had said to come about four, and it seemed to Franny the minute hand had a weight on it to keep it from making its circle. Maybe this time they would find something to prove the new principal was a spy.

She and Hannah got there a few minutes early and found a group of teachers pulling yellowed bean vines and withered tomato plants from Miss Opal's spent summer garden. Miss O'Donnell wore rolled up jeans and a baggy shirt, and her hair was tied back with a bright green ribbon. Franny wished Mr. Gregory could see her.

"Don't look now, but here comes 'Little Miss Sunshine,' " Hannah sang in a sugary voice as Dottie Crenshaw skipped into the yard. "Maybe if we ignore her, she'll go away."

But Dottie, it seemed, meant to hang around awhile. "My mama says I can help too," she said, tugging on Miss O'Donnell's skirt, "long as I don't get too dirty. I know how to dig! I buried a whole bunch of dead birds in our backyard, and a squirrel too." Dressed in blue corduroy overalls and a white puffed-sleeve blouse, Dottie wore her yellow hair in a mop of ringlets, Shirley Temple style, set off with a bright blue bow.

"Yes, yes, honey, of course you can help," the teacher said, unprying the child's hands from her skirt. "I think we can find you a little spade, but I can't promise you won't get dirty."

Hannah made a face. "Miss Opal told my mama it looked like Dottie was gonna move in with them now that she's started first grade," she whispered. "Says she's over here about as often as Oscar Stonehill, only she doesn't eat as much." Oscar Stonehill was their mail carrier, and the whole town knew he timed his visits to Miss Opal's to coincide with her baking. The whole town also knew Oscar's wife was a notoriously bad cook. Franny reckoned Miss Opal felt kind of sorry for him.

Aunt Six said if Addie Grace Crenshaw spent as much time worrying about her own youngun as she did other people's souls, Dottie wouldn't be running around all over town. Maybe she was counting on God to look after her, Franny thought.

An elbow jab from Hannah called Franny's attention to the appearance of Miss Havergal who stood to one side while everybody else pitched in to dig up the ground. When the soil was ready to plant, she took a ball of string from her pocket and told the two girls where to mark off rows.

"Is that really necessary?" Miss O'Donnell showed the principal the instructions on the seed package. "It says here just to scatter them."

But Miss Havergal silently walked off the rows, pounded stakes at each end, and stood watching while Franny and Hannah marked them with string. Franny's hands trembled, and she didn't dare look at her friend. She had never seen anybody go to so much trouble just to plant turnip greens.

"What in the world are you doing that for?" Miss Opal stood at the back door wiping her hands on her apron and looked at Miss Havergal like she'd been caught blowing her nose on a dinner napkin. "We're weeks late with this planting already. Here, let me have those seeds." She took the envelope from Miss O'Donnell, ripped it open and sprinkled a few seeds on the ground. "Broadcast them, throw them about. They don't have to march in rows! Let the children do it." And she swept back into the house leaving Miss Havergal standing in the garden with a set look on her face.

The two older girls and Dottie danced on the tilled earth, flinging seeds like rose petals, and when the package was empty, Miss O'Donnell and Miss Cochran joined them, stepping lightly to press them into the ground. Then Miss Jacobs, the music teacher, brought out her recorder and played *The Skater's Waltz*, and they all giggled and sprinkled each other with the garden hose. Miss Havergal sat on the back steps all drawn up like a rotten walnut in a shell.

"Come on, Miss Havergal," Franny said in a burst of good feeling. "Don't you want to play?" But the principal didn't answer.

Annie Tate, who worked for Miss Opal, brought out a great big watermelon and set it in the middle of the back porch. It was the good kind with green stripes that Miss O'Donnell had brought from South Georgia, and probably the last they'd get until next summer. Franny licked her lips as the melon popped when they cut into it and sweet pink juice oozed into a puddle on the newspaper.

Miss Havergal wound her string into a ball and walked inside looking like somebody held a gun to her back. "Aren't you going to have any melon?" Miss Opal asked.

"Thank you, no. I don't care for watermelon," Miss Havergal said, and the door shut firmly behind her. Franny was glad she was gone.

The following Monday Franny made a sixty-seven on a surprise test on long division. She tried not to think about it as she sat at the

counter in Maxwell's Drug Store inhaling the chili and onion perfume. Aunt Six said if the smells from Maxwell's could be bottled
and sold, she'd like to have the concession.

The big brown ceiling fan moved with a soft whirring noise, and
Franny swung her legs from the stool beside Winnie's as they
watched their hot dogs sizzle on the grill. Eating lunch at the drug
store was a rare indulgence, but they didn't have a school cafeteria,
and their mother had gone to Atlanta with Aunt Six to put Precious
on a bus to Detroit because her daughter, Daisy, was in the hospital
up there with a ruptured appendix.

Franny got back to school just in time to find Travis and Wesley
choosing up sides for war:

> *Eeny, meeny, miney mo,*
> *Catch a German by the toe.*
> *If he hollers, make him say,*
> *"I surrender to the U.S.A!"*
> *O-U-T spells out you go,*
> *You old, dirty dishrag, you!*

But for once Franny was eager for the bell to ring. Today in her
"expression" class they were rehearsing a skit for the P.T.A. meeting,
and she was going to be an ear of corn. She sat on the wall to tie her
shoe and noticed a swarm of students gathering on the steps of the
main building.

"Hey, Franny, Travis! Come see what somebody wrote on the
front door!" Hannah bellowed at them from across the playground.

Franny raced after her to the door of the building that housed the
upper grades, closed now to keep out children during the noon hour.
Somebody had written *Kilroy was here* in huge red letters on the
faded green paint.

"Monkey's names and monkey's faces, always seen in public
places!" Neely Louise Warren chanted, shaking her head so that two

pink ribbons flopped up and down.

"Betcha it was one of the little kids. Look." Travis picked up a fat red crayon, the kind used in the primary grades.

"What's this?" Miss Havergal tramped up the steps behind them, thumping a few heads to clear a path. She grabbed Travis by the arm, jerking him off his feet. The crayon went flying.

"Hey, wait a minute, I didn't do it!" Travis turned as red as the worn brick wall behind him.

"I just saw you standing there with that crayon in your hand." She gave him a fierce shake. "Don't tell me you didn't do it."

"But he didn't, Miss Havergal." Wesley's voice quivered. "The crayon was lying there. He just picked it up."

"That's right," Hannah said.

"It was already there when we got back from dinner." Franny stepped closer to Hannah as she spoke.

Travis twisted to loosen her grip on his arm. "You're hurting me. Let go!"

"What did you say?" Her voice was low and even.

They seemed to stand forever in that silent circle while the principal stared at Travis with her cast-iron face. Franny felt as though someone had kicked her in the stomach with an icy foot. "See me in my office after school," Miss Havergal said finally. "We'll see if we can't find a way to improve your manners." Her hand touched Neely's shoulder briefly as she passed.

"Hateful old bitch!" Travis muttered. And while everyone stared helplessly, he broke loose, vaulted over the banisters, and ran into the boys' restroom as the bell began to ring.

Franny's knees were still shaking as they stood backstage in the dusty auditorium waiting to rehearse the skit.

Miss O'Donnell was working with a bunch of "autumn leaves" and a few "pumpkins" from the third grade, and Franny felt a little better just looking at her in her cool blue dress with her hair all shiny in the stage lights. Now the teacher held up a slender hand. "All right, boys and girls, keep it quiet and listen for your cue." She smiled. "As you know, this will be a special night program for the P.T.A., so I want you all to do your very best."

A door squeaked open in the back of the room and the speech teacher flushed as Miss Havergal marched down the aisle and took a seat in the front row.

"I'm glad you're here," Miss O'Donnell said. "I'd like to run through our program for you . . . children, take your places." She clapped her hands, then jumped lightly from the stage to sit with the principal.

"Have you decided on a date for the meeting yet?" Miss O'Donnell asked. "I'd like to get a notice in the paper."

Miss Havergal nodded. "Last Friday in October. Eight o'clock."

"Oh, dear!" Miss O'Donnell frowned. "That might present a problem."

"I don't know why. Of course, if your class isn't ready . . ."

"Certainly they'll be ready. But you see, that's the night of the Grand Ole Opry. I doubt we'd have many here."

"There's not much I can do about that," Miss Havergal said in a loud voice. "The date has been set."

"Of course, but you see this kind of entertainment comes here so seldom . . ." Miss O'Donnell smoothed back her hair, fingered a button on her dress. "So many people are looking forward to it."

"That's not my problem. Or yours. Now, if you're going to run through your program, please do it now. I have other things to do." Miss Havergal folded her arms.

Franny's head went as empty as a soap gourd and she had to be prompted twice on lines she'd said perfectly a few minutes before. Even Betty Joyce Whitfield, who had the biggest role as Mother Nature, stumbled over her part.

The principal disappeared without comment after a humdrum finale, leaving a forlorn group on the stage.

"Miss O'Donnell, I've been looking forward to that show for weeks," Hannah said. "Can't you get her to change the date?"

"My mama and daddy won't be here, and I won't either!" R. W. Duggan kicked at the dusty floor. "I wouldn't miss Pee Wee King for nothing!"

Minnie Pearl was looking more exciting to Franny all the time now that there was a chance she might miss her. "What are we going to do now?" she said.

But Miss O'Donnell only smiled and poked a finger at Franny's nose. "Just leave it to me, Miss Franny V."

Franny nodded solemnly. She knew Miss O'Donnell had something up her sleeve. It was as good as a promise.

Chapter Nine

That night Franny came as close to liking Vance Whitaker as she guessed she ever would. She got the I. W. Harper from the pantry and sloshed about a double jigger in a tumbler. Coffee wasn't going to cut it tonight. Vance sat at her kitchen table for fifteen minutes or more holding that glass of whiskey, turning it in his hands, saying nothing. Finally he took a deep breath, looking like he wished it were his last, and swigged the drink in one gulp. "I've lost her," he said.

"Oh, Vance, I don't—"

"I don't know what to do." He shoved the glass away. The melting ice cubes clanked with a cold, hollow sound. "You know her better than anybody, Frances, tell me what to do."

"You can start by not calling me Frances," she said, getting aggravated with him all over again. "Do you have a place to stay tonight?"

He shook his head and stood. "I just took my chances and came . . . gotta get outa here . . . don't want her to see me."

Vance was right. Hannah would hate seeing him like this. "They'll be back any minute," she said. Where on earth could she put him? And then she thought of Reilly all by himself just three blocks away with one of those sleeper sofas in the living room. "Get your car," she said, "and wait for me in the driveway next door."

Faith was propped in bed reading the Herriot book Betty Joyce had brought over, and Franny asked her to please call Reilly and tell him to get out the extra sheets. "I'd better go with him just to be sure he goes to the right house," she said on her way out. "If Hannah gets back before I do, tell her I've gone to get you some clothes or something."

"Well, you could bring that cross stitch I'm working on. It's in the bag on my sewing machine—but don't you peek!" Faith waved her on and grinned.

Unfortunately Franny had already peeked. She knew Faith was making her something for Christmas, and she just couldn't stand not knowing what it was. This time she wished she hadn't. Her daughter was working on something else with geese on it. A pillow cover maybe? Franny couldn't tell for sure, and she had no idea where she was going to put it, but she would wear it on her head if she thought it would make Faith happy. When her husband died and left them the way he did, Faith was the one who got her through. The only other person Franny could think of whose name suited them better was Orville Redenbacher. But how in the world could Faith live with her all those years and not know how much she disliked goosey things? She never even went to craft shows anymore.

At least this gave her an excuse to make a trip to Faith's, and Franny was glad of it because Hannah and Gib were there when she got home. She found them in Faith's room where her daughter made "Oh, you shouldn't have!" noises over a frothy purple floaty thing Salome would have envied. Her mama stood in the bedroom doorway in her pink flannel wrapper laughing and looking ten years younger than she ought to, and Gib watched from the foot of the bed —thinking, probably, that he should've bought something like that for Wuzzy. Maybe it wasn't too late.

Faith smiled at her as she propped her bag of needlework beside the bed, and Franny knew their secret was safe. And when Vance called the next morning to ask Hannah if he could take her out to lunch, she never guessed he was only a few blocks away.

* * * * *

"How *was* your weekend with Vance?" Franny asked her friend the following Monday as they mixed punch for the Historical Society's Autumn Tea.

Hannah pried open a bottle of white grape juice (they tried hard to pretend it was champagne), and poured it into the bowl. "Actually it was better than I thought."

"Vance ask you to come home?"

"No, he didn't." She sounded puzzled. "He *says* he wants to meet Allie."

"Great. When?"

"Probably next weekend. I think we should get together before Thanksgiving, don't you? Then everybody won't feel so strange." Hannah stirred in a can of pink grapefruit juice and stood on tiptoe to see into Neely Curtis's living room. Franny knew who she was looking for.

Just about everything in Neely's house was white: walls, carpet, furniture—even the arrangement of mums on the dining room table, and Franny always felt she should slip into one of those little paper outfits they make you wear in the doctor's office. It was like stepping into a vodka ad. The outside kitchen door behind them slammed open, letting in a bracing blast of air and a familiar smell. One overpowering sniff told Franny that Shirley had brought her usual hors d'oeuvre, those little balls made of sausage, cheese and baking mix that can clog your arteries with one bite, but Shirley wouldn't try anything that took more than four ingredients. The sausage balls had been her mainstay since the Spring Garden Club Bash of 1976.

Shirley pointedly held her platter aloft while Franny mopped up a spill. "Want me to slice some oranges for the punch?" she said.

"Done," Franny said. It wasn't—yet—but she didn't trust herself in the same room with Shirley Dilworth and a sharp knife.

"Heard about Faith. She doing okay now?" Shirley smoothed the foil over her offering and watched ginger ale fizzle around the ring of frozen fruit juice in the punch bowl. "Good Lord, Hannah! You shoulda mixed that in the dining room. Now you'll never be able to lift it."

Franny hated to admit it, but she had a point. The pink contents sloshed as Hannah struggled to carry the huge bowl to the white-laid table, scattering droplets along Neely's dazzling tile floor. "Bug off, Shirley!" Hannah panted.

Shirley Dilworth shrugged at Franny and sighed. "There's a specialist in Atlanta. Dr. Radcliff just swears by her. I can give you her name if you want."

"Sure. Thanks, Shirley." Faith's doctor had already referred her to a specialist, but it was easier not to make waves. If Franny were to have an accident or something, she wanted to be able to get in to see one of the doctors where Shirley worked before she bled to death. Faith was much better now—no more spotting—but she was still confined to bed for awhile. They weren't taking any chances.

Shirley wedged her offering between Molly Gordon's tea cakes and Betty Joyce's finger sandwiches—the good kind with lemon raisin filling. "Tell Faith I'll be praying for her," she said, and gave Franny's arm the tiniest squeeze before becoming swallowed in the blizzard of the living room.

When she came to, Franny had sliced she didn't know how many oranges to float in the punch, and was starting on another. "Don't you think that's enough, Franny?" Betty Joyce stood across from her. "Neely says we can start serving now."

Franny spied her mother, plate in hand, deep in conversation with a tall, elegant woman with fashion model hair the color of summer sunlight, only carefully filtered.

"Who's that?" she asked Betty Joyce as they threaded their way through the guests.

"Janine."

"Janine who?"

She shrugged. "Janine *Somebody*. Came in with Walter Curtis."

"You mean she came with Walter, or just happened to arrive at the same time?" They had all been wondering for years if Walter would ever find anybody to meet his mother's approval. Neely had butted in on just about every would-be relationship he'd had since high school.

"Looked to me like they came together. I saw him introducing her around," Betty Joyce said. "Maybe she's a client." Walter practiced law up in Dahlonega. Had an office in their downtown tourist trap district.

Betty Joyce sipped from her brimming punch cup. "Wonder where she's from?"

But Franny wondered where Walter's companion found the exquisite mulberry suit she wore. It appeared to be silk, was simple almost to the extreme, and she set it off with a green-splashed scarf. Well, she would just have to ask.

Too late. By the time she worked her way over, the tall fair stranger had moved to another circle, and Franny's mother was suspiciously eyeing a greenish miniature quiche.

"Spinach," Franny told her. "Who was that you were just talking with?"

"Janine." She nibbled daintily.

"Janine who?"

"I don't know, but she seemed to know you. Attractive, isn't she? And smart too. Does all her own decorating, she says. Wallpaper, upholstery, everything. I believe she plans to renovate a house here."

"What house?"

"I don't think she said. Some old place in the country, I suppose." Her mother brushed crumbs from her lap and stretched a hand to one of her cronies. "Edna . . . sit here, sugar, before you spill that punch."

Betty Joyce waved from across the room and patted a place on the sofa beside her. She was telling Hannah about her upcoming trip to England.

"You've been there, haven't you, Hannah? Tell me what to take. They say Londoners can spot an American a block away."

Hannah twirled a bit of parsley on her plate. "It's been awhile, but I'd take an all-weather coat and layer if it gets real cold. Wear comfortable shoes, and you'll need an umbrella of course." She smiled. "Franny V., isn't it great? They'll be in London during the Christmas season. London! Just think—caroling and plum pudding, shopping at Harrods. Aren't you excited for them?"

With an effort, Franny smiled back. "To be honest, I'd be a lot more excited if it were happening to me, but Betty Joyce has promised to bring me a proper English housekeeper if she can stuff one in her suitcase." Franny toasted her neighbor with punch. "God save the queen, and all that. If I can't go, I'm glad it's you."

Could her neighbor tell how jealous she was? Deep-down, dark, festering jealous. And of a good, deserving couple who had saved for years for this trip. Shame on her!

"Remember your *Fun Fund* jar?" Hannah said. "You were saving your baby-sitting money for a ticket to England. Said you were going to hike over the moors. How much did you collect before you finally gave up?"

"Who says I gave up?" Franny said.

"Never mind," Betty Joyce said. "I'm saving all my brochures, and when we get back, I'll help you plan your itinerary." She rose, carefully balancing cup and plate. "More punch anyone?"

Behind her napkin, Hannah inspected the inside of her sandwich and picked out a minuscule fragment of ham fat. "Who's the model type with Walter?"

"That's what I've been trying to find out. She didn't buy that suit anywhere around here."

"There's something about her," Hannah said. "Her smile, I think. Reminds me of somebody."

"I wish you'd hurry and think who it is. I've never seen her before."

But Hannah didn't answer because they heard masculine voices—fresh masculine voices—at the door, and just about everybody turned to see who it was. An afternoon of radish nibbling didn't attract too many men in Sallie's Station.

Alma's son Fred had arrived to collect her, and since Alma wasn't ready to leave, *and* since the occasion was a fundraiser of sorts, Neely was fattening him up at the refreshment table before moving in for the kill.

Hannah took a tiny bite from a pastry and frowned. "Interesting . . . I've never thought of toothpaste filling."

But Franny guessed her forlorn expression had nothing to do with what was on her plate. The person she expected hadn't shown. "Hannah, he never comes to these things," she said in what she hoped was a gentle tone.

"What? Who do you mean?"

Franny shrugged. "Christopher Columbus, who else?" She finished off Hannah's discarded pastry. It did taste like toothpaste. "If you want to see him, why don't you give him a call?"

"After all this time? What would he think? Besides, I'm not sure I want him to know—about Allie, I mean. Didn't he and that woman he married have a son?"

"You know very well they did," Franny said, trying not to smile. "But are you really being fair? He might *want* to know, Hannah. Besides, the son went to live with his mother when they divorced. That's been . . . what? Twenty years at least."

She examined a gherkin before eating it. "How many times has he been married since then?"

"Once. No, maybe twice. But they didn't last."

"I heard he had a drinking problem. What's he running from, Franny V.?"

Franny shook her head. She doubted if he knew himself.

"What do you say we sneak into the pantry and liven up this punch with some of Claude Curtis's gin?" Hannah whispered, eyeing a gap in the crowd.

They were going to need it. As they were getting ready to leave that day, Claude Curtis came home and announced that Dottie Crenshaw had died.

Chapter Ten

October 22, 1943

The sidewalks of Sallie's Station were a patchwork of cement, and their roller skates made click-clacking noises as Franny and Hannah skated to the picture show after school.

Franny could have skated it blindfolded. The town was as familiar to her as a poem she had learned by heart, and they belonged to each other. She knew each broken slab of pavement, the oak with a twisted limb, the crumbling wall snaked with ivy. Alone, she liked to touch them, but Hannah liked to hurry. She had no time for touching.

Hannah waited while her friend sat on the Llewellyns' steps to take off her skates. Miss Willie Llewellyn had had a light stroke and was unable to get about, so Franny's mother had sent her some boiled custard.

"Miss Willie's been asking for you, honey," her mama said when Franny got home from school that day. "I ran into Miss Emmalee in the grocery store this morning, and she says Miss Willie's able to talk some now and she thinks a little visit might do her good. I told her you'd be over this afternoon."

Franny burrowed into the funny papers to see if Skeezix Wallet of

Gasoline Alley was going to get killed in the war, and pretended not to hear her. It was one of those golden late October days, and she and Hannah were going to the movies to see *The Fallen Sparrow*. Franny didn't want to go inside the dark old house that smelled of illness and age. "I'll go tomorrow," she said.

"You'll go today." Her mother took her face in her hands. "God put us here to look after each other, Frances Virginia." A visit with an old friend is only a small kindness, don't you think?" She gave her the pint jar of custard in a paper sack. "You can stop by on your way to the picture show. Now hurry, she's expecting you."

Franny rapped softly at the Llewellyns' back door, sort of hoping no one would hear her and that she could just leave the jar of custard there, but Miss Nettie opened the door and looked her over with her pebble-brown eyes. Her small hands trembled a little as she took the jar. "Sister can't talk much," she said, "but she'll be glad to see you." There was a hint of something like warning in her face, and when Franny saw Miss Willie lying there, all tiny and lost in her big bed, she knew what Miss Nettie was trying to tell her. Miss Willie was going to die.

Franny almost stumbled over Joker who lay on the rug by his mistress's bed. She didn't know where the other dogs were—outside somewhere probably. Miss Willie smiled at her with one side of her face and unfolded the fingers of her left hand which lay on top of the covers.

"She wants you to take her hand," Miss Emmalee said, and Franny did. It felt dry and cold to the touch, as if she were already dead.

"I'm sorry you're sick," Franny whispered. She didn't know what else to say. When the old woman closed her eyes, Franny gave her fingers a little squeeze and backed away. The room was gray and quiet, like a tomb. As soon as she reached the porch, she began to run.

"Let's go!" Franny didn't even put on her skates but snatched them up and raced all the way to town and through the post office parking lot to Aunt Six's safe yellow house. They would leave their roller skates there before crossing the street to the movie.

Her aunt sat in a porch rocker shelling pecans. "My goodness, what's the hurry? Your face is red as Cephus's nose!"

Franny smiled. Cephus Carmichael was right fond of strong drink, her mama said. In warm weather he slept on the porch of the town library and had even been known to wash his clothes in the fish pond and hang them on the statue of the Confederate soldier to dry.

The two girls sat on the steps while Hannah took off her skates. "Have you heard any more from Precious?" Franny asked.

Aunt Six nibbled a nut. "Called last night. They're letting Daisy go home this week, but Precious will stay with her until she gets her strength back." She leaned forward in her chair. "How you two gettin' along with the new principal?"

Franny kicked her skates aside. "Everything has been SNAFUed since that old woman came!" SNAFU meant "Situation Normal: All Fouled Up," her daddy had explained.

"Just give her a little time," her aunt said.

"Time! In time we'll all be dead," Franny told her.

"I hope you live long enough to see the Grand Ole Opry next week," Aunt Six said. "Your daddy has invited me to go along and I've bought myself a new dress. Sure hate to waste it on a funeral."

"Doesn't look like we'll even get to go now." Hannah told her about Miss Havergal and the P.T.A. "If it weren't for Miss O'Donnell, I'd skip that old play. Besides, Mama's already made my acorn costume."

"We'll get to see the Opry, Hannah," Franny reminded her. "Remember? Miss O'Donnell said we would."

"Aw, she just said that to make us feel better." Hannah started down the walk. "Come on or we'll miss the first of the picture."

"Miss O'Donnell doesn't lie!" Franny's face felt over-hot, and she almost told smarty Hannah she could go to the picture show by herself, but Franny had seen the previews, and she just couldn't bear to miss John Garfield in *The Fallen Sparrow*. It was supposed to be real scary.

The Fallen Sparrow was more than just scary. Ominous background music pushed the audience to the brink of fear, and ordinary sounds became threatening, horrifying, creating tension as tight as guitar strings. Poor John Garfield was stalked by a man with a dragging foot, haunted by the sound of a dripping water faucet.

The street was dark as they walked home, and dense shadows crept behind them. Franny looked over her shoulder as she walked. A dim light burned in the upstairs hall at the Llewellyns', and she knew Miss Willie was still alive. For now.

Franny hadn't been home more than five minutes when Hannah called.

"Franny V., you were right!"

"Right about what?" She peered around the big oak wardrobe that shadowed the hall and switched on a light. The man with the dragging foot could be hiding back there.

"About Miss O'Donnell and the Grand Ole Opry. Have you seen *The Chronicle*?"

The Chronicle was the town's weekly paper that came every Friday whether you wanted it to or not, as Franny's daddy liked to say. "Not yet," Franny said. "Why?"

"There's an article about the P.T.A. meeting. It says it starts at *seven* o'clock! Now they'll have to have it early, and we'll get to go to the Opry. Wonder how she did it?"

The next day Franny heard her speech teacher telling Miss Havergal she didn't see how the people at *The Chronicle* could make such a mistake, that she had distinctly said *eight* o'clock, and that she was so very, very sorry. Miss Havergal stomped away. She wasn't having an especially good day. That morning during recess somebody had drawn her picture on the board in bright yellow chalk with the accompanying verse:

ROSES ARE RED, THEIR STEMS ARE GREEN.
YOU HAVE A FIGURE LIKE A B-19!

It was in big block letters that covered the whole board, and it took two people to erase it.

On the night of the Grand Ole Opry, it looked as though the whole town had turned out to take advantage of the rare entertainment. Even the Gordons' wealthy neighbor, Cordelia Richardson, was there wearing her little fox neck piece that bit its tail, and the parking lot was almost full—or as Aunt Six said, "A mule was tied to every swinging limb."

It had been a warm day and the canvas had soaked up the heat of the sun. Too many people sitting too close together jammed the tent, and Franny felt sweat trickling down her neck. Her aunt dabbed her face with a handkerchief and fanned with the program.

Across the aisle, Mr. Rittenhouse kept time to the music with his cane, his white shirt as fresh as a line-dried sheet. Franny craned her neck to see who she could see. Travis, she noticed, sat right up front with R. W. Duggan. Maybe his mother had felt sorry for him and let him come after all, but she doubted it after what he'd called Miss Havergal. He'd probably sneaked out on his on.

"Franny V., looky there!" Hannah jabbed her with an elbow.

"Where?" Franny rubbed her side.

"Back there, four rows behind us. It's Miss O'Donnell and Damascus Jones." She giggled, humming *The Funeral March*.

"So what? They're just sitting together."

"Huh, bet they leave together." Hannah poked her again.

Franny slapped her hand away. "Bet they don't!"

"You two be quiet or I'll take you home," her daddy said.

It was hard not to cry when Ernest Tubb sang *The Soldier's Last Letter*. It seemed to Franny you just couldn't get away from the war, even at the Grand Ole Opry. Everybody stood and clapped when they played *Cowards Over Pearl Harbor*, and Hannah became solemn and quiet during *Searching For A Soldier's Grave*. Franny knew she was thinking of Singleton. The Kellys had finally learned Singleton was somewhere in Italy. Sometimes they would get three or four letters from him, then weeks would go by without a word. Some of the letters had black marks on them where the censor had covered words or sentences in case the letters were to fall into the wrong hands. The family never knew from day to day if Singleton was alive.

Franny was glad when Minnie Pearl came out and made everybody laugh. And she really did wear a price tag on her hat.

Franny hardly heard the rest of the show for straining to watch Miss O'Donnell and Damascus Jones. When the audience started to leave after the closing number, Aunt Six remained in her seat.

Hannah's daddy put a hand on her shoulder. "Aunt Six, are you all right? You aren't sick, are you?"

"Of course I'm not sick!" she snapped. "Just a little indigestion, that's all."

Franny stood with Hannah on the bench to watch the out-going swarm. She saw Miss O'Donnell's bright head and Damascus Jones's dark one bobbing up the aisle together, saw him take her arm in his—like she belonged to him. Hannah saw it too. "See," she said. "I told you."

Franny didn't answer. She just felt sick.

The following Monday as Franny dressed for school she heard her parents talking in low voices. "Aunt Six doesn't look well, Jonathan," her mother said. "And she seems so tired. I've half a mind to call Honey Sue."

"If you call Honey Sue, you do have half a mind," Franny's father told her with a smile in his voice. Franny stuffed books into her satchel. What was her mama so worried about? Hadn't her aunt told them she just had indigestion?

Franny gathered up her costume and started for the door. The first bell had already rung, and if she was late she'd have to stay after school and write boring, repetitive sentences.

"Not so fast." Molly Gordon tilted her daughter's chin with her fingers and kissed her forehead. "Why so glum? Late case of stage fright?"

Franny scrambled away without answering. The harvest play had been such a success the night of the P.T.A. meeting, a repeat performance was scheduled for today's assembly, and Franny wasn't looking forward to it after Miss O'Donnell had let her down by going out with that creepy Damascus Jones. Why, he must be at least thirty-five! After dating Mr. Gregory, how could she possibly bear to be around him? And him with a glass eye at that.

Later she waited in the wings with Hannah and the others listening to the tramp and shuffle as the student body filed into the auditorium. It was dim and musty backstage with the curtains closed and it made her want to sneeze. The backdrop was a huge canvas with out-of-date advertisements painted on it that raised and lowered like a big window shade.

Franny waited for the murmuring to subside but it only got louder. The chattering grew into a huge swell like a gigantic ocean wave, and she heard the thump-thump-thump of seats going up, then cries and applause. A few children ran to peep through the curtain to see what was causing the ruckus, but Miss O'Donnell shooed them back. She looked so flushed and pretty, Franny had to turn away.

"We have a special guest in the audience this morning," her teacher whispered, smiling. "So I want you to do your very best."

"Is it President Roosevelt?" Little Dottie Crenshaw wanted to know. Dottie was supposed to be a field mouse and kept stepping on her tail.

Miss O'Donnell laughed. "No, I'm afraid he couldn't make it, but this is someone who works for him."

"Who?" Franny gulped. "It's Mr. Gregory, isn't it?"

"Lieutenant Gregory now." Her teacher held a finger to her lips. "Now don't get too excited or you might forget your lines. We want him to be proud of us, don't we?"

Franny's heart thudded so she could hardly hear *The Star Spangled Banner*. Sure enough, there was Mr. Gregory—*their* Mr. Gregory—sitting in the front row right next to Miss Havergal. Franny looked at him the whole time she said her piece, and he smiled right back at her. Even Miss Havergal looked a little better in his light.

After the skit Mr. Gregory came up on the stage and gave his Red Skelton imitation. He tousled his hair, made his eyes bug out, and pranced about on wobbly legs. After the laughter faded, he put on his serious face. He would be leaving soon to go overseas, he told them and had come to say goodbye. Some of the children began to cry, and Franny felt the sneaky hot beginning of tears, but the new lieutenant laughed them away. He wanted to remember them in a happy way, he said, and he'd like for all his boys and girls to show Miss Havergal what a fine bunch of students they were.

If he only knew, Franny thought. She wanted to take him aside and tell him what a horrible person Miss Havergal was, but she knew he had troubles enough with the war and Hitler and all.

During the week to come, every time Franny or her friends saw Lieutenant Gregory, he was with Miss O'Donnell. They went to the movies together, took long walks around town, played cards at Miss Opal's, even went dancing in Atlanta, their spy sources reported. Miss O'Donnell had a different look about her: soft and sad, and vibrant like a music box song. Franny felt closer to her teacher than she ever had, felt her happiness and her fear. She wanted to put her arms around her and tell her not to worry, that Lieutenant Gregory would come back and marry her and take her to live in the house with the white fence. But Eileen O'Donnell was too fragile to touch.

That last Sunday the two of them came to church and sat in a pew at the back. The congregation seemed to sense them and nodded and smiled at each other. Couples didn't attend church together unless they had serious intentions.

Franny stood on the steps after the service waiting to tell him goodbye. A throng of people surrounded them. The men shook his hand, thumped him on the back, and wished him well with hearty voices. The women hugged and kissed him and clung to his hands. It was a bright, cold day and the wind ruffled his sandy-brown hair, swept away his laughter. He put an arm across Miss O'Donnell's shoulders and smiled down at her as if this were just another Sunday and he would be there forever.

"Franny, Hannah!" The crowd had dwindled when Lieutenant Gregory held out his arms to them. Franny felt the rough khaki jacket against her face, inhaled its wooly-brown soldier smell.

"You'll take care of her for me, won't you?" he said, smiling down at Miss O'Donnell. "Keep her out of trouble?"

Franny nodded, not daring to speak. He tossed his cap on her head and whispered in her ear. "You'll see things through, Franny Gordon. I know I can count on you."

"You can. I will," she promised, wondering just what he meant. The cap slid down over one eye, and he laughed and reclaimed it, smoothing her hair with a clumsy, masculine hand.

"Franny!" her mother called. "Come on, honey, we're waiting."

Franny stood on the steps alone. Everyone was gone: Lieutenant Gregory, Miss O'Donnell, Hannah, everyone, and she hadn't even noticed their leaving. She felt her head where he had touched it. The cap was gone, but the weight of it was still there.

Chapter Eleven

The ancient furnace, coaxed and coddled through its last seizure, gave a final shudder and quit, and Molly Gordon retreated to her frigid room and shut the door.

Franny borrowed a couple of portable heaters to keep from freezing while the heating contractor wrestled out her old elephant of a furnace and put in a new one.

Faith, snug in her own warm house, begged them to stay with her, and Betty Joyce repeated her offer so many times she said she felt like a parrot, but Franny's mother wouldn't budge.

Friends came to see her, braving the cold. "Mama, Alma's brought you some of those cookies you like with the big chocolate chunks. I'll put on some coffee, okay?" But Alma wouldn't stay for coffee because her friend wouldn't talk to her.

"She just kind of grunts," Alma said, rather huffily, Franny thought. "Sounds like my little beagle, Toby, right before he took so bad and died. You remember Toby, don't you, Franny? Heart worms it was." From the look Alma gave her as her son helped her into the car, Franny could tell she was already thinking about what kind of wreath she'd send. "If I were you, I'd call the doctor," she said.

It sounded more like her mama needed a vet, but Franny phoned R.W. instead. He brought her mother a couple of pink sasanqua blossoms from the bush at THE HOME PLACE. It was about the only thing that wasn't destroyed in the fire.

"I'm afraid it will make her cry," Franny said.

"Good. That's exactly what we want," he told her.

Franny would have liked nothing better than to have a good cry herself. When Dottie Crenshaw died, she felt relief that the woman was done with her suffering, both mentally and physically, yet her death made the grave reality Franny bore smothered inside her both indelible and irreversible. How wonderful it would be to cry it all away!

Instead she floated the fragile surviving flower in the glass leaf dish that had belonged to her grandmother, and put it on her mama's marble-topped dresser. Molly Gordon ignored it.

R.W. prescribed an afternoon at the movies—preferably a comedy—and dinner at an elegant restaurant, complete with a glass or two of wine. It sounded good to her, Franny said.

"Physically she seems okay," he said, "Just be sure she continues with her vitamins, and see if you can get her out of the house."

Franny walked with him out to the porch, which wasn't much colder than their living room. "Wouldn't hurt me either," she told him.

R.W. laughed and took her hand. "Ran into Faith in the library last week. Looks wonderful. I'm glad things are working out for her."

"So far, so good. She hasn't had any more bleeding. I try to do a little extra cooking when I can so she won't have so much to do. She's promised to take it easy." Franny smiled at him. He was a good man, a gentle man, and except for a little extra weight around the middle and a sifting of gray in his hair, he looked much as he had when he first opened his practice.

"And so should you." R.W. paused on the top step. "You're not my patient, Franny, but I don't think I'd be infringing on Dr. Winthrop's practice if I suggest you soft-pedal it some." He leaned over and kissed her cheek. "Share the burden, honey."

If only she could. "Physician, heal thyself," Franny said. R.W. had faithfully tended his wife Belinda who suffered for years with Alzheimer's until she died a couple of years ago, and everyone knew he practically supported his sorry brother-in-law. She followed him down the steps.

"R.W., Mama's driving me crazy. She feels responsible, I guess, because this happened to Dottie at her old home place. I don't think she's spoken more than ten words since we learned she died. Even Hannah can't get her to talk."

"She will, give her time." He swung his bag into the floor of his car and turned back to her. "How is Hannah? I'd like to see her."

"Then you shouldn't have to look very far. She's having the old home remodeled."

Hannah had suggested several times that she move to a motel, but Franny knew she'd be lonely there, and she wanted her to stay, especially with her mother the way she was. "If anybody can get Mama to come around, it'll be Hannah," she said. "She has more patience with her than I do."

"That could be because she isn't around her as much." R.W. shaded his eyes and looked at the lot where the old school used to be. "Wish the Baptists would hurry and get something up over there. Staring at that burned-out ruin has to be depressing for your mother." He folded his arms and leaned against the shiny black door of his Chrysler, apparently in no hurry to leave.

"You know," he said, "it kind of got to me when they tore that old school down. There was a time, though, when I would've gladly set a match to it. Remember when that awful woman was there? Back during the war. What was her name? Habersham?"

"Havergal," she said, watching his face. Was he testing her? Did he know?

"God, what a sadistic old bitch! I remember lying awake nights studying up ways to get rid of her, then all of a sudden she was gone. Remember? They say she—"

Thank heavens the van from Tara's Flower Garden pulled up about that time and the delivery boy jumped out with a huge vase of mixed flowers. Franny knew they were for Hannah because Vance had called the day before to ask her to recommend a florist.

By the time she accepted the delivery, R.W. had climbed into his car and driven away with a wave and a holler. Franny hoped he had forgotten what he was going to say about Miss Havergal.

Her mother knew the most unfortunate people. When they were small, she warned them in great detail about sticking heads or limbs out of car windows. She had a cousin who had lost an arm that way, Franny's mother said. And he had planned to be a surgeon. One of her best friends was struck by lightning as he closed a window during a storm, and a classmate had died from blood poisoning caused by mashing a pimple on her face. Franny hoped Dottie Crenshaw wouldn't become an addition to her list.

A few days after R.W. prescribed the outing, Hannah treated Franny and her mother to grilled salmon and peaches flambe at a sedate out-of-the-way restaurant in Buckhead while a Katharine Hepburn look-alike in a bright green caftan played *Clare de Lune* on the piano. Molly had eaten there once before and talked about it for weeks.

She wasn't talking now. Franny's mother endured the meal with a minimum of conversation and very little show of emotion. After coffee, she set aside her spoon and stared silently into the cup. "Poor little Dorothy," she said in a small voice that was scarcely above a whisper. "She was such a pretty little girl, remember? I hope she didn't suffer."

Franny glanced at Hannah who seemed to have found her water goblet intensely fascinating. "She was heavily sedated," Franny said. "I don't think she ever regained consciousness."

Earlier they had gone to an afternoon movie featuring Tom Hanks, one of her mother's favorites. The picture was a comedy, which they hoped would at least make her smile. But although Franny and Hannah laughed in all the right places, and even some of the not-so-right places, they never heard a peep out of her mother. To tell the truth, Franny was getting more than a little provoked with her. Tom Hanks, Molly told them over dinner, looked a lot like her friend who was struck by lightning.

Not even seeing Walter Curtis and his mystery lady friend stoked her mother's curiosity.

Hannah pulled at Franny's sleeve as they were leaving the restaurant. "Look, isn't that Walter and What's-her-name?"

"Where?"

"Going into that antiques shop across the street. Wearing a green cape . . . Quick, don't let them see us staring."

"Walter's wearing a green cape?"

"No, silly. What's-her-name."

"Janine." A green cape would make most women look like 'Mother Earth,' but on her it seemed glamorous. Franny saw her touch Walter on the arm and point out something in the window. Her every movement graceful. "Client," she said. "Has to be. Neely would've sent her packing by now."

"Not necessarily," Hannah said. "Maybe Walter's just been waiting for the right one. What do you think, Miss Molly?"

But the older woman only shook her head and started back to where they had parked the car. They drove home in silence.

Franny's daughter, Lucy, was driving home for Thanksgiving with a friend who had relatives in Chattanooga, and Faith's last ultrasound showed an active fetus. They should have a good holiday if her mother would only allow it. Franny wished she could "hocus-pocus" that old burnt-out house and make it go away.

"Why don't you ride over to Rome with me and help me pick out a light fixture for my new sunroom?" Hannah asked Franny's mother the next day. "I could sure use the help." But Molly wouldn't go. She was still tired from yesterday's excursion to Atlanta, she said.

"Good. Then maybe you'll help me make that Japanese fruitcake for Thanksgiving," Franny said. "Of course we'll have to hide it in the freezer so Gib can't find it." It was her son's favorite dessert, the very devil to make, and they only had it once a year.

"Maybe I shouldn't ask," Hannah whispered after Molly Gordon left the room, "but what's Gib planning to do for Thanksgiving? Will Wuzzy come here, or will he go there? Be a good chance for the two of them to get together."

Franny nodded. "He hasn't said, but I'm hoping. Frankly I don't care where they go as long as they try to work out some of their problems. Sometimes I feel I'm living with Eeyore. Remember the gloomy little donkey in *Winnie the Pooh*?"

And now, it seemed, Eeyore had a twin. After Hannah left, Franny went into the kitchen to drain the coconut milk before grating. Thank God for the sainted inventor of the food processor—no more bloody knuckles! In a little while her mother padded in to join her. Silently she set out eggs and shortening, then measured dry ingredients with about as much expression on her face as that old electric clock over the refrigerator.

Franny found herself gritting her teeth. Couldn't she lighten up just a little? She waited until her mother had carefully added the spices, then went over and put her arms around her. "Sure is quiet in here. If I didn't know better, I'd think I was over at Jones, Fenwick and Mullinax." Jones, Fenwick and Mullinax was the local undertaking establishment.

"I'm sorry, Frances," her mama said. "I thought you wanted help with the cake." She made like she was going to leave.

"Oh, for heaven's sake, you know I can't make a Japanese fruitcake like you can. It's just that—well, damn it, Mama, I feel bad too. I know this fire has been awful for you—for all of us, especially after what happened to Dottie, but it's getting to be downright depressing around here. Life goes on, you know."

Her mama sloshed buttermilk into a cup. "I'm doing the best I can." She attacked the batter with a mixer. Franny moved to the counter across from her and threw chunks of coconut into the food processor, then flipped the switch. They faced each other over dueling kitchen appliances.

Franny made two chicken pies for supper and took one to Faith. The short walk in the brisk November air was like an appetizer. She wanted to keep on hiking, wade through crunchy brown leaves in the hills above town, then the hills after those hills. She wanted to get away.

Faith hung her mother's old jacket by the kitchen door. "How's Gramolly?"

"Don't ask." Franny returned her hug, squelching the impulse to hang on to her sweet little smock-clad shoulders. She was *not* going to unload on this child. Not now. "She's warm, at least," she said. "The new furnace is blasting away. I left her watching those blessed soaps."

They talked about names for the baby. At least Faith talked about them. Franny had already made a list of family names—the pretty ones anyway, and as long as her daughter and Reilly avoided movie stars, national monuments, and days of the week, she would at least make an effort to keep her mouth shut.

Hannah was having dinner with a friend and wouldn't be home till later, she said. She didn't say what friend, but Franny had a fairly good idea. Hannah would tell her when she was ready.

Franny stayed longer than she meant to at Faith's. It was such a pleasure being with someone who was happy, whose life was going right—especially if that someone was Faith.

When she reached home, a light still burned in the living room, but the rest of the house was dark. Her mother dozed in front of a dark television screen, but woke when Franny closed the front door.

"Gib not home?" Franny glanced at the TV clock. It was after six.

Her mother yawned and rubbed her eyes. "Not yet. I haven't heard him come in."

Gib's car wasn't in its usual parking space behind the garage, Franny noted, when she went to warm up supper. Still, she didn't worry. Sometimes he had errands or stopped for a beer with friends, yet he always called if he planned to be late. She insisted on it. Besides, her son rarely missed a meal.

When Gib hadn't shown by seven, she and her mother ate without him. Or Franny ate. Her mother nibbled at her pastry crust and pushed bits of chicken around her plate. "You don't suppose he's had an accident, do you?" she asked.

She had supposed, but Franny tried not to think about things like that, especially after what happened to Gib's daddy. And he really wasn't all that late—just late enough to annoy her. She listened for his car in the driveway. "Probably just stopped somewhere along the way," she told her mother. Somewhere they never heard of a telephone.

At nine-thirty Franny called the radio station where her son worked, then his old college friend Shagg McKenzie, who lived in Marietta, and finally Wuzzy. She reached an answering machine at all three places.

She phoned Faith at ten, and was almost certain she woke her, but it was reassuring to speak with a live, human voice. "Did Gib mention to you what time he'd be home?" Franny asked in what she hoped was an offhand manner. "I think he said something at breakfast about a concert, but I'm afraid I wasn't paying much attention." Light laugh here.

"Mama, I haven't seen Gib for days. What's the matter? Is anything wrong?" What a suspicious child she was.

"Of course not. Sorry I woke you, honey. Now go on back to sleep."

"Maybe he left a note," her mother suggested. But Franny had checked his room. His bed had been made: Gib's definition of 'made'—the spread had been pulled partially over the pillow. His clothes were still there, and his shaving things occupied the shelf above the bathroom sink. There was no note.

Her mother started crying—that horrible, silent crying, and she tried to hide it by sitting in the big wing-back chair and holding a newspaper in front of her. Franny knelt on the floor and held her until she soaked the front of her blouse. She had been waiting for her mother to cry, wanting it, but not because of this. Pain, like a hard fist, grabbed at her stomach, and her head felt as if it might explode, spew all the dark things she carried inside all over her just-cleaned living room carpet. Franny didn't care if it did.

The State Patrol had no record of her son's having an accident, they said when Franny called just after midnight and gave them a description of his car and the tag number. Damn Gib! He'd gone out with the boys or, God forbid, maybe even another woman, without thinking or caring they might be wondering where he was. And then, of course, there was that dark fluttering fear that some fool had shot him in the parking lot.

She made her mama drink a small glass of wine and got her into bed where she tuned her radio into one of those late night talk shows. When she looked in on her a few minutes later, Gabby Gus of *The Night Shift* was still consoling "Heartbroken Herman" out on Highway 53, and her mama was asleep.

Franny curled up with their cat Sylvester and a glass of Merlot on the living room sofa to watch some old movie with Ray Milland. Sometime later Sylvester deserted her for Hannah when her friend tiptoed past and crept upstairs. The next thing she knew, it was almost four and her son was throwing up in the bathroom. Her bathroom. It didn't take Sam Spade to figure out he'd tried to drink some bar dry.

"Oh God, Mama!" he groaned. "I'd have to feel better to die."

Somehow she got him up to bed. He'd better wish he did die if he knew what was good for him, Franny thought, as she tried to get back to sleep.

Wuzzy called the next morning to ask if she'd heard from Gib. "I went to a play last night with friends," she said, "and didn't get in until late. I was afraid I'd wake you if I called."

Franny told her Gib got in late too. She didn't say how late or what condition he was in, but she supposed Wuzzy guessed.

"I'm afraid he's upset with me," Wuzzy said. "We met for lunch yesterday and I reminded him I'd be spending Thanksgiving skiing in Colorado with some old college friends. Remember Marcy, the tall blonde who was in our wedding? Well, her parents own shares in a lodge up there. We've been planning this reunion for over a year now. It was the only time we could all get together." Her voice dwindled into what sounded like a plea for understanding. "I told Gib about this months ago . . ."

The guilt thing. Thank goodness she had the backbone to reject it. Franny hoped he hadn't made a complete ass of himself and messed up his chances completely. "I don't think he's thinking straight," she said. "He misses you, Wuzzy. Gib loves you, I know he does." *Listen to yourself, Frances Hughes! You'd like to wad up that boy and bounce him off the ceiling, yet here you are defending his cause.*

Wuzzy didn't answer for the longest time. "I know," she said, and sighed. "Well . . . tell him I'll call when I get back. And Franny? I hope you have a nice Thanksgiving." She sounded doubtful.

But she meant to have a very nice Thanksgiving, thank you just the same, and Gibson Hughes wasn't going to ruin it. Franny heard him upstairs in the bathroom getting ready to go to work. He was already going to be late, and the things she had to say would take more than a few minutes. And frankly, she couldn't bring herself to look at him yet. Franny went in her room and closed the door until she heard him leave.

All day she rehearsed what she would say, and the more she thought about it, the more resentful she became.

"Gibson didn't eat a bite of breakfast," her mother said later that afternoon as she stirred up cornbread for dressing. Hannah had gone to see about new countertops for her bathroom, and the house was quiet: just the two of them and the cat sleeping in the bentwood rocker by the window.

Franny doubted if her son had cared much for lunch either, and if she could, she would have packed him a cup of lard with a hair in it.

The hot iron skillet sizzled as her mama spooned in the batter. "Says he went out with that friend of his—Shagg something or other." She slid the pan into the oven, then carefully hung the pot-holder on its hook. "Franny, I'm afraid that boy had too much to drink last night. Is Gib all right?"

"No, Mama, he's not all right." Franny told her about Wuzzy.

"He's going to lose that girl if he's not careful. Gib did a good day's work when he married Deborah." She massaged her hands with what was left of the cornbread batter—it made them soft, she said—then rinsed them at the sink. "What on earth's the matter with Gibson, anyway?"

Franny said she didn't know and started crying. She wiped off every countertop in the kitchen and started on the stove, working in widening circles with a soapy sponge. She heard her mother speaking to her, but couldn't stop crying and wouldn't stop wiping.

"Frances Virginia, if you don't stop this, I'm going to call Faith," she said, and Franny heard her on the phone with somebody at the clinic. After a while the delivery boy from Maxwell's brought her a prescription, for some kind of tranquilizer she supposed. Franny took one and went to bed.

When Gib came home that night his Gramolly was waiting at the door. "I don't ever want to see your mama as upset as she was today!" she told him. "It's about time you took a long, hard look at yourself, Gibson Hughes. It's time to grow up."

Franny smiled as she went into the bathroom to wash her face for supper. She wasn't sure what Gib's next move would be, but it sounded like Molly Gordon was back to stay.

The next morning her son's room was empty.

Chapter Twelve

"Aunt Six wasn't at church today," Franny's mother said at dinner that Sunday. "You girls take care of the dishes, I'm going to run down there and see if she's all right."

Her father helped himself to another slice of meat loaf. "I thought you said she was feeling better."

"*She* said she was. But I made her promise to see Dr. Ludlow this week."

"I think she's missing Precious," he said. "And worried about Daisy. Molly, Precious just might decide to stay up there . . . any more of those field peas?"

Her mama froze with a fork full of rice in midair. "I can't imagine Aunt Six without Precious!"

"I can't imagine Precious without Aunt Six," Franny said.

They had breadcrumb pudding for dessert. Flavored with extracts and dotted with raisins, the baked pudding was covered with tart crab apple jelly, then topped with a golden meringue. Just as they finished eating, there came a series of familiar knocks at the front door: five short raps and two louder ones. Mrs. Littlejohn's blaring voice trumpeted down the hallway. "Yoo-hoo! Anybody home?"

Franny looked at her sister and grinned. Whenever their neighbor came over it was usually about the time they served dessert, which they rarely had now except on Sundays. Franny liked Ida Littlejohn, a large bossy woman who wore her hair in a topknot and knew all the gossip in town. Once she heard Mrs. Littlejohn telling her mother that President Roosevelt did her the biggest favor in the world when he asked women to donate their rubber girdles to the war effort. Said she'd never been so glad to get rid of anything in her life, she just wished he'd asked for them forty years sooner.

While Franny and her sister scraped the plates and stacked them, their mama served a dish of pudding to their neighbor. Mrs. Littlejohn was scooping up the last bite when the phone rang, and Franny ran to answer it, wiping her hands on her mama's big apron.

"Franny, is your mother there?" It was Mr. Rittenhouse. His rusty voice sounded higher than usual and he seemed out of breath. "Your Aunt Six isn't feeling well," he said. "I think she should get down here right away."

Her mama's face turned white when she heard the news, and she asked Franny's father to drive her the two blocks to town. Franny wanted to go too, but her mother said she'd be more help if she stayed home and helped Winnie.

After their neighbor left, Franny and her sister dried the dishes and put them away. Franny even swept the floor and wiped off the stove. If she did a really good job cleaning the kitchen, maybe Mama would call and tell them that Aunt Six was fine, that it all been a big mistake. But she didn't.

It was getting dark by the time her daddy came home and told them they had taken their aunt to the small hospital in town and that their mother would stay there with her until Honey Sue arrived.

"It's her heart, isn't it?" Franny asked.

"That's what the doctor thinks," he said, pulling her close to him. "They've given her something for the pain and she's resting now.

We'll know more tomorrow."

It was hard for Franny to picture her bustling energetic aunt lying sick and quiet like Miss Willie. Her Great Aunt Six was the closest person to a grandmother Franny had, and life without her would be like life without birthdays and Christmas.

Franny crept into the dark, cold storage closet and burrowed into a mound of old quilts. In the kitchen Winnie heated leftovers for supper, and nearby in the sitting room her daddy chuckled over Senator Cleghorn on *The Fred Allen Radio Show*. Franny heard the sputter of static, the creak of the oven door, but she felt as alone as if the house had been empty. Franny had prayed for Daisy and she was getting well. She prayed every night for Singleton, and so far he had been spared. Even Miss Willie seemed to have rallied after Franny mentioned her in her nightly rituals. Now she would pray for Aunt Six. She would pray harder than she had ever prayed before, and God would listen. She knew He would because God was good. Hadn't all her Sunday school teachers said so?

Her mother came home in the early hours and was still asleep when Franny left for school, but her father said their aunt was about the same. He made oatmeal for breakfast: lumpy and gray, the way Franny felt.

They talked in whispers and the house seemed drab and hollow. Franny was glad to leave it, to have feeling return as she walked through Mrs. Littlejohn's yard taking the shortcut to school. The grass was wet with dew and the red leaves under the dogwood tree rustled where she walked.

"Franny! What do you hear from your Aunt Six?" Mrs. Littlejohn swept her porch, hefty arms jiggling with each arc of the broom.

"She's about the same, thank you!" Franny called across the yard. She didn't want to stop and talk.

Hannah waited at the edge of the playground. "I'm sure sorry about your Aunt Six," she said. "Mama said tell you she's sending a congealed salad and some rolls for your supper. Reckon she's gonna be all right?"

"I don't know. She hasn't changed. And Honey Sue's there now." Franny frowned. That could make her aunt even worse.

The two sat on the low stone wall in silence until they heard squeals from a cluster of girls on the steps of the main building.

Hannah frowned. "What's that all about?"

The noisy circle grew as others ran to join them, shrieking and jumping about as though they waded in boiling water. "Come on, let's go see!" Hannah jumped up, pulling Franny along beside her. Travis ran to meet them. "Miss O'Donnell's engaged! She's got a ring—a real diamond! Hey, didn't I tell you? Didn't I?"

Franny wrenched free and snaked through the bubbling crowd to where Neely Louise stood gushing over her teacher's left hand.

Miss O'Donnell smiled and made room for her on the step beside her. "Well, Miss Franny, how do you like it? I don't expect you're too surprised."

She touched the tiny diamond, a single stone set in platinum like a miniature star. "It's beautiful. Just right." And it was. Franny grabbed her teacher in a clumsy hug. Why did she want to cry?

A sharp elbow dug into her shoulder, somebody stepped on her toe. Shirley Puckett forced her way between them. "Get outa the way, Franny! I wanna see."

Something warm and sweet stirred inside her chest, welled behind her eyes. Franny stumbled to her feet and pushed past her. No one must see her tears. She ran to the other side of the big oak, the one at the edge of the playground, and put her arms around it, felt its rough, familiar texture against her face. If only she could become an invisible part of it, stand there forever. For months Franny had hoped this would happen, and now that it had, something held her back. Tears slipped down her face and soaked into the bark of the tree.

It was Aunt Six. Her illness had ruined everything! She should have listened, admitted that she was getting old and sick. It was her fault for being so stubborn.

"Franny? I just heard about your aunt." Miss O'Donnell stood beside her. How long had she been there? "I know it must be hard for you. She's a special lady, isn't she?"

Her teacher traced the bark of the tree, but didn't try to touch her. If she had, Franny would have broken in two. Franny nodded and tried to wipe the tears away with the back of her hand. "It's not that I'm not happy for you . . . I am. Really, I am."

"I know you are." Miss O'Donnell spoke softly. "Feelings are unpredictable. Sometimes they come tumbling out upside down. It's human nature."

"It is?"

She smiled. "Of course it is." She touched her then—lightly on the shoulder. "Now, better hurry and rinse your face. It's almost time for the bell."

That night Franny heard the front door close when her mama came home from the hospital and hurried downstairs to meet her. Her daddy was still up reading. A light came from under their door. Her mother hung her coat in the hallway. She looked tired and pale in the darkness and her bright hair was coming loose. Franny put her arms around her. "Mama?"

"Franny." Her mother's hands were warm on her face. "You should be asleep, honey. You have school tomorrow."

"I couldn't, Mama. I was thinking about Aunt Six. Is she . . ."

"Well, she's complaining, so she must be getting better." Her mother smiled and wrapped a strand of Franny's hair around her finger. Franny followed her to the kitchen where she switched on a light and pulled one of the green wooden chairs away from the table. Her mother sank into it with a sigh and pulled Franny onto her lap.

"Is Aunt Six going to die?" Franny asked.

"I don't know, Franny. I don't think so." Her mother wrapped her arms around her. "We'll just have to wait and see."

"I've been praying," Franny said. "I prayed for Daisy and Singleton—Miss Willie too—and now for Mr. Gregory."

"That's good, honey. You just keep on doing that." Her mama sounded like she was going to cry.

"Do you pray, Mama?"

"Well, of course I do." Her mother kissed her cheek and rocked her back and forth like she did when Franny was little. Franny liked it.

"Do you think God listens?"

"He always listens, Franny, but sometimes His answer isn't what we'd like it to be."

"You mean like in *The Lord's Prayer*? 'Thy kingdom come, thy will be done . . .'?"

"Something like that," her mother said.

"Then why pray at all?" Franny studied her mother's face. "Why bother to ask?"

"Frances Virginia!" Her mama frowned. "Where on earth do you get such notions?"

Franny shrugged. "It just doesn't seem to make any sense to pray for God's will to be done when He's gonna have His way whether we like it or not."

Franny didn't get to see her aunt until she came home from school a few days later to find her mother waiting on the porch. Her stomach did a flip-flop. Something was wrong!

"Franny, Winnie and I are going over to the hospital. Hurry and wash your face and hands and you can say hello to Aunt Six." Her mother wore her good black coat, the one with the pretty braid buttons. Now she hurried her up the steps.

Franny played with the hook on the screen door. They always called in the family when people were dying. "Oh, Mama!" She started to cry.

"No honey, it's not like that." Her mother smiled, and Franny knew everything would be all right. "She's much stronger today.

Your aunt has something called angina, but it can be controlled with the right medicine. Dr. Ludlow thinks this was a warning—probably brought on by fatigue. Aunt Six is just going to have to slow down, that's all."

Franny threw water on her face and wiped the dirt on a towel. Her prayers *had* worked. Aunt Six was going to get well. She knew God had a lot to do with it and was willing to give Him credit where credit was due, but hadn't she—Franny—had a part in it too?

The hospital had dingy green walls and a smothering antiseptic smell. They found Honey Sue and her husband sitting on a bench at the end of a long hallway, and the two rose when they saw them.

Franny's mother drew in her breath. "Honey Sue! Is anything wrong? Is Aunt Six—"

"Resting," Honey Sue whispered. "Sleeps all the time." She drew Molly aside. "Cousin Marjorie, you're going to have to help me talk her into coming home with us. I can't do a thing with her!" She fumbled in a huge black purse for a handkerchief and dabbed at her eyes. "She's too old to live alone, and I can't stay here forever. I don't know what to do."

"I know, I know." Franny's mother patted the woman's arm. "But things will work out. Precious called this morning, and she thinks she'll be able to leave Daisy in a day or so." She put an arm around Honey Sue to keep her from turning away. "Why, she can stay with us at night until she's stronger. You know she's like a mother to us, and the girls adore her."

"But you and Precious can't be with her constantly. What if she has another one of those attacks when she's alone?"

"Your mother just needs to learn to pace herself," Molly said soothingly. "Dr. Ludlow thinks she'll be more at ease in her own home right now."

"Humph!" Honey Sue sniffed. "That old man's in cahoots with her, but she's *my* mother, and I worry about her."

"Of course you do," Franny's mama murmured. She turned to

Leon. "Why don't you and Honey Sue go on now and have something to eat? We'll stay here with Aunt Six."

Leon unfolded his long frame from the bench, his mouth drooped at the corners. He seldom acknowledged Franny with more than a nod, and when he did, he looked as if he knew something bad about her that she didn't know. Now he edged silently past Franny and her sister to stand beside his wife. "She's right, Honey Sue. It'll do you good to get away for awhile."

Honey Sue threw up her hands like she was trying to fight off mosquitoes. "Oh, all right, but see if you can get her to eat. She complains about the food something awful."

After the couple left, Franny's mother opened the door a crack. Aunt Six lay propped against pillows, her head turned to one side. She looked asleep. "Don't wake her," her mama whispered.

Aunt Six drowsily opened one eye and sat up. "Is she gone?"

Her niece nodded. "We thought you were asleep."

Aunt Six smiled and winked at Franny. "So did Honey Sue. It's the only way I can get her to leave me alone."

"Why, Aunt Six, you ought to be ashamed," Franny's mother scolded. "Honey Sue loves you. She worries about you."

Their aunt blinked at her toes and sighed. "And I love Honey Sue, she's the only child I have, but I love her more at a distance. I don't want to *live* with her." She reached for the hairbrush on the table beside her and fluffed up her tousled blue locks. "She can't cook, you know. I'd starve to death down there. And that stingy Leon—says he's a vegetarian. He's just too tight to buy meat—even if we could get it." Aunt Six drew up her long, bony knees and shook the brush at Franny's mother. "Why, he wouldn't spend a dime to see Jesus Christ ride a bicycle around Woolworth's!"

"Aunt Six!" Franny's mama acted like she was shocked. Franny didn't know why. She had heard her say it before.

"Well, it's true and you know it. Marjorie, you've got to help me stay here in Sallie's Station." Aunt Six reached out and took

Franny's hand. "Sugar, I can count on you, can't I?"

Franny leaned over and kissed her to let her know she was on her side, but the familiar words frightened her. Mr. Gregory had asked her the same question only a few days before. What did they expect her to do? Didn't they realize she was only ten?

A nurse entered with the supper tray, cheerfully lifted the lid, and tucked a napkin around their aunt. Aunt Six took one sniff and pushed it away. "Pig slop," she said. "Hellcat wouldn't eat it."

"But *you* will," Franny said, "if you want to get out of this place." She picked up the fork and put it in her aunt's hand.

Aunt Six gave her a funny look, made a face, and dug in.

Chapter Thirteen

The note on the refrigerator said, *Call Dr. Weinstein*, and gave a telephone number over in Rome. It was the week before Thanksgiving. Franny and Hannah had just returned from a hilly, three-mile walk before breakfast, and Franny was starving. She poured herself a cup of coffee while Hannah put skim milk and cereal on the table. They were both dieting before an anticipated holiday of blimping out.

"Who's Dr. Weinstein?" Franny asked her mother when she sat down to her toasted English muffin and orange marmalade.

"Doctor who?"

Franny waved the message in front of her. "Dr. Weinstein. This is your handwriting, isn't it? Says call Dr. Weinstein."

"I don't know. Some woman just left a message for you to call him."

"But I don't know any Dr. Weinstein. Are you sure they had the right number?"

Her mama stirred sugar into her coffee. "Asked to speak with Frances Hughes. That's you, isn't it?"

She couldn't argue with that. After breakfast Franny called the number and got one of the biggest shocks of her life. The mammogram she'd had the day before showed a small suspicious area, and they wanted her to have another at the hospital.

Franny stared out the kitchen window at the big spruce between their house and the house next door where Betty Joyce and Hubert now lived. She and Winnie had played dolls under that tree. It was a familiar part of her life. Today it didn't look any different. She didn't feel any different.

"Probably nothing to worry about," the radiologist said. "But just to be on the safe side, we'd like to take a second look—make us feel better all around."

To hell with that, Franny thought. She was feeling fine before he called, but she dutifully phoned the hospital and arranged to go in that afternoon.

The two people at the breakfast table, having heard one side of the conversation, stared at her. "Some people will go to any lengths to get me on the cover of *Penthouse*," Franny said in an effort to solicit a smile. It didn't work. "Oh, come on," she told them. "It's probably a thumb print on the X ray. Cancer doesn't run in our family, and none of our relatives has had lumps on their breasts—unless you count those socks Winnie used to stick in her bra."

Her mother left the table and shut herself in the bathroom, and Hannah became so cheerful she was just plain obnoxious. They both insisted on going with her to have the mammogram. They were going to feel pretty silly, Franny told them, when they found out they'd confused her X ray with somebody else's.

The three of them marched into the Radiology Department at Floyd County Hospital in Rome twenty minutes before the scheduled appointment and waited. The whole time she sat there, Franny felt oddly detached, as if this weren't happening to her.

Franny didn't know about most women, but by the time she had reached the age of thirty, she had very little modesty left. If those fun little visits to the gynecologist didn't take away the teaspoon of decorum remaining, the procedure for a mammogram should. She was rather heavy-breasted, and every time she was told to sling one up on that cold plastic plate, she felt like they were weighing hamburger. *I'll take a pound and a half today, please, and are you sure this is sirloin? Looks like a lot of fat to me.*

Today's technician was pleasant and efficient. And kind. A different radiologist would read the X rays and compare them with the others, she told her. The woman smiled a crisp, clean smile. "It won't be long now. I don't think you have anything to worry about."

That's when Franny started to worry: when somebody told her she didn't have anything to worry about. And it was the second time she'd heard it that day.

A few minutes later the technician poked her head in the door and told Franny she could get dressed, that the doctor would see her in a couple of minutes. Franny found a stack of dog-eared magazines on the window sill and chose the most recent and appealing. It featured an in-depth article about the first family's vacation retreat. George and Barbara's, that is. Franny read the whole thing. The couple of minutes stretched into five . . . ten . . . fifteen. Had they forgotten her completely? Or, protected by stacks of out-of-date magazines, had she survived a nuclear explosion that had wiped out an entire population? Franny was just about to find out when the woman returned for her.

The doctor was about Franny's age, short, with a bristly mustache and square bifocals. He showed her a display of a series of her mammograms against a lighted background. She hadn't had a man take this much interest in her breasts since . . . well, since Will died.

"I apologize for taking so long," he said, after offering her a seat. "But I'm sort of on the fence here. This could go either way." He pointed out five almost microscopic dots on the left breast. They looked as if somebody had dipped a ballpoint in white ink and scattered them in an area smaller than a pea. "Could be just calcium deposits," he said. "And most likely that's what they are, but if you were my wife or daughter, I'd want you to have a needle biopsy just to be sure."

Needle biopsy. Not two of her favorite words. No wonder he wanted her sitting down. "It's a fairly simple procedure done in out-patient surgery, but you'll want to confer with your doctor, possibly get another opinion."

The doctor's voice was gentle as he put his arm around her, gave her shoulder a pat. "I don't usually like to give odds, but in your case I'm about ninety-eight percent certain they won't find a thing. Really, Mrs. Hughes, I don't believe you've anything to worry about."

Franny's own doctor, John Winthrop, didn't seem seriously concerned when she called him later that day. In fact, she thought he could've sounded just the least bit distressed about it. "I've had several patients biopsied for spots about that size," he told her. "Turned out to be just calcium deposits about every time." He paused. "I don't want you going through this unless it's really necessary, Franny. First I'd like you to see Dr. Kirkland, a radiologist over in Cartersville. Patricia Kirkland went to Emory with my nephew, Tim. She won't guide you wrong."

And of course she would expect payment up front, Franny thought, taking note of the doctor's phone number. Her insurance would cover eighty percent of the cost, but she'd had to write a check for a hundred dollars for her afternoon session at the radiologist in Rome. Christmas was a-comin', and the turkey was looking more and more like a partridge in a bare tree! But Franny made the appointment, taking some comfort in the theory that Patricia Kirkland, having breasts of her own, wouldn't be too hasty to advise cutting on hers.

For supper the three watched a game show on television while eating a last-minute meal of scrambled eggs and grits. Nobody wanted to talk about how they had spent the afternoon. Franny didn't even want to think about it. They had agreed earlier they wouldn't say anything to Faith unless it seemed absolutely necessary. Nobody wanted to define necessary.

But Lucy would have to know, and it wasn't going to be easy.

Something good had happened to Lucy. Franny could tell by the look on her face as soon as she walked in the door, and she shoved her grim news behind her. Lucy had a *paying* job as assistant stage manager and a small speaking part in a play that would open after Christmas in New Jersey. "I'm getting closer, Mama," she said. And after hugging her mother and grandmother, ran the few blocks to share the news with her sister.

Hannah had left to spend Thanksgiving with her family, and that night after her mother went to bed, Franny had her younger daughter all to herself. Still, she couldn't bear to bring up the subject of the radiologist's findings, although the knowledge of it hovered like a rain cloud at a Sunday School picnic.

Even after the tiresome drive from Connecticut, Lucy had energy enough to keep them up talking till one in the morning. That was when it occurred to her to ask about her brother. Franny hadn't had the heart to tell her Gib wouldn't be there for Thanksgiving.

Lucy was small and blonde like her daddy's side, but she had the Gordon temperament. When she was small, she was either weeping or sunny. Her daddy called her "April." "What do you mean, he won't be here?" she asked. The two sipped tea by a feeble lick and flicker of a fire, and Sylvester made himself at home in her daughter's lap as though she'd never been away.

"We had a small problem in communication," Franny said, and told her about Gib's "good ole boy" experience.

Lucy looked at her with that superior little disapproving expression the younger generation reserves for doddering parents. "Gib's a grown man, Mama. He's used to staying out as late as he wants."

Franny returned the look—or tried to—over her cup. "So it's okay if he ends up smearing himself and whoever happens to come along all over the highway? That's a *grown* man?"

"Well, the drinking's stupid, but you're not responsible." She stroked the sleeping cat and wouldn't meet her mother's eyes. Gib was her big brother, her champion and defender. Now it was her time.

"Interesting word *responsible*." Franny set her cup aside. "That's the whole point, Lucy. Your brother is not responsible." She told her of her concerns about Wuzzy, their future together. "Don't you see? Coming in drunk, not telling us he'd be late—that was only an added worry and inconvenience. Gib is twenty-eight years old. I keep hoping he's going to mature, take stock of his life. But when? I'm getting too old to baby-sit."

"Gramolly always said he took after her great uncle Tobias," Lucy said.

"The one who traded his horse for a fiddle and joined a traveling tent show? Thanks for reminding me. Your brother was having a rough time, but he seemed to be handling it okay until this happened. Wuzzy didn't go along with his plans for the holidays. One little snag and he ties one on! To put it mildly, I kind of flipped out over this last episode, and it's upset your grandmother too. It happened so soon after THE HOME PLACE burned, and that tragedy with Dottie. She lost her cool with your brother I'm afraid."

"What do you mean?"

"More or less told him to shape up or ship out."

"Gramolly?" Lucy's eyes were as round as her teacup.

Franny smiled. "The very same. Your brother shipped out, so to speak."

"And you went along with this?" Her daughter seemed on the verge of shock.

"Lucy, dear, my only regret is *I* didn't say it sooner."

"Do you know where he is?"

"With a friend, he says. Shagg, I suppose—for now, at least. He's taken all his clothes—all but that tweed jacket Winnie gave him last Christmas. He never did like it."

When Gib was nine he had tied his new sneakers, his football jersey, and a couple of peanut butter sandwiches in an old towel and run away from home. Faith trailed him at a discreet distance for a few blocks until he ate the sandwiches and wandered home to watch his favorite cartoon show. This time it was going to take more than Popeye to get Gibson back on track.

Lucy examined the dregs of tea in her cup. "When did all this happen?"

"Last week. He must've left early Saturday morning. When I went up to change his sheets, I found an empty room and a message scrawled on the back of a bank deposit slip."

She frowned. "What kind of message?"

"Said he thought it best to go away for awhile, and that he'd call."

"And did he?"

"Yes, that same day as a matter of fact. Said he was staying with a friend and would be in touch. I didn't talk with him. Your grandmother answered the phone."

"You know Gib, Mama, he's always been his own person. Who knows what he'll do next?" Lucy shrugged. "It would be kinda nice, though, if he thought of somebody else for a change."

Franny went over and sat on the arm of her chair, put her arm around her. "We're not going to let this ruin our Thanksgiving, honey. We have too much to celebrate: your new job, Faith's pregnancy. Your brother's facing a difficult challenge. Let's think of it as a crossroad, an adventure."

Tomorrow, she thought as her daughter kissed her goodnight. She would tell Lucy tomorrow.

But her mother spared her the trouble. "Your mama's got a lump in her breast," she announced to her granddaughter the next morning at breakfast.

"What?" Lucy froze with a glass of orange juice halfway to her mouth.

Franny set the kettle down so hard the stove shook. "Why did you tell her that? I was going to do it in my own good time."

"When? I know you, Franny. You'd let the holiday get past us.

Not telling Faith is one thing, but Lucy needs to know. You need for her to know."

"I meant to wait and tell you when I saw Dr. Kirkland on Friday," she said to Lucy, who came and locked her arms around her.

"Then I plan to go with you," she said. "Faith's always been the one in charge. Now it's my time to be bossy."

That afternoon Franny was in J.J.'s Super Mart with Lucy buying oranges for tomorrow's spiced punch when she heard somebody call her name. There, standing between the broccoli and the new potatoes, was Travis Kimbrough's daddy. Only she knew it couldn't be him because Travis's father died about ten years ago. It had to be Travis himself. Darned if he didn't look just like him! That just showed how long it had been since the two of them had seen each other, Franny thought.

"Frances Virginia! Come over here and give us a hug! And who's that gorgeous thing you have with you?" He tossed a couple of apples aside and held out his arms. His paprika hair had turned almost white and his freckles had run together, but Travis Kimbrough's smile was still big. And so was his stomach. When she hugged him, Franny almost bounced.

Travis was spending the weekend with his son, Jimmy, and his family, he told them. Franny helped him pick out some apples and they carried their produce to the mile-long line at the express register. The three of them were standing there talking when in walked the statuesque Janine, this time in a jaunty blue tam and matching sweater and without Walter Curtis. She smiled and waved as if she knew them, then moved off into the pyramids of cranberry sauce.

"Travis, who in the world is that?" Franny asked. "She acts like we're old buddies, and Mama says she's renovating a house around here."

He frowned. "The leggy blonde? Never saw her before. Believe me, I'd remember!"

"Name's Janine. Seems cozy with Walter Curtis."

"So she's the one! Wyndie—you know, my Jimmy's wife—says she's opening a dress shop at the new mall. Janine's Boutique it's called. I think Walter has an interest in it."

"And in her," Franny suggested.

"You think so?" Travis craned to see over the head-high shelf of confections by the check-out counter. "Must be somebody special then. Neely's vetoed all the others."

Travis grabbed at an apple that was about to roll to the floor. "Say, how's your mama? Heard about the old place burning. God, what an awful thing! Poor old Hollywood Dot."

"It hasn't been easy," Franny said. "Having Hannah around has helped."

"Is she still in town? Heard she was staying with you."

"She's spending Thanksgiving with her family," Franny said, making room in her basket for the bag of nuts and some tangerines Lucy thought they needed.

"I'd sure like to see her. Look, you're going to this dedication thing in February, aren't you? For the new school, I mean. Maybe we can have a reunion or something. Be fun to get together."

"Why don't you come by the house sometime this weekend and we'll talk about it," Franny said.

"Great. I want to see Miss Molly anyhow." Travis glanced behind him and lowered his voice. "Do you all still have *real* ambrosia and Japanese fruitcake?"

They were finishing dessert the next day when Travis stuck his head in the door and hollered. Franny's mother made a big to-do over the yellow roses he brought, although where he got them, Franny couldn't imagine. They had always been her mother's favorite, and not everybody remembered that. Her mama loved Travis. He was "one of hers," she said, and she forgave him in turn for breaking her porcelain candle holder—the one shaped like a lily—spilling permanent ink on her kitchen floor, and riding his bicycle over her iris.

Faith made a place for Travis at the table and Lucy served him a generous dish of ambrosia, along with a thick slice of cake, which he happily devoured. "Can heaven be any better than this?" he asked, scraping up the last smidgen of pineapple.

"I doubt it," Franny said, "but probably neither of us will ever find out."

Later, while Reilly and the girls played hearts with her mother, Franny and Travis went out on the porch. It was a mild afternoon, what Molly Gordon called "sweater weather," and the two sat on the steps in the sun. The porch, Franny noticed, needed painting again, and that sagging spot in the corner would soon have to be replaced.

"If you and Hannah will try to get in touch with the rest of the class—" Travis frowned. "How many of us are left now anyway?"

"Twenty-seven last count."

"Not bad, considering, I guess." He looked over at where the grammar school used to be. "If you can locate whoever's left, we can have the party out at our cabin. I've still got that little place at the lake Daddy built back in the fifties. Joan and I used to bring the kids there weekends, turn them loose."

"I'm sure Neely Louise will help," Franny said. "And Shirley." Lord, she'd better not forget Shirley! Self-preservation is a strong incentive.

Travis stood and held out his hand. "Let's walk around the block. It's depressing looking at the school that isn't there—and that charcoaled house on the other side of it. How do you stand it, Franny?"

She shrugged. "Do I have a choice? Anyway, it's temporary. They're supposed to bulldoze it any day now. The Baptists have bought the old home place lot for future parking." And wouldn't her Methodist grandmother whirl in her grave if she knew?

Except for the school and the blackened remains of her mother's old home, that part of Sallie's Station looked much as it did when

127

they were children. The Canfields' place on the corner was yellow now instead of white, and the rambling frame house where Travis grew up looked almost the same in spite of the luxurious new pool that took up most of the backyard. They circled the area on the other side of the school and took a shortcut along the narrow alley that ran behind it.

Travis leaned over to inspect the culvert that intersected the road, then pointed toward what used to be the school playground. "Look Franny, they've covered it."

"Covered what?" She was in a hurry to get back home. Too much coffee at dinner.

"The drainage ditch. Remember?"

"How could I forget? They covered that old thing years ago, thank goodness. It was dangerous."

"We used to pretend there were monsters in there. I think I halfway believed it," he said.

"Maybe there were." Franny walked faster, not waiting.

Travis hurried to catch up with her. "Don't tell me you're still afraid of the tunnel troll, Frances Virginia."

When she looked up at him, his smile slowly faded. "You mean the thing that happened that day?" The face that had been animated only seconds before seemed to shut down as though the power behind it shorted out. "Hell, Franny, how were we to know? We were just kids! If I could change things, don't you think I would? Besides somebody had to do something—you know that." He looked at the ground as he walked. "Is it true, Franny, that she . . . you know . . . had a thing for girls?"

"From all I've heard, I'm pretty sure of it," Franny said. "Thank goodness I wasn't her type!" The thought of it made her Thanksgiving dinner squirm unhappily in her stomach.

"Guess we never will know that whole story," he said. "Wouldn't it be good if we could erase the parts of our lives we didn't like?" Travis said. "Get rid of them once and for all. I reckon it would take a pretty big eraser, though, to rub out a blot like Havergal."

A blot. A mistake. The description suited, Franny thought. She hadn't consciously thought of the woman in ages, now suddenly within the last few months, she seemed to be back in their lives like a bad stomachache.

Chapter Fourteen

November 20, 1943

Franny stopped at the corner to watch a convoy of khaki-colored trucks rumble past. It was the Saturday before Thanksgiving, and she was free, free, free! For a little while anyway. Young, fresh-faced soldiers called and waved to her as she waited to cross the street on her way to visit Aunt Six. Franny waved back, smiling. Once one had tossed her peppermint, and another, chewing gum.

Even Winnie had abandoned her hit-and-miss efforts at *Humoresque* on the upright and sprinted outside to wave when she heard the drone of the troop-laden trucks. She was still corresponding with a tall, blond boy named Larry who had thrown her his address back in September.

Miriam Thatcher, walking to town with little Tommy in his stroller, stopped and lifted the baby in her arms. Tommy had never seen his father, a gunner with the Eighth Air Force over in England, but his mother kept a big picture on her dresser and showed it to Tommy every day so the baby would know him when he came home. The two of them lived a few houses up the street with Tommy's Grandmother Thatcher and a maiden aunt, and Franny's mama said it would be a miracle if that baby wasn't spoiled rotten with three women fussing over him.

Franny found her aunt and Mr. Rittenhouse at the kitchen table eating apples and cheese. Mr. Rittenhouse pared the fruit with a steady twist of his fingers and gave Franny the corkscrew of pink, transparent peeling. "Throw it over your shoulder and it will tell your sweetheart's initials," he said.

The peeling flopped behind her chair, curled in what looked like the letter "R." Franny couldn't think of anybody whose name began with an R except for R. W. Duggan, and he certainly wasn't her boyfriend. "Huh!" she said.

Mr. Rittenhouse whittled a sliver of cheese which he sandwiched between two wedges of fruit, then popped the whole thing in his mouth and chewed for a long time. Aunt Six did the same. She looked rested now, but had shrunk somehow. She'd been to the beauty parlor and her hair was a vivid blue. She patted it between bites.

"Honey Sue called this morning," she said, feeding Hellcat a crumb of cheese. "Wanted to know if I *slept* well last night." She whacked a slice of apple. "I said of course I slept well, I always *sleep* well . . . it's the getting up that's hard to do."

Mr. Rittenhouse smiled. "You're not staying alone?"

"Molly's with me at night this week," Aunt Six explained. "And Precious stays during the day—just until I get my strength back, Dr. Ludlow says." She poked her friend's bony arm with a scarlet-tipped finger. "I'm younger than you are, Double-A. A lot younger. You live by yourself just fine."

He nodded. "Indeed I do, but there may come a time when that's not possible."

Aunt Six leaned across the table. "And then what?"

Mr. Rittenhouse concentrated on his apple. "I'll worry about that when the time comes."

"Uh-huh!" Aunt Six moaned. "And you don't have a Honey Sue

131

pestering you all the time, treating you like you don't have enough sense to put on your drawers in the morning."

Franny looked to see what his reaction would be to the mention of underwear, but he seemed not to have heard.

Her aunt poured steaming brown tea into cups and Franny dribbled milk into hers. Mr. Rittenhouse took lemon. He offered a slice to Aunt Six.

"Thank you, but I take my coffee, my tea, and my liquor straight," she said.

Franny giggled. The only time she had ever seen her aunt drink whiskey was in eggnog at Christmastime.

Precious rumbaed past them down the hall pushing a dust mop and singing *Brazil* at the top of her voice, and Mr. Rittenhouse put a hand to one ear. "What's that Precious is singing?"

"That's her song for the week," Aunt Six said. "Kinda catchy, isn't it?"

"I like it," Franny said. "Makes me want to dance. Wonder what she'll sing next week."

"Probably *Don't Get Around Much Anymore.*" Her aunt sipped tea. "Staying here with me every day ties her down pretty much I'm afraid. She won't say so, but I know she's had to give up a lot of her church work."

"Then be glad she thinks you're more important." Mr. Rittenhouse set aside his cup. "Now, Miss Frances Virginia, if you'll go find the Parcheesi board, I'll challenge you to a game."

But her old friend seemed not to have his mind on playing. She had won three games out of five when they heard voices in the hall, and Precious poked her head in the doorway. "Company!" she said, leading little Tommy Thatcher into the kitchen by one finger. "Look who's come to see us."

Mrs. Thatcher followed with a crusty brown loaf of bread that filled the kitchen with its warm yeasty smell.

Aunt Six had to have a piece at once. "Miriam, it's just what I've been wanting." She cut thick slices for everyone. "How do you find the time?"

"I have too much time as it is," Miriam admitted. She smiled. "And it's such a messy job, nobody dares come into the kitchen. It's about the only time I get to be alone."

"I know what you mean." Aunt Six offered Tommy a cracker which he smeared all over his face. The baby laughed and reached for Hellcat, who seemed just as intrigued as he was.

"You scratch that baby and you'll end up in a gunny sack in Salacoa Creek," her aunt threatened. But the cat allowed Tommy to stroke his fur, and with a sudden twitch of his long black tail, curled into a ball under the table.

They played a couple of more games of Parcheesi after the Thatchers left, but it didn't take long for Franny to see the old man's heart wasn't in it.

"A penny for your thoughts, Double-A?" Aunt Six said, noticing his preoccupation.

He blinked and smiled, then finally rattled the dice in the cardboard shaker. "Sorry, afraid I'm not much competition today."

"Something on your mind? Nothing serious, I hope."

Mr. Rittenhouse shook his head. "Not if I can help it." His blue eyes gleamed as he rolled the dice.

Franny remembered what he had said about wanting a blue balloon. It was hard to guess what Mr. Rittenhouse was thinking.

She didn't see Mr. Rittenhouse again until Thanksgiving Day. Her mother had invited her old friend to a special holiday dinner, and Franny helped her sister set the table with their grandmother's delicate gold-scalloped china, and silver, polished to a gleam on a crisp white cloth. Between basting the turkey and chopping celery and onion for the cornbread dressing, their mother fashioned a centerpiece of fruits, nuts, and autumn leaves. Franny stood in the doorway admiring it. A coal fire glowed orange in the fireplace, and a shaft of sunlight struck a water goblet like a magic wand.

She wandered into the kitchen where her mother stirred eggs and stock into the dressing. "When are the others coming?" Franny asked.

"In a little while." Her mama opened the Frigidaire, looked inside with a blank expression, then closed it again. "Your daddy's gone to collect Aunt Six, and Mr. Rittenhouse is probably on his way. Why don't you put on your coat and meet him?"

Franny ran through dry brown leaves on Salacoa Street and up Wisteria Hill. Maybe Mr. Rittenhouse would ask her inside for a tour of his treasures. Franny never tired of looking at the shelves lined with pottery with geometric designs, shells and shark's teeth, colorful beads, scary masks, and the dainty carved ivory called scrimshaw.

"Come in, come in! What a nice surprise." Mr. Rittenhouse met her at the door, black tie in place as usual. "I was just about to leave, but I do want to take your mother a bottle of my mascadine wine." He waved her into a crowded little study. "Why don't you have a look at some of my curiosities while I run to the basement and get it?"

Franny browsed happily among the relics, examined a shell called a "bleeding tooth," touched the tip of a bluish-brown arrowhead. It wasn't nearly as pretty, she thought, as the one she had found.

Franny looked about and liked what she saw: a rocking chair by the window with an open book in the seat . . . a bowl of rosy apples. She liked the little brown house, the stone fireplace, the narrow casement windows. A short hall led from the study to a bed-sitting room at the back, and Franny glanced through the open door. The paneled walls were painted a soft yellow, and books lined one side of the room. Framed documents, maps, and brownish photographs covered the other walls.

Curiosity drew her inside. A younger Mr. Rittenhouse posed in front of a crude hut. Another smiled down from an elephant. *An ele-*

phant! Franny smiled too. The shelf above his desk was lined with a collection of large bright mugs. Franny picked one up and looked on the bottom: *Made in Germany.* A yellowed parchment framed in black verified that Albert Adolf Rittenhouse had successfully completed the course of study at Emory College in 1881.

Could that have been his father? No, Mr. Rittenhouse would have been a very young man then. She jumped, startled at the sound of his footsteps on the basement stairs, and fled into the study.

Albert Adolf. *Adolf,* like Hitler. No wonder he used the initials Double-A!

Later that afternoon, after Mr. Rittenhouse had left for home, Franny told Aunt Six what she had seen.

"I know," her aunt said quietly.

"You mean you knew all along? You knew his name and didn't tell?"

"Frances Virginia, if Mr. Rittenhouse wanted us to know his name, he would use it. Apparently he doesn't care for it. You can certainly understand that."

"But Adolf!" Franny made a face. "Sounds like Hitler."

"I suppose it's an Austrian name," her aunt explained. "Or German. Mr. Rittenhouse is of German extraction."

"He is? How do you know?"

Aunt Six took off her bifocals and looked at her. "Franny, Rittenhouse is a German name; so is Weber, Bessemer, Westinghouse . . . My goodness, he's made trips to Germany at least twice before all this came about. He has relatives over there." She shook her head at Franny's shocked expression. "It's nothing to be ashamed of. He doesn't try to hide it. Double-A was born in this country. He's a loyal citizen and a very good friend."

But the fact that their old friend shared a name with that horrible man was like a pebble in Franny's shoe. She told Hannah about it the next day.

Hannah only shrugged. "So what, Franny V.? Mr. Rittenhouse

was born before old Hitler, wasn't he? How did his mama know that nasty man would come along and ruin the name?"

The two had crawled into the drainage ditch behind the school—to see if Cephus had left any whiskey there, Hannah said, but mostly because there was no school the day after Thanksgiving and they didn't have anything else to do.

Franny and her friends thought of the ditch as a secret tunnel, but their parents called it a sewer and warned them to stay away. The deep gutter, open for several yards, ran alongside the school and between the Whitfields' house and Miss Opal's where it was screened by a fence on both sides. From there the covered ditch ran under Salacoa Street and emptied into a connecting system behind the Thatchers.

There were creatures in the tunnel. Hideous creatures. Franny, having invented them, knew them well. One was the Tunnel Troll, a hunched, hairy gnome with burning eyes, ferocious claws, and a nose that could sniff out children. Another was the Slimy Sewer Snort, a cross between a giant lizard and a bat. Green, with a wingspan wide enough to block the passage, he attached himself to the ceiling and snorted before attacking. He considered fingers and toes a great delicacy.

In the tunnel's eerie darkness, the monsters became a reality. Franny sensed their presence, heard the blood-chilling sniff of the Troll, the warning snort of the green bat-lizard. Sometimes she even felt the disgusting brush of his wings.

Franny was glad when they reached the Whitfields' yard where they could climb the slippery sides of the gutter and cut across Mrs. Littlejohn's yard to home. She was struggling for a toehold when Hannah grabbed her arm. "Wait, I hear somebody!"

Franny stood still and listened. *We-e-e gath-er to-ge-e-ther to ask the Lord's ble-e-ss-i-i-ings* . . . She peeked through the shattering sumac. On the other side of the fence Mrs. Whitfield rehearsed her solo for Sunday's church service while taking her wash from the line.

He has-tens and chas-tens his wi-i-l-l to make knownnn . . . One at a time she snapped a jillion dish towels and folded them into her big wicker basket.

"We can't let her see us," Hannah said. "We'll have to go through the tunnel to the Thatchers."

Franny nodded. If Betty Joyce's mother saw them, she was sure to tell their parents. Silently they entered the dark passage, trying to avoid the slick, filthy sides. In the darkest stretch of the ditch they crawled over slippery rocks until they reached firmer ground. Franny thought of snakes and spiders, listened for the suspicious grunting of imaginery demons, and tugged the sleeves of her navy cardigan around her fists. The damp gutter smelled like a garbage can in August and she'd just as soon not know what she was sliding through. Their feet made sucking sounds as they walked, and ahead of her, Hannah stumbled over a pile of loose rocks. The grating rattle echoed through the passage.

Franny heard traffic overhead when they reached Salacoa Street and knew they were almost there. A few more feet and she could see light at the end, only there wasn't as much of it as there should be. It was getting dark.

In her rush to get out, Franny stepped into a crevice between two rocks. The rough granite tore into her ankle, and when she tried to pull her foot away, the larger rock rolled onto her shoe, wedging it like a vise. Hannah whirled about at her cry. "What's wrong?"

"Foot's caught. I can't get it loose! See if you can move this rock . . . and hurry, it hurts!"

Hannah tugged at the stone. "I can't budge it, Franny. Can't you pull your foot out?"

"Every time I try, it cuts even more." Franny touched the back of her ankle and it felt sticky and warm. The weight of the rock was crushing, and pain throbbed like the devil's own heartbeat. "My foot's smushed!" she cried.

Hannah squeezed her hand. "I'll go for help."

"No! Don't leave me. Try again, you can do it."

"No I can't, Franny V. The rock's too big. I'll have to find somebody to help." Hannah gave her arm a pat. "I'll be right back."

"Hurry! Please hurry." Franny closed her eyes and heard her friend moving away, slipping, scrambling over rocks. Shivering, she crouched, listening to the slosh of sluggish water. Somewhere above her it dripped from a drain in the side. *Plunk! Plunk!* Franny almost forgot her pain for remembering John Garfield in *The Fallen Sparrow* who had been threatened by the same terrifying sound. Would the man with the dragging foot come after her? Was he here, now, in the sewer?

A shadow loomed behind her. Did it move? Was that a snort? Franny held her breath. She wished she had listened to her mother. Miss O'Donnell would have to write Lieutenant Gregory about her unfortunate end, and he would be sad. She wondered what her old principal would do in her situation. "You'll see things through," he had told her. "I can count on you." She was glad he couldn't see her now.

The stench made Franny's stomach turn. It smelled like something dead. A rat? Blackness surrounded her. All she could see was a speck of gray light at the end. A witch—if there was such a thing—could be standing right beside her. Travis said Miss Havergal was a witch, said she shed her skin at night and turned into a cat. Witches knew everything, he said, and could go everywhere.

Did she know how much Franny hated her?

Chapter Fifteen

"I don't know." Dr. Kirkland peered at her mammogram. "Whatever it is, there isn't much of it, but there's something . . . something about it that bothers me." The lump hadn't shown up in ultrasound, nor had she been able to locate it manually. Franny couldn't see the reason for all the hoopla over five puny dots.

The doctor sat across from her studying the file in front of her. Patricia Kirkland could be any of the young mothers Franny saw in the grocery store, running in at the last minute for milk and bread before collecting a carpool of first graders. Blonde and pretty with a hint of pink lipstick, she didn't look much older than Faith.

Now she looked up at her. "I recommend you go ahead with it," she said. "I'd rather not take a chance."

"You think I should have the biopsy?"

She smiled. "I don't think there's any reason to be concerned, but if by some slight chance they do find something, we'll be getting rid of it before it gets any larger." Dr. Kirkland took her hand in both of hers as Franny got ready to leave. "You will ask your surgeon to send me a report, won't you? I want to know how this turns out."

Surgeon. *Her* surgeon? The last time she'd had surgery was when she had her tonsils out at eight, and Dr. Ludlow, dead now for at least twenty years, had been a general practitioner. Franny didn't know any surgeons.

But John Winthrop did. He gave her the name of a group in Rome. There were about eight of them, and every one of them was competent, skilled, even brilliant—all those things doctors say about each other. Franny made an appointment with the grouchiest one. Of course, she didn't know that at the time.

Dr. Herman. Leonard Herman. He had close-cropped gray hair, a long nose that looked as though it had been caught in the crack of a door, and talked with sort of a hiss. Eventually she came to call him Lennie, and in time, even Lennie Baby. Behind his back, of course.

Without changing his expression or tone of voice, the surgeon explained the procedure and drew a diagram of what he planned to do. Franny could tell he thought he was wasting his time on her. She agreed.

The doctor had a cancellation on Monday, his nurse told her, and if the hospital hadn't already filled that slot, she would get them on the schedule. Franny thought of those old Westerns where the damsel in distress screams her head off while the runaway stagecoach careens toward the cliff. This stage was moving too fast for her, but she didn't dare jump.

Actually it worked out for the best because Lucy, who planned to drive back on Tuesday, could be there with her, leaving Hannah to stay with her mother. Aside from the family and Betty Joyce, Franny didn't tell anyone else what she was going to do. Faith thought her mother and sister were in Rome shopping for the boots and coat Lucy planned to take back to New Jersey.

That morning she waited for Lennie in her chic little gown and cap. The radiologist who inserted the needle—or wire—that protruded from her breast, (covered by a cone of sorts, thank goodness!) said the white dots were so small he had trouble finding them, and he had performed this procedure on only one other woman whose spots were smaller than hers. They took a series of films to help guide the surgeon's hand and sent her back to wait.

The pain was minimal. They gave her a local anesthetic and something to make her drowsy, but she knew what was going on. The surgery took less than an hour.

Lucy waited with her mother until the drowsiness wore off and the nurses were satisfied with her vital signs. They were reading aloud to each other from one of the more sensational women's magazines—something about making a love nest out of your bathroom—when somebody said, "Knock, knock!" and the blue-striped curtain parted. R. W. Duggan stepped inside. Dr. R. W. Duggan in his wrinkled green outfit of the kind Franny's surgeon had worn.

"You'll get rid of that thing if you're smart," Franny said. "I hear the warden's been looking for you."

He smiled and spoke to Lucy, then leaned over and kissed Franny's forehead. "One of my maternity patients delivered a little while ago. I saw them wheeling you out of surgery as I was going in. Franny, why didn't you tell me about this?"

"Women have babies as outpatients now? I'm surprised you don't just set up a tent on the lawn."

"Don't change the subject. When did all this come about?"

She told him. "The lab report should be back by Wednesday, but I don't think Lennie Baby expects any trouble."

He raised his brows. "Lennie Baby?" Then laughed when she explained. "Oh, Franny! Nobody else but you." R.W. looked at his watch. "How about if I treat you two to lunch? When are they letting you go?"

"Soon," Franny said, "but I'll pass on the hospital cafeteria, thank you just the same. I'm suspicious of their liver."

"Me too. We'll go across the street to Martha's Kitchen. Good home cookin'—clogs your arteries, but it tastes great. I think they get a kick-back from the cardiac people."

"Sounds good to me," Franny told him. "But I warn you, I haven't had breakfast."

After R.W. left, Lucy helped her dress. Franny could have done just fine by herself, but she could tell this was something her daughter wanted to do. Slowly Lucy brushed her mother's hair, then put her arms around her. "Mama, I hate leaving you like this. I wish I could stay."

"Don't you dare," Franny said, holding Lucy's face in her hands. "You go up there and knock 'em dead. I'll be fine. Besides, I have Hannah. We'll call you as soon as we know anything."

"I wish you'd let me tell Faith." She tied first one shoe, then the other, just as Franny had for her.

"No use worrying over nothing. You know how Faith is."

Lucy frowned as she helped her with her coat. "When I get a hold of that Gibson Hughes, I'm gonna slap him into Never-Never Land! Where on earth do you think he could be?"

Franny didn't know. She hadn't heard from Gib's friend Shagg, but he was due home sometime the past weekend his mother had said, and Franny planned to call until she chased him down. The day before, Lucy had talked with somebody at the radio station where her brother worked who told her Gib had taken a short leave of absence, but she had no idea where he was. How like her son to do something like this, Franny thought. She had always been healthy, so he had no reason to believe she might be otherwise, but what if something happened to his grandmother?

Betty Joyce brought over cornbread and a big pot of homemade vegetable soup for their supper. Hannah served it, and Lucy washed the dishes. Franny was beginning to feel like Lady Astorbutt until Lucy announced the pipes were leaking underneath the sink. They had replaced so much of the plumbing, there shouldn't be any of the original left, but it always managed to squirt out in a different place. Franny put in a call to the plumber and got on his waiting list. When he finally got around to them, she might as well get him to do something about that upstairs toilet that wanted to run night and day.

Again Franny tried to call Shagg, but he still wasn't in. She was hoping he might be able to give her some clue as to why her son would take a leave of absence this close to Christmas, especially since he was having trouble with his marriage. She was tempted to phone Wuzzy, but was afraid she might not want to talk with her. After all, she *was* Gib's mother.

Lucy was polishing off the last piece of cornbread when the phone rang, and she took her last few bites into the hall to answer it.

But the cornbread remained uneaten when she returned after several minutes and tried to get Franny's attention behind her mother's back. "Telephone, Mama." Her voice sounded flat, not like her Lucy at all. "Wuzzy," she whispered as Franny walked past her to the phone.

"Franny, do you know where Gib is? I've been trying to get in touch with him since I got back from skiing." Wuzzy sounded both annoyed and worried. Gibson did that to people. "Nobody seems to know where he is. Have you talked with him?"

"He called the day after he left," Franny told her. "We knew not to expect him for Thanksgiving."

"Did he say where he was calling from?" she asked.

"No, I just assumed he'd be going home to Savannah with Shagg." And frankly, Franny didn't care if her son had feasted at the Golden Arches after taking off the way he did. "Did you try the station?" she asked.

Of course she had. Franny swallowed and felt the familiar gnawing of fear in her stomach. Damn him for doing this to her!

"All I got was an answering machine. I left three messages. Nothing! Finally spoke with the receptionist there. She says Gib hasn't been in, and nobody answers at Shagg's." Wuzzy was quiet for a minute. "You don't suppose he's sick, do you?"

"No, of course not. I'm sure there's some explanation. Try not to worry." A lie. She not only thought he was sick, she thought he was tossing about in some barren motel room with a raging fever and nobody there to care. Or worse still, he'd been mugged, stripped of his identity, and was lying in Atlanta's Grady Memorial Hospital with tubes in his body.

"Wuzzy, you're not keeping something from me, are you? I mean, did anything happen between you and Gib—other than the misunderstanding about the ski trip—that would cause him to do something . . ." *don't say, stupid, Franny . . .* "drastic?"

She could almost see her shrug. "Not that I can think of. I told him we had to talk when I got back. I guess he thinks—I don't know what he thinks! But if you hear from him, please tell him to call."

Franny promised she would and asked her to do the same. She looked at her mother smiling at something Hannah said. Lucy sat on the arm of her chair, and now and then Molly Gordon absently stroked her granddaughter's hand. How could she tell her mother her only grandson had disappeared?

Gib and Shagg McKenzie had visited back and forth since their freshman days at the university, and Shagg's parents came to the wedding when Gib and Wuzzy married. Somewhere Franny had their address in Savannah.

She found it in the little box of index cards stuck back on her closet shelf and was relieved to find it listed a phone number as well. Her mother's hearing wasn't as good as it used to be, still Franny called from the upstairs phone.

Geraldine McKenzie was delighted to hear from her, she said, and inquired after everyone's health. Franny told her they were fine and asked about theirs, although, to be honest, she really didn't give a fig. How do you ask a relative stranger if she knows where your son is?

Franny had known Geraldine since their sons roomed together their freshman year. She dressed in what Lucy called "expensive old lady clothes," had her hair done every Thursday, and divided her time between charity work and bridge at the club. Whenever Franny spent time with her, it almost wore her out trying to think of something to say, and she couldn't bring herself to admit why she'd called. In the end, she made light of it.

"That scalawag Gib's gone off somewhere and I need to get in touch. I wondered if he might be with Shagg. And did they happen to mention where they'd be?" *Oh, silly, silly me! I don't have sense enough to get in out of the rain. Won't you please take pity on me and help me find my son?* She would dearly love to slap people who talked like that, but when it came to her children's welfare, Franny Hughes had no pride.

This was met by a silence that lasted nearly as long as the Ice Age. "Oh. Dear. My goodness, Frances, I'm afraid we haven't seen him. Shagg was here for most of the weekend—wouldn't miss Thanksgiving here at home—or so he says." The woman laughed. "Frankly, I think the real attraction is Esther Lynn's tipsy trifle.

"Shagg left last Saturday for London. Some kind of business meeting . . . something about software." She cleared her throat. "I don't believe he's due back until the end of the week. To tell you the truth, I haven't the faintest idea where he's staying over there, but if he should call, I'll ask him about Gib if you'd like."

"I'd appreciate that," Franny said, hoping she didn't sound as desperate as she felt.

And maybe it was just as well. With Gib on her mind, she didn't have time to worry too much about what the biopsy would reveal.

Chapter Sixteen

November 26, 1943

Franny's legs ached from crouching in the same position, and her foot hurt so she couldn't think of anything else. Each time she tried to move, the hateful rock pressed and grated until she was sure her foot looked like the bloody meatloaf her mother smushed through the grinder. And she couldn't feel her toes! Were they sliding around inside her shoe in a puddle of blood? Would she be like President Roosevelt who was paralyzed from polio and have to spend the rest of her life in a wheelchair? Franny didn't even want to think about her shoe, probably ruined beyond repair, and her parents would have to use precious ration coupons to get her another pair.

And where was Hannah? Hit by a car? Dead? And Franny would die, too, because no one knew to look for her in the tunnel. Franny clung to the slippery sides and yelled.

"Franny? Franny Gordon? Where are you?" Somebody answered, but it wasn't Hannah. It was a man. She heard his footsteps crunching through the sewer, saw the yellow circle of flashlight bobbing in the darkness.

"Over here!" Franny yelled. "I can't move, and it hurts!"

"I'm coming!" he called. "Keep talking so I can find you."

The beam of light grew wider, bounced off the walls, streaked across the muddy water. Franny couldn't see the man's face. Maybe Hannah had brought her daddy. That was why it had taken her so long—she had gone home for help.

"Here!" she shouted. "Over here by the wall . . . oh, please hurry!"

The light struck her face. Franny closed her eyes. "I see you!" the man shouted. "Hold on, Franny, I'm coming."

His voice . . . it seemed familiar, but it wasn't Hannah's daddy. The man with the flashlight approached from the other side of the water, his long legs jumped the stream in one leap. "It's all right now, Franny. I'll get you out of here." The light crisscrossed the rock on her foot, cast wavering circles on the walls, and Franny saw his face. *Damascus Jones.* She screamed.

"Here, here, you're going to be all right." His cold hand touched her face.

I'm dead, Franny thought, and Damascus Jones is going to carry me away and do those awful things Travis says undertakers do to people. "I'm not dead!" she shouted, flailing wildly with her fists. "I'm not dead!"

"I should hope not." He grasped her firmly by the shoulders. "Now be still, Frances, be very still and hold on to me. I'm going to move that rock."

"Where's Hannah? I want Mama," Franny cried, still struggling.

"Hannah's gone to get your parents." The man's voice was calm, almost soothing. "Now, Franny, I want you to pretend you're a statue. You've played slinging statues, haven't you?"

"Yes." She gulped. Was he going to swing her against the sides of the gully, bash her head on the stones?

"If you keep on thrashing about, you could dislodge that rock, wedge your foot even deeper."

"Don't hurt me! Please don't hurt me. I want to go home."

"Then be still." His voice was sharper. "Hold on to me like I said. I'm going to try and lift this rock." Damascus Jones loosened his hold on her arms. "Now, it might hurt some when I move it because your foot is probably numb, so remember—you're a statue. Be as still as you can." He waited. "Okay?"

"Okay," she said finally.

Franny felt a sharp, cold pain as he lifted the heavy rock, but she clenched her teeth and shut her eyes as tightly as she could. Her breath came in deep, jagged gasps as the rock rolled to one side.

"All right, Franny, that's fine." She opened her eyes to discover she had both arms around his neck. "Just keep holding on," he said. "I'm going to carry you out of here." He lifted her foot and eased her up in his arms. "Hang on now," he said. "We'll have to go slow so we don't jar you. Wouldn't do for both of us to fall." There was a hint of a smile in his voice. "You're a brave girl, a good soldier, but don't tell anybody or they might draft you."

Franny tried to laugh just to show him she was a good sport, but all she could manage was a stiff smile which seemed dry on her face.

"Why, they might even take me in the army when they find out I can see in the dark with one eye," he added.

So what Hannah said was true: Damascus Jones really did have a glass eye! "Maybe they will," Franny said.

"Afraid not." He stepped carefully over a tumble of stones. Just ahead Franny saw the blessed gray light from the Thatchers' backyard, heard her mother call her name. "I've tried to enlist," Damascus Jones said, panting slightly, "but I guess I'll just have to stay here and rescue young ladies."

"I'm glad," Franny said and meant it.

The next day Damascus Jones brought Franny a whole box of chocolate-covered cherries. Dr. Ludlow had to take seven stitches in her foot and Franny wore one of her daddy's big socks over the bandage. She had to wear a bedroom shoe until the swelling went down and was still hobbling around a little when they heard the news about Miss Willie.

* * * * *

Franny laughed when Miss Willie Llewellyn died. She didn't mean to. Miss Willie was her friend and she knew she would miss her, but Franny had never seen a dead person before. Shirley Puckett said they were flabby. She had touched her great aunt Ethel, she said, and she had been soft, and kind of cold. Of course Shirley said a lot of things, and most of them were lies, but as Franny stood beside the casket—to tell Miss Willie goodbye, her mother said—she thought about what Shirley had said, and giggles oozed out like jelly from a doughnut. Horrified, Franny slapped her hands over her mouth and ran from the room. Her mother thought she was crying.

The funeral was held right there in the Llewellyns' front parlor so Miss Willie's dogs could attend. She had wanted it that way. The four of them sat there just as good as you please and never barked once, although Joker looked like he was crying inside. It was the first time Franny had been allowed in the front door at the Llewellyns' and she had never seen the parlor. She hoped she'd never see it again. The room was dark and cold and smelled like a basement. Everyone sat on folding chairs Damascus Jones had furnished and whispered to one another.

Later Franny thought about going to the cemetery to tell Miss Willie she was sorry for laughing the way she did, but her old friend probably couldn't hear her buried as deep as she was. Franny wondered what it was like being shut in a box like that with dirt piled on top of you. Winnie had taught her a song about worms crawling in you when you died: *The worms crawl in, the worms crawl out, the worms play pinocle on your snout . . .* It made her sick to think of them crawling on Miss Willie.

Miss Willie would never dry her hair in the sun, never eat popcorn again. Franny's mother explained that the spirit didn't die, but went to live with God, and that Miss Willie was in heaven with Jesus.

Franny knew Miss Willie would go to heaven because she was

good. She tried to picture Miss Willie sitting in God's parlor having hot chocolate. Miss Willie liked hot chocolate. And she would get to see what God looked like. Franny wondered about that a lot—what God looked like. The Bible said man was made in His image, so he must look like one of them. She thought he probably looked like old Mr. Boggs up the street who had hair so white it hurt your eyes and a great hooked nose with a hair on it.

God knew everything you did, Franny's Sunday School teacher said. Even the bad things, and if you were really sorry, He would forgive you. If Miss Willie were with God, she must know everything too, which meant she knew what Franny had done when she looked into her coffin. Franny hoped she would forgive her, but then everybody wasn't as nice about that as God was.

For a long time after that, every time Franny walked past the Llewellyns' house, she got a hard, hurtful knot in her chest and had to look away. And when she went to the picture show, the smell of popcorn almost made her cry.

Franny was glad a few days later when Aunt Six called and asked her to run an errand. Dr. Ludlow had removed the stitches from her foot and she was wearing outgrown shoes of Winnie's until they saved enough ration coupons to buy a new pair.

Aunt Six had painted a watercolor picture of the stone arch Mr. Rittenhouse built that marked the town limits, an early Christmas present for her friend, she said. Now framed and wrapped in red tissue, it waited to be delivered.

Franny and Hannah took the gift to Mr. Rittenhouse in the brown cottage on Wisteria Hill while on their way to Scouts. The old gentleman let them in with a worried smile, then excused himself from the room, explaining that he was on the telephone. He slipped into the little back room where Franny had seen the diploma and pulled the door almost shut. While Hannah looked at the relics, Franny edged closer to listen.

"I see . . ." Mr. Rittenhouse spoke softly. "And when may I expect the plans?"

Franny held her breath so long it hurt, heard him whisper something about it being urgent, not having much time. Quietly she hurried back into the other room where Hannah examined an Egyptian bracelet.

"Hey, wonder how old this is? Reckon it came out of a tomb?" Hannah frowned. "What's wrong? You sick?"

Franny shook her head. Maybe she could leave the present on the big oak table by the window.

"*Something's* the matter. What is it?"

"Tell you later." A large book sat in the center of the table. It looked very old. Franny put the gift beside it.

Hannah wandered over to see what she was doing. "Look at that! Must be a Bible. Did you ever see one so big?" She opened the cover, ruffled a few pages and shrugged. "Can't read a word. What kind of language is that?"

Franny stared at the brown-spotted pages. She had seen enough movies, read enough posters to know the book was written in German.

"I see you've discovered the old family Bible." Mr. Rittenhouse stood in the doorway. "It belonged to my grandparents. My father brought it all the way from Munich." He walked over to stand behind them. "I'm sorry I took so long on the phone, but it was long distance, something I had to take care of."

Franny bit her lip until it stung. Her heart beat faster. Did he know she knew? "We brought you a present from Aunt Six," she said, inching toward the door. "It's there—on the table."

"How nice. But please stay. It's always pleasant to have company on such a dreary winter day. Let's go into the kitchen where it's warmer. Maybe I can find enough sugar to make cocoa."

"We have to go to Scouts," Franny said, dragging Hannah after her. "We're collecting scrap metal today—so we can beat the Germans." Still holding tightly to Hannah's hand, she turned and fled.

"Franny V., slow down, will you? You've about pulled my arm clean off and I've got a pain in my side." Puffing, Hannah sank onto a stone wall at the bottom of the hill. "Why'd you run off like that? You hurt his feelings, I could tell." She pulled her beret down around her ears. "Why are you acting so crazy?"

Franny told her about the old man's relatives in Germany and the phone conversation she'd overheard.

"I'll swear, you *are* crazy!" Hannah said. "We've known him all our lives. Why, Frances Virginia Gordon, Double-A Rittenhouse wouldn't hurt a fly!"

It bothered Franny that neither Hannah nor Aunt Six would believe Mr. Rittenhouse was a spy. And it bothered her even more that she did.

Most of the families in Sallie's Station had been in the States so long they were either vague about their mixed ancestry or didn't care—except for Mrs. Haywood C. Greer III who claimed to be descended from British royalty. Their nationality was American, and they never thought of themselves as anything else.

A second generation American, a comparative newcomer, Mr. Rittenhouse wore his German heritage like a second skin, an evil, clinging spider web that wouldn't wash away. Franny wished she had never seen his name on that diploma. She wished she could forget.

Chapter Seventeen

What might have been the longest period in her life turned out to be an adventure. Franny was changing the drip pan under the sink about mid-morning the next day when the doorbell rang. Faith and Reilly had left with Lucy about an hour before to meet her ride in Chattanooga, and she hoped it wouldn't be her youngest coming back for something she'd forgotten. Hastily she dumped rusty water out the back door and replaced the pan. Could it possibly be the plumber? He'd led her to believe it would be an all day wait. Oh, glory! Had she moved up on his list?

Franny heard her mother open the door, then the soft murmur of voices. Definitely not the plumber. Wiping her hands, she hurried into the living room, hoping she didn't jiggle under her baggy sweat shirt. She couldn't wear a bra just yet.

Her mother stood looking at the woman in the doorway as if she were trying to figure out who she was. Franny knew who she was. "Please come in," she said, and held the door open wider. "I'm Franny. Franny Hughes, and this is Molly Gordon, my mother."

The stranger smiled as she gripped her hand. "I know. I'm Allie. I came to find my father."

I came to find my father. Just like that. She announced it in the same way you might say, *I came to collect for The March of Dimes.*

"Your mother's just up the street waiting for the tile man," Franny told her. "And your father—well, that's another kettle of fish." By that time she had Allie seated at one end of the living room sofa while she tried to explain to her mother, as tactfully as she could, who Allie was. She had no idea how much her friend's daughter knew about her father. Drat Hannah for getting her into this!

"Does your mother know you're coming?" Franny asked. With all the running from doctor to doctor, she hadn't heard a report from Hannah about her Thanksgiving weekend, other than it went well and that Vance was on his best behavior.

Allie shook her head. "No, it was a spur of the moment decision. Suddenly I just had to know . . . so here I am." Her smile was wide like her mother's, and she wore her dark hair in a short, stylish cut reminding her of Hannah's, but her smoky hazel eyes came from her father.

"Franny, why don't you take Allie on up to Hannah's?" her mama said. "I'll wait here for the plumber."

"Bless you," Franny whispered as she kissed her goodbye. "I won't be long." This was one problem of Hannah's she wasn't going to deal with, not if she could help it.

"How do you know your father's here in Sallie's Station?" Franny asked as they walked to Allie's car.

She grinned. "That's the impression I got from some of the things Hannah's said."

"But she hasn't told you who he is?"

"Only that he was special and that they loved each other. They must've been hardly more than children themselves." Allie drove slowly, concentrating on the road. "Franny, do you know who my father is?"

"Yes." She couldn't get around it. Allie would know if she lied. "Here's the house on the left, the red brick with the big sycamore in front.

"And Allie?" Franny put a hand on her arm as they turned in the driveway. "As far as I know, your father isn't aware you exist. Your mother never told him she was pregnant."

She fingered her car keys, slid them around the ring. "Why not? Why wouldn't she?"

"They were only eighteen, and there were . . . circumstances. He was going away to school—to West Point. Hannah knew if she told him, he'd throw it all away."

"Dear God!" Tears filled her eyes. "She loved him that much."

"She loved him that much, so go easy on her, okay?"

Just for a minute, Franny closed her eyes. *Please God, we could use a break here!* What if Allie's father doesn't want to see her after all these years? What if he doesn't care?

Franny stood at the window as Hannah pulled into her drive later that afternoon. Allie wasn't in the front seat with her, so where was she?

"Home. I sent her home." Hannah waved away her offer to help and carried the groceries inside.

"For heaven's sake, Hannah! Why?"

"*Because he doesn't know.* I couldn't very well drop in on him and say, 'Looky, looky! Guess who we have here? Surprise!' "

Franny put away milk and eggs, tore open a package of Oreos. "So, when do you plan to do it? Or do you?" She offered Hannah the open pack, which she ignored. "You're not being fair to either of them keeping this to yourself."

"I know, I know. I've been putting it off, but I'm going to, I promise."

"When?"

"Today. I'm going to tell him today. Will you get off my back now, Franny V.?" Hannah hurled frozen vegetables into the freezer and slammed the door. They stared at each other across the table. Franny realized her friend was on the verge of crying.

"Oh, Franny V., I'm sorry. I didn't mean to be such a scratchit hatchet." Hannah came over and put her arms around her. "Like you need this on top of everything else. But I'm scared. I'm just plain scared!"

Franny smiled at the words they had made up in the third grade. "It'll be okay. You'll see."

"I've tried to tell him a couple of times. Like when we went out to dinner the other night, and last week when we walked up on Hickory Hill—but you know how he is. I could never figure out how his funny mind works."

"It's none of my business, I know," Franny admitted. "But is it still there?"

"Is what still there?" She accepted a cookie after all.

"The feeling you had for each other." Franny stopped short of calling it love, although she didn't know what else it might be.

She smiled. "It's funny, but I think it is—only in a different way."

"What about Vance?"

"That's what worries me the most." Hannah pulled out a chair and sat at the kitchen table, the same table where they had struggled with homework, giggled over boys, planned first Franny's wedding, and then Hannah's. It was there Hannah had coaxed Molly Gordon into eating the day after her husband died. Now Franny sat next to her, her arms resting on the scarred maple surface.

"Vance and I haven't gotten along this well in years. He's really trying, Franny. Honest to God, I think the man cares—at least as much as he can care. I don't want to hurt him." She ran the tip of one finger along the dent where Winnie tried to crack a hickory nut with a hammer. "I've ordered a few basic pieces of furniture; they're supposed to deliver them by the end of next week, and I've asked about a part-time job at Blackwell and Parker."

Franny frowned. "Blackwell and Parker? But that's an accounting firm."

"And they need an accountant, silly! At least through tax season.

I'm moving back into the old house, Franny V., for a little while anyway, until I decide what to do."

"But you know we love having you here." Especially now, Franny thought. *Please don't leave me now.*

Hannah read her thoughts as usual. "I'm not leaving you, Franny V. I'll be in and out as much as ever. I just need a little space, and so do you." She gave her shoulder a poke. "Don't worry, you can't get rid of me."

Franny poked her back. "So who's worried?"

How do you tell somebody he has a daughter who's over forty years old? Do you lead up to it gently: *Remember that night we parked behind Bohannons' Mill?* Or, *How would you feel about being a grandfather?* Better Hannah than me, Franny thought. Yet, after Hannah left that evening, she couldn't get her off her mind. At least not until the telephone rang.

Her mother had already gone to bed and she hurried to answer so it wouldn't wake her. It was after ten and Franny was always a little jumpy about late night calls. At her age, ten was a late night call. The dark side of her took over. They had found her son's car at the bottom of a cliff; Faith was in early labor; Lucy had an accident on the drive to New Jersey. And then she thought of Hannah. Had there been drastic repercussions?

Her heart did a belly flop when she heard Shagg's voice.

"Mrs. Hughes? I apologize for calling so late, but I just got in from London. Look, I really feel awful about this, but there's a message from Gib on my answering machine that's been there over a week. Guess he forgot I wasn't coming back here after Thanksgiving. I was hoping he'd gotten in touch with you by now, but from your calls, I take it you haven't heard from him."

"Not since before Thanksgiving. Shagg, do you know where he is?" She leaned against the wall, trailed a finger across the telephone shelf. It needed dusting.

"Somewhere down on the coast of South Carolina, I think. He was either going there or to Florida, he said. It was one of those places that got hit so hard by the hurricane back in September. Gib went down there with a bunch of volunteers to help out. You know, paint, repair some of the roofs, things like that."

Gib? Franny thought about their back step that was being held up by cement blocks. Forgive me, God. Gibson Hughes knew how to use a hammer and paint brush? It was news to her!

But good news. Franny couldn't stop smiling. "What brought this about?" she asked.

"His radio station sponsored it, along with some of the churches in the area," Shagg said. "Gib told me close to fifty volunteers were going, but he wouldn't know exactly where he'd be until he got there." He groaned. "I was supposed to call you, let you know not to worry. Wuzzy too. Kind of late, I'm afraid. I think he's due back tomorrow."

"That's okay, I'll call Wuzzy," she told him. "And thanks, Shagg." Thanks for giving me the first goodnight's sleep I've had all week. Franny dialed Wuzzy's number. Maybe there was hope after all.

She woke the next morning with somebody sitting on her bed. "Wake up," Hannah said. She was smiling. Franny yawned and sat up, shoving a pillow behind her back. She heard her mother puttering about in the bathroom, brushing her teeth, washing off all that cold cream. No wonder they had plumbing problems.

"What time did you come in?" she asked. She had crashed before the late show went off.

Hannah flopped across the foot of the bed and raised up on one elbow. "Not too late—a little after midnight."

"So, what did he say? You did tell him, didn't you?" Why did Hannah always make her drag things out of her?

"You'd have been proud of me, Franny V. It took awhile to work up the courage, but I did it. I finally told him. He didn't believe me

158

at first. Thought it was a joke. We'd rented a video, he made lasagna. I waited until I'd had a couple of glasses of wine . . . Wesley doesn't drink anymore, you know. We never did get to the video."

Hannah sprang into a sitting position, lithe as a monkey. "Finally I brought out the pictures," she said. "The ones I made last summer of Allie and the boys, and she'd given me a couple of baby pictures too. It was the pictures that did it."

Franny nodded. Those eyes.

"He was furious," Hannah said. "I thought he was going to start throwing things. He turned as white as that lamp shade over there. Said he'd never forgive me for keeping it from him. She was his daughter too. We could've kept her, raised her together."

"Sure, that sounds good now," Franny said. "But you were eighteen, and he had that appointment to West Point."

"Don't think I didn't remind him of that." Hannah slid from the bed and frowned at herself in the mirror, ran fingers through her hair. She wore a baggy yellow running suit and dirty sneakers. "Well, he'll just have to work through it—like I did. He missed seeing his daughter grow up. So did I. But he cried, Franny. He just held on to me and cried."

Franny shoved the covers aside and slid her feet into slippers. "Sometimes you have to weep away your yesterdays so you can start on tomorrow."

Hannah turned and looked at her. "Who said that?"

"I did. Does he want to see her?"

She nodded. "I'm driving her out there this afternoon."

"Good. I couldn't imagine him reacting any other way. Do you think he still resents you?" Franny reached for her robe at the foot of the bed. It was good to feel rested.

"Yeah. Probably always will, but not as much as he would if we'd married and he was earning five dollars an hour at the carpet mill." She jogged in place in the bedroom doorway. "Coffee's ready if you want some. Feel like walking this morning?"

"Absolutely." If she had the wind for it, she would have felt like racing around the block. Franny told her about Shagg's call, whispering so her mother wouldn't hear. She had never told her she didn't know where Gib was.

Hannah grinned. "This calls for a celebration. What about lunch after church at that new place downtown—the one where Peabody's Dry Goods used to be? What's it called? *The Pink Petunia.* Just you and Miss Molly and me. My treat."

She hadn't seen Hannah this happy since . . . well, it had been a long time. She fairly glowed through a longer-than-usual church service, and was even halfway civil to Neely Louise Curtis who asked her to serve on the telephone committee for the Arts Council.

The Curtises sat in the pew in front of them: Neely Louise and her husband Claude, with Walter and Janine. Today Janine wore her thick, sun-spun hair in a simple twist. Gold loop earrings dangled from perfect pink lobes. When they stood to sing, Franny noticed how the fitted jade jacket nipped her small waist. She also noticed how Walter leaned toward Janine to sing, their arms linked. This time, she thought, Neely Louise might as well plan to fork out big bucks for the rehearsal dinner.

Franny was surprised when after the service, Walter, usually reserved, put a chummy hand on her shoulder as they walked up the aisle.

"Mrs. Hughes, I don't think you've met my fiancée, Janine Hendricks."

"I believe our paths have crossed," Franny said, "but it's nice to meet you at last. Welcome to Sallie's Station."

Janine smiled as Franny took her well-manicured hand. "My mom grew up here," she said, "so it's a little like coming home."

"Your mother? Then I must have known her. When—"

"Walter, we really must hurry along." Neely gave her son's sleeve a white-knuckled pinch. "Your father's made reservations at the club for lunch."

Neely turned to Franny with a spurt of a smile. "There'll be plenty of chances to visit later."

Franny ignored her. "And will the wedding be here in town?" she asked Janine.

"By all means," Walter said. "Around Valentine's Day—if I can wait that long." And he gave his bride-to-be an affectionate squeeze. Franny couldn't be sure, but she thought the young woman blushed.

Out front her mother was deep in conversation with the minister's wife, whom she thought was distantly related to her through her grandmother on her father's side, and Hannah was trying to escape from Alma Cranford. Alma had been pestering her for weeks, Molly said, to find out about Hannah's marital status. Frankly, Franny was curious herself.

Although it was early December, the sun was warm in spite of a fitful breeze, and Franny thought of that long ago November Sunday when Lieutenant Gregory told them goodbye.

The skeleton shadow of a maple now zigzagged over the walkway where he had left her, and as Franny stood waiting for her mother and Hannah, she saw Janine Hendricks and the Curtises get into Claude's sleek, black Lincoln at the curb.

Her mother had grown up there, Janine said. What was it about her that reminded Franny of someone? And for a second she thought she knew. But surely not. That couldn't be.

Chapter Eighteen

December 2, 1943

The Whitfields' smokehouse smelled of old clothes, mice, and musty love letters long forgotten. A single bulb dangled from the ceiling, casting eerie shadows in the corners of the room. The building wasn't really a smokehouse anymore. It had a wooden floor, and the family used it as a storeroom, but it still smelled faintly of cured meat.

The little house adapted to any setting: It made a handy cave when Betty Joyce and her friends acted out *Ali Baba and the Forty Thieves*, served as a western jail for rustlers and outlaws, and was once the palace of the beautiful Aztec queen who schemed to destroy Tarzan. Neely Louise Warren was the beautiful Aztec queen.

Travis licked the end of his stubby pencil. He had given up taking minutes of the meetings in lemon juice after the paper caught fire when he tried to read it.

Wesley had trailed Miss Havergal to the park on one of her early morning runs, he said, but the only other person there was Cephus Carmichael, and he was asleep on that old settee they kept on the porch of the library.

"My daddy says Cephus sells black market liquor," Betty Joyce said. "Moonshine too. You sure she didn't buy anything from him?"

But Wesley shook his head. "I don't think she even knew he was there. Besides, Cephus does all his business in the drainage ditch. Everybody knows that."

Travis didn't know it. "Aw, you're making that up."

"Am not. I've seen him hiding bottles in there," Wesley said. "Too bad Miss Havergal doesn't drink. They'd get rid of her in a minute." Wesley's father was chairman of the school board and he knew what was and wasn't expected of teachers in Sallie's Station, Georgia.

Hannah shrugged. "I don't think she's going to meet anybody. She doesn't drink whiskey and she's not a traitor, she's just mean!" And she slammed a fist into the arm of Mrs. Whitfield's wicker rocker.

"The only two people she likes are Shirley and Neely Louise," Travis said. "They get to do anything they want."

"Miss Havergal's always telling Neely how nice she looks," Hannah said. "Like she doesn't know it already." Hannah lowered her voice in an imitation of the principal. *Your hair looks very nice today, Neely, and what a pretty new dress* . . . Shoot, I guess I'd look good too if my mama spent a million hours a day at the sewing machine like Neely's does!"

But Franny was glad Miss Havergal didn't talk like that to her. The sound of the woman's voice made her feel like she'd walked through a spider web.

Betty Joyce smeared a soda cracker with peanut butter. "I don't like her, either. Nobody in my class does, but I think we should give her a chance. She never seems to have any fun. I think she's kind of sad."

Franny found herself nodding in agreement. It was hard not to go along with Betty Joyce. She was a year older than the rest of them and had read nearly every book in the school library. She had sharp blue eyes and a plain, thoughtful face, and Franny knew she would never condone something she didn't believe in.

"Well, it's not my fault the old witch doesn't have any fun," Hannah said.

Travis spoke in a sepulchral whisper. "Once when I was over at Miss Opal's, I heard her and Annie talking. Said Miss Havergal didn't have any family. Said she was raised by a lot of different people." He snickered. "Coulda been wolves, remember? Like that statue of those two little boys they used to have over in Rome."

The Italian city had presented the statue of Romulus and Remus to its Georgia namesake, but the gift was banished to storage when the two countries went to war.

"How do they know who raised her?" Wesley asked.

"I reckon old Havergal told them," Travis said. "You know how the other teachers go home for Christmas and stuff? Well, Miss Havergal told Miss Opal she'd be staying right here in Sallie's Station. Doesn't have any place else to go.

"Poor old thing!" Travis made a long, sad face. "Don't you feel sorry for her, Frances Virginia? Why don't you invite Miss Havergal over to your house? How'd you like to come downstairs and find her sitting under your tree? Ho! Ho! Ho! Looky what Santy Claus brought!"

"And how'd you like to go stand on the corner and stack greasy BB's?" Franny kicked at him and missed.

"But I guess we could try being nicer to her," she said. Her Sunday School teacher had done a real job on them about the Golden Rule that week and Franny's conscience gnawed at her.

Wesley frowned. "Come to think of it, I never have seen her laugh."

"It might work," Betty Joyce said. "What've we got to lose?"

"Not me!" Travis shuddered. "I'd die before I was nice to that old ha'nt!"

The next week Travis brought Miss Havergal the biggest, reddest apple Franny had ever seen. Franny offered to wash the blackboards after school, and Hannah presented the principal with the last of her mother's yellow chrysanthemums. She accepted the offerings without comment.

Miss Havergal had stopped forcing Junior Massingill to read aloud after his mother paid her a visit, but she made up for it in other ways. She asked him to sharpen pencils for her, empty the wastebasket, raise or lower the shades. Anyone else would have jumped at the chance just to get out of his seat, but it gave Junior the jitters to get up in front of people. He broke the points off pencils, jerked the shades until they flapped at the top. Watching him, Neely Louise developed a silly giggle. Franny couldn't figure out what had come over Neely Louise. She reminded her of Charlie McCarthy who was on the radio every week with the ventriloquist Edgar Bergen. Edgar Bergen's words came out of Charlie's wooden mouth, only when Neely Louise spoke, she sounded like Miss Havergal, and her face mirrored the principal's expression. Franny just itched to vault over her desk and slap her.

War and Miss Havergal. They went together like castor oil and stomachaches, and it seemed they would have to put up with her until it was over.

It wasn't getting any easier to be nice to Miss Havergal, but they had given their word, and Franny was determined to try. And then something made them change their minds, and it was because of what happened to Wanda Culpepper.

Wanda Culpepper had spent two years in the fourth grade and no telling how many in the first. She was smaller than her classmates, but her pinched face and weary expression made her look much older. Wanda was a "kick-me" kind of person. She had grayish skin and lank, greasy hair, and wore dresses that were either too large or too small. She wasn't teased or made fun of—not intentionally, anyway. She was just ignored, like a scrawny kitten nobody wants to pet. And Wanda accepted that. She wasn't afraid of her classmates. But she was afraid of Miss Havergal.

The class had their school pictures made that morning and Wanda's hair was frizzy-curled. She wore a new dress, blue with red flowers, that bagged at the waist and hung well below her knees.

Miss Havergal had assigned busy work—three digit multiplication—while she shuffled papers at her desk, and Franny glanced up as she tried to remember seven times nine. Wanda sat two seats in front of her, across the aisle and to the left, and as Franny watched, the girl squirmed in her seat, twisted from side to side, and shook the desk in front of her until Carol Delaney turned around and told her to be still. Wanda sat on her foot.

Finally she raised a thin arm, shyly at first, then as Miss Havergal took no notice, waved it about. Miss Havergal frowned at somebody's paper—probably hers, Franny thought, red-pencilled it with methodical zeal, and progressed through the stack.

Franny cleared her throat, coughed, and dropped a pencil on the floor, hoping to get the woman's attention. Couldn't she see the girl needed to go to the bathroom? Franny ached for Wanda Culpepper, although her habits repulsed her. She forgot to wipe her nose, brought fat back in a huge white soda biscuit for lunch, never knew her spelling words, and read in a halting whisper that made Franny want to tug the words from her.

The Culpeppers lived in an unpainted shack on Icehouse Road. Franny and her friends passed their place on the way to Scoggins' Store where they bought their licorice whips, Moon Pies, and jawbreakers when they had a nickel to spend. The year before, Franny and Hannah had "adopted" Wanda for a while, coached her in spelling and reading, played with her after school, but it hadn't helped a bit.

If only she could get Wanda fattened up on some of her mama's good cooking, Franny thought, let her soak in a hot tub for about an hour, scrub and cut her hair, and get her into some decent clothes, she would be a different girl.

Wanda didn't seem to mind when the two girls abandoned her.

In fact, she seemed relieved. It took Franny a while to get over her disgust with her for not going along with their plans. Now she just ignored her like everybody else, but it was hard to ignore somebody in such obvious discomfort.

Franny knew Miss Havergal sometimes helped Neely Louise with her math before school began. Once she'd come early and seen the two, heads together, at the principal's desk, and Miss Havergal was explaining a problem just as nice and patient as could be. Maybe if she were kinder to Wanda, Franny thought, the girl might do a little better. But their math teacher didn't like Wanda Culpepper and it was becoming even more obvious she wasn't going to pay her any attention.

Franny was struggling with the last problem when she heard a suspicious trickle and saw the yellow puddle in Wanda's seat trickle to the floor.

"Miss Havergal, Wanda's done peed in her pants!" Shirley Puckett held her feet off the floor as if she were afraid the puddle would become a wild, raging river and wash her away. Franny wished it would.

Wanda put her head on the desk and covered it with her arms. Hands on her hips, Miss Havergal glared down at her. "Why on earth didn't you ask to be excused? A girl as old as you!"

"Yuck! It's all over the floor," Neely Louise pointed out as she skipped-hopped up and down the rows collecting papers for the principal. She made a face as she tiptoed around the damp spot.

The principal continued to glower at Wanda who shook with silent sobs. Finally she grabbed a handful of tissues and threw them on the girl's desk. "Here, wipe your face and get a mop from the broom closet. Hurry up now!"

"Miss Havergal," Franny said, "I'll get the janitor if you want." Wanda hiccupped into her tissues.

"Esau has other things to do. Wanda can clean up after herself—then maybe this won't happen again." Miss Havergal turned her back and dashed the homework assignment on the board—pages and pages of it. "We have about five more minutes of this period," she added with a curt nod to Wanda. "I want to see that floor clean before the bell rings."

When Mrs. Hightower came in for science and found Wanda mopping under her desk, her face went all tight and pale. She sent Wanda to the girls' restroom, and Franny to find some clothes for her from the "Bundles for Britain" they kept in the storeroom. Franny finally got to clean up Wanda and dress her in different clothes, but it wasn't any fun. She cried the whole time.

And that was when they all knew that, orphan or not, Miss Havergal had to go.

It happened a few weeks before Christmas. Bing Crosby was already dreaming of a white one on the phonograph at Goldman's Five and Ten. Franny and Hannah, in town for some preliminary price checking, strolled from store to store, coats buttoned to the chin, their breath making little clouds of smoke in the air. This year the two had agreed to exchange boxes of chocolate-covered cherries. The year before their gifts had been plastic heart-shaped pendants with pink sachet inside. Once they had given each other a miniature oil lamp filled with green perfume, but their mothers wouldn't let them wear it.

The stores bustled with shoppers. A uniformed soldier, home on leave, walked hand in hand with his girlfriend looking in all the windows. It was Saturday, and people from the country had come to town to do their weekly shopping. Men in overalls lounged against the sunny sides of buildings and sprayed tobacco juice. Once one of them had hit Hannah on the leg; now she walked on the edge of the sidewalk with one foot on the curb.

At the Five and Ten, Franny fingered a green glass ashtray, admired a set of salt and pepper shakers shaped like roosters, and glanced longingly at the candy counter where two sailors teased

Lottie Mae Upshaw who measured out jellybeans. She watched the girl ring up a sale.

"Gosh, wouldn't it be wonderful to have a job in here?" Hannah sighed at the wonder of it. "Especially at Christmas."

Franny nodded. She couldn't think of a more exciting place in December than Goldman's Five and Ten: the continuous holiday music, the smell of popcorn. As the season grew nearer, all these things swelled into a tingling, "getting-ready-for-it" feeling that grew until Franny thought she might explode.

"Look!" she yelled, temporarily forgetting her fantasy. "There's Miss O'Donnell."

The speech teacher lingered over the stationery supplies where she selected a pad of tissue-thin air mail paper with red and blue borders that folded into an envelope. They called it V-Mail.

"I'll bet I know who that's for," Franny said in greeting.

"And I'll bet you're right." Miss O'Donnell smiled down at them.

"Did you hear from him today?" Hannah asked breathlessly.

"As a matter of fact, I did." Their teacher patted her blue knitted bag. "And he asked to be remembered to you as always."

Franny had written a long letter to Lieutenant Gregory, and earlier their class had chipped in to buy him a "Surprise Package for Servicemen" from Maxwell's Drug Store. The kit contained a plated, steel-covered Bible, billfold, talc, cologne, shaving lotion, a pipe and tobacco pouch. Lieutenant Gregory didn't smoke, but would be well-equipped if he should decide to take it up.

Miss O'Donnell frequently shared snatches of his letters with her students and encouraged them to write as well. Once Mrs. Hightower had made it a class project for English.

Franny was worried about Miss O'Donnell. Miss Havergal had taken to dropping in on her expression class, then standing at the back of the room with her arms folded and a grim look on her face. It made everybody uncomfortable, especially Miss O'Donnell, who had enough to trouble her with Lieutenant Gregory off fighting somewhere. At times, Franny noticed, her teacher's eyes had a lost, faraway look.

Hannah wandered off to look at comic books, and Franny to examine the price of an orange-striped pitcher she thought her mother might like when Miss Havergal stormed past, looking neither to the right nor left, her face as white as a Pepsodent smile. She didn't speak to Franny but marched right to Eileen O'Donnell and backed her up against the notions and patterns a few counters away.

"I just happened to drop by *The Chronicle*," the principal said.

Miss O'Donnell tried to step back, but there was nowhere to go. Bright circles burned on her cheeks.

"The man at the front desk over there—the one who edits the local news—told me something you might find interesting," Miss Havergal said. Her smile reminded Franny of the way the wolf smiled at Red Riding Hood.

The young teacher attempted to smile back. "Oh, and what was that, Miss Havergal?"

Franny felt a light touch on her shoulder and almost yelled out loud. Hannah stood behind her with a finger to her lips. Together they crept closer, crouched behind a display of men's blue work shirts.

"I spoke to him about getting the time wrong on the notice you gave him for the October P.T.A. meeting," Miss Havergal said. "And from what I understand, it was printed *exactly as written*. Now, what do you have to say about that?" She wasn't smiling any more.

"I really don't know what to say. There must have been a mix-up of some kind, a misunderstanding. I'm sorry." Miss O'Donnell tried to straighten her shoulders and stand tall, but the other woman loomed over her.

"Oh, there's been a mistake all right. Your mistake."

Franny could tell the speech teacher was getting really mad now. She held her little blue handbag in front of her like a shield. "I said I was sorry, Miss Havergal. Why can't we just put this behind us? After all, this happened almost two months ago. What can it matter now?"

"It matters because you went behind my back. You defied me. You arranged it so those children could attend that ridiculous country tent show." The principal spit out her words. Franny could imagine her standing on a balcony next to Adolf Hitler spewing hate. Franny bit her lip and reached for Hannah's hand.

"You're going to be very sorry, my dear, before I'm through with you." The principal spoke softly now so the girls had to lean closer to hear. "I'll have your job for this. You can count on it."

Chapter Nineteen

Sunday. Only a few more days and then she would know for sure. And what time would the doctor call? On his lunch hour, maybe. That would make it another half day before Franny learned the results of her biopsy. She tried not to let her mother know she was even allowing herself to think everything might not turn out all right, but that pesky little doubt was like a tickle in the back of the throat. And it wouldn't go away.

The lunch with Hannah was a welcome diversion, followed by the excitement of Allie's arrival soon after they got home. She rushed inside looking like a Christmas tree in green wool pants and a holiday sweater, only Allie didn't need any lights.

Hannah's daughter stood in their living room shifting her bulky bag from one shoulder to the other. She was idling on high, eager to scratch off, but her mother insisted she sit.

"What's the matter? He is expecting us, isn't he?" Allie sat on the edge of her chair. "He hasn't changed his mind?"

Hannah knelt on the floor beside her. "No, he hasn't changed his mind. I just thought we needed to talk first. There are a few things you should know."

Franny looked at her mother and the two of them started to leave the room, but Hannah called them back. "No, please stay. You were the friends who helped me through all this, the ones I relied on during that awful time when . . ." She held out a hand to Molly, her second mother. "I'd like you both with me now.

"Your father's name is Wesley Fuller and we started dating the summer before our senior year in high school," Hannah told Allie. "After that, neither of us even looked at anybody else. The next spring, when I found out I was pregnant with you, Wesley had already been accepted at West Point. I knew if I told him about you, it would put an end to that, so I didn't.

"After graduation," Hannah said, "my parents sent me to stay with an aunt in South Georgia until you were born in December. As you know, I put you up for adoption, and after Christmas began my freshman year a semester late." She laughed. "An all-girls school, naturally."

Allie bent her dark head to her mother's, one hand rested on Hannah's shoulder. "But what about my father? Didn't he wonder where you were? Didn't he ask?"

"I broke off the relationship after high school graduation," Hannah told her. "He didn't know where I was. Everybody thought I had started school a quarter early—at least that's what we hoped they thought." She shrugged. "Things were different then. Babies born to unwed mothers weren't included in the weekly birth announcements in *The Chronicle* the way they are now. It was something you only whispered about.

"Allie, your father didn't learn until yesterday that he had a daughter. In fact, it was years before he'd even speak to me again. I hurt him when I left that summer. He didn't understand, but it was the only way. I had to do it like that, or he would have come after me, thrown it all away."

Hannah stood and pulled her daughter to her feet. "Now, of course, he's furious—only not with you." Gently she placed a hand on either side of Allie's face as a sculptor might give a last loving pat to a finished work. "I guess I'm ready whenever you are."

For an answer, Allie drew her smaller mother into her arms and cried. Franny did the same with hers.

After the two of them left for Wesley's, Franny phoned and invited Faith and Reilly over for supper. She wanted her family around her too—the ones she could find. They would have something hot and nutritious, something time-consuming to prepare. While her mother napped, Franny chopped celery and onions for a chicken casserole while watching Doug Bolding, who lived behind them, teetering on a ladder to string tiny lights on the big cedar in his yard. This year she hoped they wouldn't blink.

The casserole was ready to bake and Franny had just shoved acorn squash into the oven when Wuzzy called. She was out when Franny had phoned the night before; she'd gone to her parents for the weekend, she said, and had Franny heard anything from Gib? Wuzzy hadn't heard a word, and to tell the truth, she was getting worried.

Franny's news about Shagg's call was met with silence, then sort of a choked, muffled sound. "Oh, Franny, I can't tell you how relieved I am! I was so worried . . . I thought—well, I don't know what I thought. I didn't want to frighten you, but I was afraid of what he might've done."

Franny couldn't remember ever being as glad to hear another person cry. Wuzzy's tears meant she still cared, or Franny hoped they did. "Shagg was supposed to have called you," she told her, "but he didn't get the message until he got back from London. This mission of Gib's to Florida or wherever must've been a last minute decision." She made a joke about her son's carpentry skills and Wuzzy laughed.

"Please tell him I want to hear from him if you talk with him before I do," she said. "This trouble between us—well, it isn't all his fault, you know. We both need to grow up some."

Franny lived off that for the rest of the day, and when Faith came later, she wanted to know why her mother was smiling. Faith looked tired and said her back ached some, but her appetite was good. If only they could just get her through the next few weeks!

Lucy phoned as Franny was getting ready for bed to let her know she'd arrived safely in Newark and was staying in a friend's apartment until she found a place of her own. Franny tried not to think of dark subways and muggings and people shooting each other on the street. And it was getting almost as bad in Sallie's Station. Why, just the other day somebody ran off with Willadeen Hicks's pocketbook in the parking lot at the mall. Knowing Willadeen, it probably contained the first dollar she'd ever earned.

Franny went back to see the surgeon the next day so he could check the incision on her breast. It looked fine, he said. He didn't. His mouth looked like a bad mending job, all puckered and pulled down at the ends. She asked him again when she might hear from the biopsy and he told her again that it would probably be Wednesday, and did she want to make an appointment to come in? "Why would I want to come all the way over here for something you could just as well tell me over the phone?" Franny said. Driving home she realized doctors probably preferred giving bad news face to face.

"And how was Lennie Baby?" Hannah asked her later.

"Baggy trousers—cow plop brown. The man has no behind whatsoever. And there was a little adhesive bandage on his chin where I suspect he'd cut himself shaving."

"Comforting to know his hand's that steady," Hannah said, and they laughed. In fact, they laughed about a lot of things that day.

After an awkward beginning, she told Franny, the afternoon with Allie and her father had blossomed into something good. "She fell in love with his library—you know all those books Wesley has. And there's his collection of Civil War memorabilia. That's her specialty, you know. Allie wrote her dissertation on that." Hannah grabbed an apple from the bowl on the coffee table and polished it on her pants. "When they got into dates and battles, I left." She grinned. "I don't think they even realized I'd gone." She sighed. "And frankly, I don't think he's quite forgiven me yet."

* * * * *

"Gib called while you were gone," Franny's mother announced later. "Said he'd call again either tonight or tomorrow."

"He didn't say exactly when? How was he, Mama? How did he sound?"

"Sounded like Gibson Hughes," she said, giving her one of those looks most mothers are born knowing how to use and never seem to forget. Of course, she didn't know about his disappearance into the Twilight Zone.

"You didn't tell him anything, did you? About this breast thing, I mean?" Why did she avoid using the word *cancer?* Would not using it make it not be there?

"I thought you should be the one to tell him," she said. "You made such a fuss when I told Lucy. Besides, you know I don't like to talk about things like that over the phone."

Tuesday Franny got out her Christmas china. The pattern featured Santa Claus and his sleigh—even Rudolph, and every child who came there loved it. So did Franny.

And since it was getting into December, she decided to haul out some of the decorations. It seemed to Franny that people seemed to decorate for Christmas earlier than they used to. It hadn't really been that long since Thanksgiving, had it? But she hummed "Deck the Halls" as she set out the little nativity scene Faith had made in Scouts from plaster of Paris. The ethereal renaissance angel Franny had bought on sale the year before now ascended or decended—she couldn't decide which—from the sideboard in the dining room, and Lucy's baby doll, the one she'd seldom played with, sat in her usual little red chair by the fireplace. Franny was rummaging in the buffet drawer for candles when somebody rang the doorbell.

Her mama had gone with Hannah to see what she'd done with her house, so Franny hurried to the door thinking it might be Betty Joyce with some things from her refrigerator that wouldn't keep, since she and her husband were leaving in a couple of days for England. But it wasn't Betty Joyce standing there with what looked like a plate in her hands. Through the curtained glass of the front door, the person looked a lot like Shirley Dilworth. Franny was afraid she must've gaped when she opened the door, because darned if it wasn't Shirley Dilworth! Shirley poked the plate at her and put a hand on one hip. "Well . . . aren't you gonna ask me in?"

Franny looked from the plate to Shirley and found herself being backed inside. "Well, sure, come on in, Shirley. I'll make coffee. I'm ready for a break anyway. I was just getting around to putting out some Christmas things."

"Oh, I did that the day after Thanksgiving," she said, noticing Franny eyeing the plate. "Muffins. Oatmeal raisin. Got 'em at the bakery. They're supposed to be good for you. Thought you could use them with Hannah here and all." She looked about. "Lucy gone back?"

"Left last week." Shirley trailed after her to the kitchen and sat at the table as Franny filled the coffee pot.

"Hannah not here?"

"She and Mama have gone to look at the house. You should see it, Shirley. It looks like a different place." Franny measured coffee. Shirley Dilworth wasn't a casual drop-in friend. What did she want? Franny looked at the clock hoping her mother and Hannah would drive up and save her, but they hadn't been gone that long.

The two ate muffins as the coffee perked: *plop, plop,* measuring seconds, minutes. Shirley asked all about Lucy's new job, how Faith was feeling now, and had they decided on a name for the baby? And there was something in her eyes. More than interest. Understanding? Who was this person? Franny found herself telling her about Gib's volunteering to help hurricane victims, laughing over his lack of building experience. They drank coffee, ate another muffin. Shirley told her about her son's second wife and getting adjusted to being a stepgrandmother. Franny asked about her newlywed daughter who planned to go back to school at night. She was beginning to *almost like* Shirley Dilworth! But why was she there? Why this sudden concern?

The phone rang as Franny poured a second cup of coffee and she excused herself to answer it.

"Mrs. Hughes, this is Dr. Herman. I have the results of your lab report." Why was he hesitating? "Is anyone there with you?"

Franny looked at Shirley and knew. So this was why she'd come.

Chapter Twenty

December 11, 1943

How long had they been standing there? Franny buried her face in the scratchy shirts, smelled their stiff new smell. Miss Havergal was gone. She had stalked from the store in the same manner she entered. The Ice Queen. The room itself felt colder.

Hannah tugged at her hand, but Franny held her still. Their teacher mustn't see them here. Miss O'Donnell looked small and pale. Her mouth quivered and she opened her bag for a handkerchief, then stood for a minute with her hand over her eyes. Franny thought her hand trembled a little. She watched her walk past, the paper sack with the writing paper in it clutched in one hand. Franny wanted to hug her teacher, say she was on her side, but it wasn't the time.

"Wesley," Hannah said. "Let's get Wesley. He'll know what to do."

Franny agreed. They couldn't handle this alone. They ran home without speaking, past the boy selling mistletoe on the corner, the stuffed Santa in the window of Lottie's Fashions, the lighted tree in the park. But it didn't seem like Christmas anymore.

It was freezing in the Whitfields' smokehouse, but they didn't dare go inside the house. Betty Joyce's mother was visiting with Addie Grace Crenshaw, and little Dottie was on the prowl. Travis had already run her off once—told her the smokehouse was haunted by the ghost of Betty Joyce's great aunt Bertha who had hung herself in there.

"Betty Joyce never had a great aunt Bertha, silly!" Hannah told him, but Travis only shrugged. "Dottie doesn't know that," he said. Franny wondered how long it would take the little pest to find out.

Franny wrapped a musty quilt about her and beat her mittened hands together. Travis pulled a knitted cap over his ears and shivered; Hannah stamped her feet. Only Wesley seemed unaffected by the cold. He stood in the doorway, hands in his pockets—his only concession to the temperature. "Betty Joyce said she'd be here in a minute," Wesley said. "She's finishing a scrapbook for her uncle Hiram. He's leaving for Fort McPherson in the morning."

Betty Joyce's uncle Hiram had reddish brown hair like hers and could whistle just about any tune you wanted. He worked in Peabody's Dry Goods where Franny's mother bought her cloth, and once he had given Franny remnants to make doll clothes, but she never did. She was sorry she hadn't told him goodbye.

Every month more and more of their men were leaving. Window after window in Sallie's Station displayed the white banner with a blue star that meant a member of the family was in the armed services, or a gold star for the one who would never come home. Franny got to where she hated to see the boy from Western Union ride by on his bicycle. Telegrams meant bad news. Soon there wouldn't be anyone left.

"Maybe we could get Mr. Kennedy at *The Chronicle* to say he made a mistake," Betty Joyce suggested when she arrived a few minutes later. Her mother had made gingerbread and it was still warm. Franny held hers between her palms and nibbled a little at a time.

"Too late for that," Wesley said. "Miss Havergal's out to get her. Don't you see? She just needed an excuse."

"Shouldn't we tell our parents?" Hannah asked. "If they know what she means to do, surely they'll help us."

Travis gulped the last of his gingerbread and wiped the crumbs on his sleeve. "They haven't believed us before." He turned to Wes. "Your daddy's head of the school board. Can't he do something?"

But Wesley shook his head. "He can't go over the principal's head—not for something like this. Miss O'Donnell broke a rule. She didn't do what Miss Havergal asked."

Franny thought about what Lieutenant Gregory had said just before he left. "You'll take care of her, won't you, Franny? I can count on you." He had meant for her to look after Miss O'Donnell. Franny hated to think how disappointed he would be.

"What if *Miss Havergal* broke a rule?" Franny asked.

Travis balanced on an old piano stool. It tilted from side to side. "What kind of rule?"

"An important rule. Something that would get her fired."

"Like what?" Wesley frowned.

"I don't know." Franny shrugged. "What if she stole something? Broke the law?"

"There's a rule against teachers drinking," Hannah said. "Remember that science teacher they fired at the high school? Singleton said he passed out over his Bunsen burner."

Travis made a rude noise. "Old Havergal doesn't drink," he reminded them.

"Even if she did, we couldn't prove it," Betty Joyce said. "Besides, it's not a crime to drink."

"That doesn't matter," Wesley told them. "It's against the rules for teachers, and if the school board ever found out, they'd be in trouble." He looked at Travis and smiled. "Big trouble."

Franny heard Hannah draw in her breath. She knew what Wesley was proposing, but nobody wanted to say it.

Wesley stood and folded his arms as he spoke. His voice was calm and low. "So . . . I guess we'll just have to make sure they find out."

* * * * *

Franny had never experienced anything like it, this cool, slick gray feeling. This must be what it's like being shot from a cannon, she thought, carefully pouring her father's I. W. Harper into an empty jelly jar. She was being propelled toward some kind of end, and she couldn't help herself. It wasn't a bad feeling. In fact, she kind of liked it.

Franny held the jar to the pantry light. This would have to be enough; it wouldn't do for her father to miss it. She had taken what looked to be about half a cup, maybe a little more, and she hadn't spilled a drop. Wesley was to borrow the same amount from his father's private supply, and Travis said he knew his Uncle Willie kept "shine" under the floor of his tool shed where his Aunt Myra wouldn't find it.

If Travis Kimbrough's mama, who was at that moment giving the devotional at the Ladies' Missionary Society, knew what they were doing in her kitchen that Sunday afternoon, she'd be thinking about turning somebody else's cheek. And Travis would have to learn so many Bible verses, he might as well take up preaching.

Hannah and Betty Joyce had found two empty liquor bottles in the trash can behind the Peacock Cafe, and with their combined booty, they were able to fill two half pint bottles enough to make a good slosh and a convincing smell. The next afternoon, while the principal presided over an hour-long teachers' meeting after school, the girls would find some way to plant one bottle in Miss Havergal's room at the boarding house—where Annie Tate would be sure to find it. Miss Opal's housekeeper was a notorious gossip. Travis and Wesley were responsible for slipping the other bottle into the principal's desk drawer in the school office.

What would her parents think, Franny wondered, if they knew what an awful thing she'd done? Of course her parents shouldn't be too surprised, but poor Betty Joyce hardly ever did anything wrong. Her mama and daddy would probably make her spend the next fifty years in church. Franny could just picture her sitting in the last pew, her bright braids all turned to gray, wearing a black hat with an old squished rose on it, kind of like Miss Emmalee Llewellyn's.

The next day Franny stood watch in Miss Opal's upstairs hall while Hannah planted the evidence in the principal's dresser drawer, leaving it partly open so the bottle would show. She had first poured an inch or so in Miss Havergal's toothbrush glass, and soaked a saucer-size area of the embroidered dresser scarf. Later they learned it took off the varnish. Miss Opal was making bandages at the Red Cross and all the teachers were at their after-school meeting. Only Annie remained in the house singing hymns as she ironed in the kitchen.

Franny gripped the banister and held her breath. She could have sworn she heard somebody in Miss Opal's fig bushes as they sneaked in the back way. Is this how a soldier felt on patrol? If she'd had to choose between facing her principal and Adolf Hitler, Franny would have had to give it serious thought. She knew this was the afternoon Annie ironed for some of the teachers for a little extra money, and now and then Franny heard the thump of the iron as the housekeeper paused for breath between verses. Franny allowed herself to relax a little as the woman finished *When the Roll is Called Up Yonder* and began *Amazing Grace*. As long as she could hear her deep, rich singing, she was safe. Before Annie started supper, she would collect the dresses, skirts and blouses, smelling of sun and starch, and hang them in the appropriate rooms. This could be any time.

A paralyzing weakness spread from Franny's stomach to her legs, and she'd begun to wonder how much longer she'd be able to stand when Hannah came flying out of the principal's room, almost knocking her downstairs. Together they fled down the empty front hall and out the side door that faced the Whitfields' where Betty Joyce was supposed to be keeping watch in the shadows.

"What ya'll been doing in there?" A small dirty face appeared from behind an azalea, and Dottie Crenshaw crawled out with grime on her knees and leaves in her hair.

"Nothing," Hannah said. "Go on home now. It's late."

"You can't make me. You're not my mama." The child shifted a wad of gum the size of a walnut from one side of her mouth to the other.

"I'll bet your mama doesn't even know where you are," Franny said. "How long have you been playing back there?"

"I saw ya'll go in Miss Opal's and she's not even home. She and my mama are down at the Red Cross." Dottie skipped in a circle around them. "I'll bet Miss Opal doesn't even know you were in there, does she? I'm gonna tell!"

"It's none of your business, you nosy little brat!" Hannah moved a few steps toward her, and Dottie darted around a peach tree and let a limb smack her pursuer in the face. "Don't let her get me!" Dottie begged as she saw Betty Joyce emerging from the hedge.

"What's going on?" Betty Joyce looked like she'd seen a ghost.

"I thought you were supposed to be watching," Hannah whispered. "No telling how long she's been back there."

"How was I to know? I didn't know she was there." Betty Joyce looked from Hannah to Franny. "Honest! I was watching. I never saw her."

"So what do we do now?" Franny asked.

"Here come Wesley and Travis," Betty Joyce said as she watched the two boys sprinting across the street. "Maybe we oughta get out of sight or something before Miss Ha—before somebody sees us."

"What are you all doing out here? Are you crazy?" Panting, Wesley slipped behind a cedar tree and melted into the shadows behind Miss Opal's garage. "What's the matter? Did something go wrong?"

"*She* went wrong." Hannah nodded her head in Dottie's direction. "She was hiding in the bushes, saw us go in."

"Aw, she don't know nothin'!" Travis said. "She's just a little squirt. Go on, get outa here, Dottie, before your mama comes looking for you."

"I know you all have been up to something!" Dottie giggled, hopping on one foot. "And I'm gonna tell."

"We were just fixing up a surprise for Miss Opal," Betty Joyce said in a sugary voice. "If you tell her, it won't be a surprise anymore." It was probably the first time in her life that Betty Joyce had ever lied. Franny thought she did it well.

"I don't believe you. I'm telling!"

"You do, and we'll throw you in the drainage ditch with the Slimy Sewer Snort." Wesley's face was solemn, and he kept looking over his shoulder as if the monster might be lurking close by.

"You don't scare me. I'll tell who I please! What have you all been up to, anyway?" The child frowned as she backed away.

"The Tunnel Troll just loves little tattletale girls," Franny told her. "And he hasn't had his supper yet."

"It's cold in there, and dark." Hannah said. "You won't like it."

"Look, Dottie, if you can keep a secret, I'll give you a nickel," Travis said, digging in his pocket. "You can buy a candy bar."

The little girl shook her head. "I want two candy bars."

"I think I have a nickel left from Christmas shopping." Betty Joyce took off her glove and checked her coat pocket. "Okay, you can have two, but you have to promise." She offered the coin on the palm of her hand.

"I promise!" Dottie said as she snatched it away. Then, "I'm telling, I'm telling!" she sang. "I know a secret! I know a secret! Ya-ya-ya-ya-ya!"

Franny lurched forward, hands out, itching to shake the obnoxious brat, swat her skinny little fanny. Miss Addie Grace would have a fit if anybody messed with her precious "lambie," as she called her, but just now Franny didn't care.

"Quick, grab her, Wesley!" Travis yelled. "The Sewer Snort's stomach's growling!"

185

Afterward, Franny would try to recall how it happened, but it was like a film run too fast. Dottie dodged away from them, zigzagged across the lawn like a frightened rabbit. Franny heard the horrible screech of the car's brakes and a scream that came from somewhere deep inside her. Then Dottie Crenshaw lay in the street with her eyes closed and blood all over her face while the five of them crouched over her.

"Oh Dottie, I didn't mean it! We didn't mean it. We weren't really gonna throw you in the ditch." Travis knelt beside the child and cried. "Why'd you have to go and run in the street?"

Mattie Williamson, who had been driving home from the dentist's in the pre-dusk, stumbled from the car. "Precious Jesus! I didn't see her," the woman said. "She just ran right out in front of me. God knows, I tried to stop!" She wasn't crying, but she trembled so Franny thought she might shatter right there in the street. "Somebody run quick! Tell Damascus Jones to send his ambulance," she said, spreading her coat over Dottie's small form.

"Dottie, please don't die," Hannah said. "Please, God, don't let her die."

Wesley touched Dottie's limp wrist. "She's not dead. She has a pulse. Don't just stand there, Hannah! Get Mr. Jones *now*. Hurry!"

"Somebody needs to call Miss Addie Grace." A small voice spoke behind her and Franny turned to find Betty Joyce standing there, as still as stone, and groggy, like she'd been in a deep sleep. "I mean, shouldn't we? Her mama oughta know."

"Yes, yes. Of course we should. But, oh dear God, I just can't do it." Mattie Williamson sat on the cold pavement beside the injured child and touched Dottie's cheek. "One of you, please, see if Miss Opal's there, or Annie. Ask somebody to call."

Betty Joyce looked down at Dottie with a quiet porcelain face. "I'll go," she said, and ran.

"It's our fault," Wesley said. "If she dies, it's all our fault." Franny had never seen Wesley cry before but he was crying now, silently,

186

crouched there in the street, his head on his knees. And she was crying too. Would she have struck Dottie Crenshaw if she could have caught her? She wanted to, but she didn't. She didn't touch her. And what did it matter now? The little girl was bleeding in the street because of them, maybe dying. This was worse than Aunt Six being so sick, worse even than Mr. Gregory going to war, because they were to blame. "I'm sorry," Franny sobbed. "I'm so sorry, Dottie. We didn't mean it."

"Well of course you didn't mean it!" Mrs. Williamson spoke up. "I hope you don't blame yourselves for this. The little girl ran right in front of me. It wasn't your fault at all."

The three of them looked at each other. But nobody spoke. And as they waited there for help, Franny saw the gleam of a nickel where it had rolled into brown leaves by the side of the road.

Dottie Crenshaw lay in a coma in the hospital in Rome with her leg broken in three places, a fractured collarbone, and internal bleeding. Doctors had given her two blood transfusions, they said, and most of the population of Sallie's Station, Georgia, prayed for her through the night. Franny prayed too. Mrs. Williamson had said they weren't to blame for what happened to Dottie, but Mrs. Williamson didn't know what made Dottie run in front of her car. God knew though, and Franny spent a lot of time talking to Him about it.

The next day at school, Wesley told them at recess that his dad had received a telephone call from Miss Opal the night before. It looked as though Annie had taken the bait.

Miss Havergal's face was pasty white, like she'd scrubbed it with Old Dutch Cleanser and let it dry there. She walked stiffly into the room, thumped her satchel onto the desk. "Turn to the review section on page fifty-eight of your workbooks, do as many as you can."

For forty-five minutes the principal sat rigidly turning a pencil in her fingers. The sun glinted off her glasses as she stared blankly at the deserted swings on the playground. Beside her in the corner, the class

Christmas tree, festive with paper chains, tilted on its wooden cross-piece, and filled the room with a spicy cedar smell. At the end of the period, Miss Havergal rose and left the room, gray serge back stiff as a tree trunk, arms strained with the weight of the satchel.

As she was leaving the building after school, Franny heard Miss Jacobs, the music teacher, whispering to Miss Hightower that she'd seen several members of the school board meeting in the office.

The office. That was where Wesley and Travis had left a half-filled pint of "shine" the day before. During the faculty meeting it had been on display to anyone passing the open door. Just before the teachers dispersed for home, Wesley shoved it to the back of the principal's desk drawer behind two confiscated comic books and a wooden whistle. Later, they would learn, that was exactly where Mr. Fuller found it.

"She *cursed*," Wesley told them, quoting his father. When they confronted her with what they had found, Miss Havergal cursed and threw a bottle of ink halfway across the room! It narrowly missed Mr. Alfred Maxwell, the pharmacist, whose suit always looked recently steamed and pressed. Wesley didn't know what the curse words were because his dad didn't repeat them, but Mr. Fuller said they were words no lady should use. And she had yelled and hollered too. Said it was all a conspiracy and they were all just too stupid to realize it.

After two days Dottie Crenshaw had stabilized but was still in a coma, and Franny felt oddly removed from the everyday things going on around her. Somebody else was wearing her skin. The four of them in Mrs. Hightower's room looked quickly away whenever their eyes met. They had promised—no—sworn not to mention their secrets again. It was over now, and there was nothing else they could do. The waiting had begun.

Miss Havergal waded through the week before the holidays, a mechanical presence in a stiff mask. Franny knew the woman disliked them, but the fire behind it was gone, leaving a cold, black lump. They had won. She knew they had won, but Franny found no glory in their victory, no elation. She couldn't hate the principal anymore, and she missed that—having someone to blame, someone she could see. Not like Hitler.

During the Christmas play on the last day, the principal sat alone in the front row. The chair beside her that Mr. Gregory had occupied in October looked bare, expectant, as if he might dash in from some Pacific island, helmet in hand, and slide into place.

It was rumored that Lieutenant Gregory was somewhere in the South Pacific, but nobody knew exactly where. That bothered Franny. She liked to put her finger on things.

"They can't tell us that, Franny V.," Hannah told her. "We never know where Singleton's going to be. Loose lips sink ships, you know."

Franny knew. She kicked a twig on the sidewalk as they walked to town. They had pooled the Christmas money they were going to spend on each other to buy Dottie Crenshaw a paint set for when she came out of her deep sleep. If she came out of it. Franny sighed. Why couldn't war and troubles take a Christmas vacation like everybody else?

On the way to Goldman's they stopped at Mr. Sanderson's Butcher Shop to find Franny's neighbor Mrs. Littlejohn hunched over the glass counter. "Doesn't your mouth just water for some good old pork?" Mrs. Littlejohn bellowed when she saw her.

"Yes, ma'am, it sure does." Franny handed the butcher the family's collection of drippings. They were used in making explosives for the war.

"I'll swear, I can just taste it! But all those coupons for just a few little chops!" Her neighbor gripped the clasp on her worn brown handbag as if to keep the precious ration stamps from escaping.

The shop smelled of sawdust that littered the floor behind the counter, and of a raw, salty odor that had to do with the butcher's grisly operations behind the swinging door.

Mr. Sanderson poured the contents of Franny's can into a bucket with a sickening *glump* and gave her back the slippery container.

"Tell your mama I heard Peabody's is going to have stockings in tomorrow," Mrs. Littlejohn whispered to Franny. Well, it really wasn't a whisper, but was more like a soft yell. She shifted her bundles and thumbed once more through her ration book. "Tell her to get there before they put the sign in the window. There'll be a line all the way around the block."

Franny thanked her neighbor and left her to decide about the chops. She found Hannah at the collection center at the end of the street where she'd gone to drop off a bag of ragged stockings. A sign over the door of the center said: *Junk can win the war!* And Franny felt that as many times as she'd been in there, they should have won it already.

"I'll bet Lieutenant Gregory's already on one of those islands over there getting ready for the next battle," Franny said as they started home, but Hannah didn't answer. Because of Singleton, Hannah didn't like to talk about the fighting.

The Americans had taken Tarawa and Makin. Franny had read about it in the papers. They called it "island hopping," which made her think of a giant playing hopscotch.

Since their principal left for overseas, Franny tried to keep up with what was going on, although she didn't understand a lot of it. When the weekly *Chronicle* came, she devoured every line.

Most of the contents pertained to the war. At Sallie's Station High School the students had helped distribute ration books . . . a group of junior and senior girls enrolled in a first aid class . . . the results of a poll taken at the school determined that *Miss You* was the current favorite song among the girls . . . *This is the Army* was playing at Martin's.

Advertisements, too, were patriotic: "HAS YOUR SOLDIER'S SUBSCRIPTION EXPIRED?" asked *The Chronicle*. "Keep Morale High—Send That Army Boy Your Picture!" urged Dawson's Photographers.

If there was some way not to think about the war, Franny wished she knew what it was. Even the Burma Shave signs, placed at intervals along roadsides to advertise shaving cream, had taken up the effort:

Let's make Hitler
And Hirohito
Look as sick as
Old Benito
Buy Defense Bonds
Burma Shave

At a war bond rally a few days later some of the boys from Winnie's class hung Benito Mussolini in effigy from the redbud tree on the courthouse lawn. The crumpled wreckage of a German plane, shot down over Sicily, was displayed right next to the monument for Echota County's World War I dead. Franny touched the cold, gray wing tip. It had a sweet, metallic odor and smelled of death.

Chapter Twenty-one

"If you're going to have breast cancer, I suppose this is the best kind to have," Dr. Herman said, in what seemed a pathetic attempt to make Franny feel better. The name of it sounded like something you might have to take your freshman year in college: *intraductal carcinoma*. (I managed to scrape by intraductal carcinoma 101, but this 102 is the pits!)

"What you have is a precancerous condition," he told her. "Right now the cells are contained in the milk ducts, but if they break out into the surrounding tissue, they become invasive." Franny's was in the last stage before doing that, he said, and according to the lab report, these cells extended to the margin of the resection.

"You mean there might be more in there?"

"Very possibly. We removed the cluster of calcification that showed up in the mammogram, but there could be some that didn't."

She found herself shielding her breast with one hand as they talked. "So what can we do?" Franny glanced at Shirley who sat looking into her coffee mug, both hands wrapped around it.

He cleared his throat. "Unfortunately, ductal carcinoma in situ doesn't respond well to radiation or chemotherapy. In your case, I'd recommend a modified radical mastectomy, but of course there are other options. We'll talk about these when you come in."

Franny made an appointment with his receptionist to come in the next day—or she thought she did. She didn't remember doing it. Other options, he'd said. What other options? How much would they have to cut out before she got rid of all those nasty little cells crammed inside her milk ducts?

From her window she saw Betty Joyce pull into her drive and dash inside with an armful of packages, last minute purchases, she supposed, for her trip to London. Her neighbor was going Christmas shopping at Harrods, and she was going to have her breast cut off. Tears welled in Franny's eyes. It just wasn't fair!

Somebody touched her shoulder and Franny turned to find Shirley standing behind her. "You knew?" she asked.

She nodded. "The FAX came in for Dr. Winthrop this morning with the lab report. I knew they'd be calling you soon, and I just didn't want you to be alone when you heard. I've been there, Franny. I know."

"You had breast cancer, Shirley? When?"

"Almost five years ago. Had a mastectomy, then radiation and chemo. Made me feel like hell for a while, but—hey—so far, so good!" Shirley put an arm around her. "Go ahead, cry if you want to. Say 'shit.' It's allowed."

Franny was too numb to cry, but not too numb to say shit, so she did. It didn't help a lot. "I'm sorry, I didn't know," she said. "Why didn't you tell me?"

She grinned. "It's not something you put in *The Chronicle*, you know. And it happened before I married Bud. We'd just started seeing one another, and I thought, 'Well, this is it for him!' But damned if he didn't surprise me. Bud's always been a leg man, he says.

"Look, you're going to think of a lot of questions when the shock wears off," Shirley said. "And when you do, I'll be glad to answer them if I can." She lowered her voice, although there was nobody else there to hear. "Your doctor will try to explain this crap to you the best he can, but it helps if you can talk to somebody who's been there."

Franny made a face. "Doctors!" She told her about Lennie Baby with the sewed-up mouth and fence-post personality and discovered that she could still laugh. But she did have questions. Did it hurt? And what about reconstruction?

"Not as much as you'd think," Shirley told her. "I did have to take a little physical therapy to regain the use of my arm." And she gave her the name of a good plastic surgeon. In spite of her then-fiance's objections, she said, Shirley had decided on a saline implant. "It's more affordable and it works for me, but Franny, you should see what they can do now. Why, this doctor can even build a titty out of your stomach!"

Franny was laughing when they heard Hannah's car out front. "You don't want me here when you tell your mama," Shirley said on her way out. "But before you decide *anything,* Franny, get a couple of other opinions, and read up on this as much as you can. I've got a book I'll be glad to loan you—tells you all about it." She paused at the door. "And for God's sake, don't tell Dr. Winthrop I've been here. We're not supposed to do this, you know. I could lose my job."

Franny promised as she walked with her to the porch. Hannah, crossing the yard with Franny's mother, gave them a quizzical look.

"What was that all about?" Hannah asked as Shirley drove away. Franny brought them inside, sat them down, and told them.

Her mama's lip trembled and Franny could tell the flow was about to begin. "Don't you dare cry," she told her. "We don't have time for that right now. Besides, it's not as bad as it sounds." She explained about the cells being noninvasive. "It's not even cancer yet," she bragged.

"But your breast . . . you might have to lose your breast!" Her mother crossed her arms in front of hers.

"Well, it's not like I walk on it or anything. Shoot, it can't even write a letter or carry a sack of groceries! And to tell you the truth, it hasn't been much good at all for a long time now—except to balance out my blouse."

Hannah still sat with her jacket thrown over her lap where she'd removed it when she came inside. With one hand she worked the zipper up and down while staring into the empty fireplace. "It's all that pork fat," she said. "All that cooking with streak o' lean. It's a wonder we don't all have it."

That wasn't exactly what Franny wanted to hear just then, and she told her so. Besides, she still liked a mess of green beans or turnip greens cooked the right way once in a while, although she had cut down on using fat.

Hannah stood and put her arms around her. "I wasn't thinking, I'm sorry. Oh, Franny, I hate it that this has happened to you! Do you really think you might have to . . . have this done?"

She wasn't thrilled, either, Franny told her. And she meant to find out a lot more about it before she did anything drastic. "But there's one thing I'm certain of," she said. "Faith mustn't know. Not yet, anyway."

"What about Winnie?" her mother asked. "Don't you think you should call your sister?"

"I will, Mama, but after I talk with the doctor and know more than I do now. I can't even answer my own questions, much less hers."

After supper Franny went by Shirley's and brought home the book she'd told her about so she would know what to ask the surgeon the next day. Later she read aloud from it to her mother and Hannah and showed them the illustrations. She wanted them to know what was going on too.

That night Franny dreamed of booger bears. It was late, almost dark, and she was a child again walking home from school. Franny's booger bear was dark gray and furry. It walked upright and its ears stuck up on top of its head. In her dream it stalked, stealing quickly, quietly from tree to tree. But Franny knew it was there behind her, she could see the tip of its long, bushy tail, the gleam of sharp white teeth.

She hadn't thought of booger bears in years. They were a part of her childhood, a game played at twilight just before dusk. *Ain't no booger bears out tonight, 'cause my daddy killed them all last night!* they would sing. And then the one who was *it*, the "booger bear," growling horribly, charged after them, usually catching the child who couldn't run very fast, the youngest one. Franny. A scary version of tag, it was a game filled with delicious terror played in those dark precious minutes before their mothers called them in for baths and bed.

Waking with the covers knotted about her, Franny enticed Sylvester into her bed and slept with the cat's warm body next to her breast.

The next day Lennie wore slime green trousers and a smile that didn't quite make it. The bandage on his chin was gone. Good. He told her what she had already read in Shirley's book and drew pictures on the back of a prescription pad. According to her surgeon, and to the book she'd read, Franny had three options: A wide excision of the affected area, in which there was a ten-to-twenty percent chance of subsequent cancer; a wide excision plus radiation, which helped reduce recurrence by about five-to-ten percent, or a radical mastectomy, usually about a one-hundred percent cure. Franny said she would think about it and let him know.

"Don't take too long," he told her with his usual gracious aplomb. "One patient put it off for seven months. It was too late." He did offer to present her case before a board of physicians at the hospital there. The group was composed of specialists in several areas who reviewed each patient as an anonymity, then decided on diagnosis and treatment.

Dr. Herman agreed to schedule Franny for what they called a

"blind" biopsy the following week to see if any of the threatening cells were in her other breast. Shirley's book advised it, the surgeon said he thought it was a good idea, and it made sense to Franny. Of course—to use a clichéd (and painful) expression, it was more or less a stab in the dark.

When in Rome, do as the Romans do, to paraphrase a quote, and since everybody in Rome, Georgia, seemed to be doing their Christmas shopping, after she left the doctor, Franny went shopping too. She had her list, a little money in her checking account, and the rest of the afternoon. It was cold enough to be bracing, carols rang through the malls, and store lights twinkled through gilded greenery.

For a person who felt the first shiver of Christmas spirit when red felt stockings competed with plastic jack-o-lanterns at K-Mart, Franny was having a major problem, and she didn't like it. Would this be her last Christmas? Would she miss watching her first grand-child grow up?

The new dictionary she had bought for her crossword-cheating mother seemed suddenly heavy. Was that a pain in her stomach? Her hair hurt. Franny didn't feel so good anymore. She dragged past a frozen yogurt shop without even considering treating herself. She wasn't hungry. Too weak to eat, to shop, to smile back at the tired, flustered lady in the gift wrap department, Franny rested on a bench by the fountain. An old black man sat across from her and stared solemnly at his feet. Had he been to the doctor too?

If only this were a solid thing, maybe she could deal with it. But how do you fight those sneaky little cells that won't show themselves in a lump? They could be anywhere. Everywhere. Franny examined her hands, her fingernails. Were they swimming around underneath the skin? Would they find them in her other breast too?

Finally she worked up enough stamina to shop for a soft green blouse for Faith and a small table lamp for Lucy's apartment. If she croaked before Christmas, Hannah would just have to do the rest of her buying. Franny had purchased her friend's gift a few weeks before: a print of the old grammar school building by a local artist. And, of course, a box of chocolate-covered cherries.

As they were eating supper that night, Betty Joyce came over with the keys to their house, most of a quart of milk, and the only African violet she hadn't managed to kill. Franny put it in her kitchen window and said she'd do her best but wasn't making any promises. She wasn't going to tell her about the lab report but her neighbor asked, and Franny couldn't think of a lie.

"It could be worse," Franny said, and told her what she'd learned.

"Oh, Franny!" Betty Joyce stood behind her chair and put her face next to her's. "I'm so sorry, but I'm glad they caught it when they did. I hope you're going to take care of this, get it out of the way." She hugged her then. "Who needs the silly old things, anyway?"

Franny felt a giggle rising in her throat that wouldn't be restrained. It was a minute before she could talk.

Hannah thought she was crying. "Franny, what is it?" She rose from her chair. Her mother reached for her hand.

Franny wiped her eyes with her napkin. "Remember those silly book titles we made up in junior high? *Under the Grandstand* by Seymore Butts . . . *The Tiger's Revenge* by Claude Balls . . . ? I guess I'll have to read *The Broken Brassiere Strap* by One Hung Low!"

She and Hannah were cleaning the kitchen after Betty Joyce left when the doorbell rang. Hannah had her hands in soapy water and her mother wasn't dressed, so Franny propped the broom against the wall and went to see who it was. Maybe Betty Joyce had found something else in her refrigerator that wouldn't keep, but their neighbor usually just stuck her head in the door and yelled.

The first thing she saw when she opened the door was an enormous bunch of red roses, then two arms came from behind them and lifted her off her feet. "Mama, I love you," Gib said. "Just tell me what you want me to do."

"I want you to grow up," Franny said. "I want you to stick with one job and one wife. I want you to *never* do something like this to us again."

And while I'm at it, she thought, *I want people to stop killing each other and for chocolate not to be fattening.*

Franny held her son with one arm and the roses with another and took a deep, long sniff of their summer garden smell. "And I want you to fix that loose board on the back steps."

Maybe, if she were lucky, she'd get a couple of wishes out of the lot.

Chapter Twenty-two

Late December, 1943

Three days before Christmas Dottie Crenshaw awoke from her coma and demanded ice cream. Because of her shattered leg, it would be weeks before she could come home from the hospital, but otherwise, she seemed to be recovering as everyone had hoped. Franny thanked God every night in her prayers. And although she didn't admit it to Him, she was also thankful that Dottie didn't seem to remember anything about the accident or what caused it.

Franny wore Christmas like a cape, whirled it about her: a bright, sequined cloak of vivid red and green days, navy, star-splashed nights. With the Junior Epworth League, she went caroling in shattering crystal air, giggled on porches, stuffed herself with nut bread and ginger cookies. Franny stored up smells to last a year: cedar from the tree, pungent fruit cake wrapped in cheese cloth and soaked in wine with half an apple tucked in the hole—to keep it moist, her mother said. And now and then she stopped to remind herself that had Dottie Crenshaw not improved, the season wouldn't be festive at all. If Dottie had died, they might as well have skipped Christmas altogether. But Dottie didn't die. God was good, and everything was going to be all right.

By the end of the holidays, Franny had read her two new *Nancy Drews* and used up all the litmus paper from the chemistry set Santa Claus brought. A few days before school started, Franny used one of the dimes from the roll she'd found in her stocking to see Abbott and Costello. Lou Costello was a funny little fat man who was always being chased by gangsters, hit over the head, or getting stuck in revolving doors. Bud Abbott was his tall, thin partner who got him into all those messes, and then got mad at him for being so stupid.

Today's feature was preceded by *The March of Time: News of the World*, and followed by a continued serial that went on for weeks and weeks and always left the hero or heroine in some perilous situation from which it seemed impossible to escape. But they always did.

Halfway through the newsreel somebody kicked Franny's chair from behind. The film showed the rubble of London after a bombing raid and she felt as though they had destroyed her own backyard. She was almost afraid to watch, afraid she might recognize a building from a story she had read, or one of those enchanting little cottages with a garden in back like she'd seen in picture books. They had evacuated the children to safer places, Franny had heard. But someday she was going there.

The oaf behind kicked her again. "Cut it out!" She turned to give him a dirty look.

It was Wesley, just back from his grandmother's in Chatsworth. "Got something to tell you," he muttered through a mouthful of pickle.

"What?"

" 'Bout Miss Havergal." He wiped juice from his chin. "Tell you after the movie."

"Shh!" Betty Joyce curled one foot under her. "Be quiet, the picture's starting."

But Franny lost track of the plot. What did Wesley mean? Did Miss Havergal find out what they had done? Would she be waiting for them when they went back to school with that thick paddle with the hole in it? Was she having them all put in jail?

Franny had heard her mama and Mrs. Littlejohn talking about Miss Havergal's ugly scene with the ink bottle. Franny's mama said she was shocked and disgusted that the school board hired a *common* person like that in the first place, and Mrs. Littlejohn said she could have told them the woman had a screw loose when Annie Tate said she put sugar on grits. Surely they wouldn't have her back.

After the movie they saw a film featuring Bugs Bunny selling war bonds, and finally Franny's favorite, an Our Gang comedy, but even that wasn't as funny as usual. As soon as the comedy was over she raced up the aisle. It would be just like Wesley to say something like that, then disappear without explaining. But he and Travis waited in front of the ticket booth.

"What do you mean about Miss Havergal?" Franny demanded.

He drew them to one side over by the glass-enclosed poster that advertised coming attractions: *Humphrey Bogart in "Casablanca"—Tuesday, Wednesday and Thursday.* "She's not coming back," Wesley said. It was good to see him smile again.

Betty Joyce frowned. "How do you know she's not?"

"Because I heard Dad talking about it over the phone," Wesley told her. "He said she would never teach *anywhere* again if he could help it."

Wesley's father, as chairman of the school board, should know. Franny looked up at the blue lighted star on top of city hall and said, "Thank you, God!"

"Who's gonna take the old ha'nt's place?" Travis wanted to know. But Wesley shrugged. He hadn't heard that much, he said. They didn't find out until the following Monday who their new math teacher would be.

"Coming in on a wing and a prayer . . ." Travis sailed around the school yard, arms outstretched, and made a crash landing into Betty Joyce.

"Stop it, Travis!" She picked up her books and started to tell them again about how her uncle Hiram had seen Bette Davis and Linda Darnell at the Hollywood Canteen. He was stationed at a naval base in California and the Whitfields had his picture in their living room in a white sailor suit.

"What's all this?" Miriam Thatcher stepped up behind them, coat pulled tightly around her, cheeks flushed from the cold. "Sounds exciting!"

"Oh it is!" Betty Joyce pounced on the opportunity to recite her story to a new listener. She added another movie star each time, it seemed. "What are you doing here, Mrs. Thatcher?" she asked when she finished her tale.

"I'm going to be your new math teacher." Miriam Thatcher smiled. "Don't look so surprised. I majored in math in college, taught two years in Atlanta before I married Tom."

"But what about Tommy?" Hannah asked.

"Oh, he's well taken care of. His grandma and Aunt Minnie will see to that."

Travis grinned as he walked away. "Hey, this is gonna be fun! I bet we won't hardly have to do any work at all." And he ran to tell Wesley the good news.

That afternoon during math class Travis demontrated his skill at making paper airplanes. Since he enjoyed working with paper so much, Mrs. Thatcher told him, he could help her grade workbooks after school. And she gave the class homework too, but she always assigned Wanda the easier problems, Franny noticed, and never called on Junior Massingill to read aloud. By the end of January it seemed almost as if Miss Havergal had never been there at all, and Franny thought she was out of their lives forever.

They heard it first from Wesley. He was late to school that morning and his eyes had lost the light behind them. They didn't look like Wesley's eyes at all.

Mrs. Hightower glanced at the homework he tossed onto her desk and then at Wesley, who shambled to his seat as if he wasn't quite sure where it was. "Wesley, you didn't complete your essay. Are you sure you want to hand this in?"

At his desk, he lifted a white face. "Ma'am?"

"Your assignment. If you've been sick, I can give you an extension.

"Wesley, is anything wrong?" Franny sensed alarm in their teacher's voice.

He sat so rigidly it shook the whole row of seats. "Miss Havergal's dead," Wesley said.

There was never the slightest doubt in Franny's mind that Wesley was telling the truth. It was war time and you didn't joke about death, not even Miss Havergal's.

"What happened?" Mrs. Hightower leaned forward, arms braced against her desk, dislodging a couple of papers that drifted to the floor. She didn't seem to notice.

Franny couldn't remember a classroom being this quiet. And the awful thing was, she thought of the trouble it would have saved them if they'd only known the principal was going to die. Franny stared at Hannah's back, the way the round white collar of her blouse was half-tucked under her green cardigan. Hannah didn't move.

"How, Wesley?" their teacher asked again. Her voice was soft, almost flat.

Mrs. Hightower doesn't really want to know, Franny thought, and she twisted the chipped red birthstone ring on her finger. She didn't want to know, either. Wasn't it enough the woman was gone?

Wesley folded his hands in front of him and stared straight ahead. "She killed herself."

"Oh." Mrs. Hightower sat, hands to her face. "Wesley, are you sure? Couldn't it have been an accident?"

"She shot herself," Wesley said. "In the head."

And that was the last thing he said that day. To anybody.

It was a bright, windy day, and Franny spent morning recess with her back against the building trying to absorb warmth from the sun, strength from the sturdy old wall. Hannah crouched on the ground beside her, chin on her knees. Some of the girls came over and asked them to jump rope, but neither felt like playing. They watched Wesley on the bench by the water fountain, history book in his lap. He appeared to be scrutinizing every line, but he never turned a page.

Travis came out of the boys' restroom with a blotchy face and sat beside his friend, but Wesley didn't acknowledge him. Finally Travis stood, hands in his pockets, and kicked at the bench where Wesley sat. Franny could tell he was good and mad, but she couldn't hear what he said. Wesley never lifted his head. Seeing the two girls against the wall, Travis plodded over, wiping his nose with the back of his hand. "I reckon we might as well've pulled the trigger."

"I know," Franny said. Was this really happening? If only they could have another chance! She would crawl through the drainage ditch on her hands and knees if it would bring Miss Havergal back to life, make Dottie's leg whole again.

Travis looked over his shoulder at the two statues behind him: Wesley on the bench, and the Indian on the water fountain. "It was his idea, remember? Wesley was the one who thought of it."

"But we all did it," Hannah reminded him. "And it's our fault Dottie ran in front of that car. There must be something wrong with us. We're just the same as murderers—all four of us."

"Five," Franny said. Somebody was going to have to tell Betty Joyce.

Betty Joyce Whitfield stayed out of school the rest of the week. With a sore throat, her mother's note said, but the other four knew it wasn't her throat that hurt.

Each morning when she woke, Franny tried to pretend it hadn't happened, that it had been a bad dream; but reality soon pounced with its awful weight, and she had to drag it around another day.

Franny squinted her eyes shut tight and strained to squeeze out the tears, but they wouldn't come. She was sorry for what she'd done, sorry for the unhappy child Miss Havergal had been and the joyless adult she'd become. She tried to imagine the principal as an orphaned child being shunted, unwanted, from one place to another, but she only saw the woman's embittered face with eyes that held no room for hope.

The next week they gathered in the empty school yard after everyone else had gone home and sat on the cold back steps where Miss Havergal often stood. What they had done was wrong, Wesley said. They'd made a terrible mistake, and since he was the one who thought of it, he reckoned he was most to blame.

Maybe so, Hannah told him, but that didn't make her feel any better. Having lost her appetite, she was skinnier than ever. Soon, Franny worried, there wouldn't be anything left of her friend but two big, sad eyes and a tuft of dark hair. "And there's Dottie," Hannah added. "We're lucky she didn't die too."

"I heard she's coming home from the hospital next week," Travis said. "Sounds like she's gonna be okay."

"But she'll walk with a limp, might even have to use crutches," Franny said. "Miss Addie Grace told Mama her leg hurts an awful lot."

"I never meant for her to run into the *street*," Travis said. "Heck, we were just teasin'."

But Dottie Crenshaw's leg was just as broken and Miss Havergal was just as dead. For atonement Franny had given the walkie-talkie she got for Christmas to Wanda Culpepper. It was all she could think to do. She had eyed it for months in the toy section of her daddy's hardware store and it was the present she wanted most. Now she didn't ever want to see it again. Nights she lay in bed listening to her sister's deep-sleep breathing and prayed that numbness would come. She wished she could cry, but all she did was ache, ache, ache. Franny couldn't remember the last time she slept all night.

"Coulda been somebody else who shot Miss Havergal," Travis suggested. "You know how mean she was. How do they know for sure who pulled the trigger?"

"They know," Wesley said. And nobody asked for details. Wesley had learned of the principal's suicide from his father, who heard it from the local superintendent. The last check they'd sent had been returned and he was told of her death when he called to inquire.

"I reckon we'll all go to hell." Hannah sounded mournful.

"Not me." Betty Joyce tugged her coat around her. "I'm going to confess at prayer meeting tonight. God will forgive you if you ask Him."

"You just have to blab it to everybody, don't you?" Travis jumped to his feet. "We promised, don't you remember? Betty Joyce Whitfield, don't you *dare!* Besides, what good will it do?"

For once Franny agreed with him. She hadn't said a word to anybody, not even her mother who trailed after her like a shadow with a long, worried face, but it festered like a sore inside her.

"Travis has a point," Wesley said. "Telling won't bring Miss Havergal back, and it won't heal Dottie's leg. Besides, you don't have to go to church to tell God you're sorry."

"I guess not," Betty Joyce said. "But you have to *mean* it." This to Travis.

"We could do it now, right here," Franny said. Surely God knew she was sorry. She'd already told Him about a million times, but she'd say it a million more if she thought it would make Betty Joyce keep her mouth shut.

"My mama dragged me over to see Dr. Ludlow, then made me swallow a whole lot of that nasty brown medicine because she thinks I'm bilious—and I still didn't tell her a thing." Hannah scowled at Betty Joyce. "You can just stick it out like the rest of us!"

Wesley looked from one to the other. "What's done is done. Telling can only hurt us, and I don't know about you, but I hurt enough already. It's like my grandma says—we made our bed, now I guess we gotta lie in it . . . for the rest of our lives. Maybe that's punishment enough."

Franny thought of Mrs. Hightower's favorite quote from the Bible about reaping what you sow. It looked like they were going to be stuck with a bitter crop.

"You mean *never* tell?" Betty Joyce asked.

"Not anybody?" This from Travis.

"Not anybody. Not ever." Wesley held out a square hand, palm up. "Promise."

Silently Hannah put her hand on his. Betty Joyce, crying, followed; then Franny, and last of all, Travis.

"Can we pray now?" Betty Joyce said. And they did.

"You reckon God will forgive us?" Travis said.

"He already has," Betty Joyce said.

Franny wished she could be so sure.

Chapter Twenty-three

"Look, Ma, the sooner we do something about this cancer thing, the better," Gib said. "Promise me you're not going to be one of those silly women who thinks a breast is more important than living."

Just what was this *we* business, Franny wondered. She didn't see that he had the physical characteristics to be in a position to judge, but was so glad to see him, she let it pass. "How did you find out?" Franny looked him over. He was a tall, skinny nuisance, but he was her nuisance and she loved every scruffy inch of him. Her son was sunburned and needed a haircut, but he looked happier than she'd seen him in a long time.

"Hannah called." She should have known. "How long were you going to wait before telling me, Ma?"

She shook her head. "Had to find you first."

Gib gave his mother another brief squeeze before deserting her for the refrigerator. "Wuzzy and I have decided to give it another go," he said between bites of cold chicken. "Had a long talk last night . . ." Gib grinned at her. "Guess we both have a lot to learn."

Franny smiled. It seemed like she'd heard him say that before, but at least it was a start.

Because it was so late, Gib spent the night and they stayed up after midnight talking about the time he'd spent in Florida. "I actually got to be passably good with a hammer, and I promise I'll come back one day soon and do something about those back steps," he said.

Maybe she should be pleased at hearing this, even excited, but somehow it didn't matter.

"I think you should tell Faith," he said. "It's not right to keep this from her. She's gonna be mad as all get-out when she finds out."

"Let's wait and see what happens," Franny told him. "I'm going back to see Dr. Kirkland, find out what she thinks I should do. And my surgeon said my case would come before the board next Tuesday. If and when I do have surgery—and it's looking like I will, it won't be until after Christmas. I promise I'll tell her then."

Faith had seemed unusually tired for the last few days, and Franny knew she was worried about the baby. She wasn't going to add to her problems any sooner than she had to.

"I'll be back the weekend after this one to get the tree," Gib promised when Franny told him goodbye the next morning. "We are going to have Christmas here, aren't we? When's Lucy coming home?"

"I don't know if she is. It costs a lot to fly, and this job doesn't pay enough to sneeze at." In spite of Lucy's objections, Franny had written a check to help tide her over, but doubted if there would be any left for plane fare.

"She'll be here." Hannah spoke from the landing, wrapping her familiar white terry robe about her, feet swallowed in pink fuzzy slippers. She was on her way downstairs to make another of those disgusting blended vegetable drinks she'd been dosing Franny with all week. "I'm giving her my frequent flyer points.

"Oh, hush!" she said when Franny started to protest. "Where am I going to use them? I'm exactly where I want to be. For now."

"Call when you know something," Gib said, kissing his mother's cheek on his way out. She noticed he still had the fancy red car.

"You didn't tell him about having the other biopsy," Hannah

said as they watched Gib drive away.

Franny shrugged. "I can only stand to sling just so much shit at a time," she said.

A low, mama bear-like rumble erupted behind her. "Frances!" her mother said. "You're getting to sound downright coarse." This last word was whispered. "When did you start talking that way?"

Franny hugged her and laughed. "Blame it on Shirley Dilworth, but I think I'm getting attached to the word."

Fortunately, she didn't have to sling any. The biopsy didn't turn up any more of those dark, sneaky cells hiding in her other breast. But that didn't necessarily mean they weren't there, Lennie Baby took pains to explain, and recommended a mammogram every six months in case more white dots appeared.

The hospital board unanimously recommended a modified radical mastectomy, which meant they would remove the breast and many of the lymph nodes, but not the muscles beneath. Patricia Kirkland agreed, as did Franny's family doctor, John Winthrop. "It's as close to a one-hundred-percent cure as we have right now," he said. "Of course you might live for years without it and have nothing develop. There's just no guarantee." He patted her shoulder. "I can't make the decision for you, Franny. I can only advise."

"What if this happened to your wife?" she asked him. "Your sister? What would you say to them?"

"I'd say, 'Cancel your plans for the next few weeks and make an appointment with a good surgeon.'"

"Is Leonard Herman a good surgeon?" She told him about the man's gruff temperament.

"One of the best." He smiled. "Would you prefer a hand-holder or a top-notch physician, Franny?"

"Isn't there such a thing as a combination of both?"

He did refer her to a plastic surgeon whose specialty was breast reconstruction. He was the same doctor Shirley recommended. Hannah went with her to read the brochures and watch the video in the small cubicle set aside for prospective patients. Franny preferred the procedure called the TRAM flap in which the surgeon builds a breast completely from the patient's own stomach tissue, tunneling it beneath the midriff with muscle still attached. It didn't contain any foreign substance and would lose or gain weight just as the other breast did. Also, she'd get a tummy tuck in the bargain. The drawbacks were, it was very expensive and she wasn't sure her insurance would cover it. It was also a major operation, lasting sometimes seven or eight hours, and would put her out of circulation for about six weeks. She didn't have to make a decision right away, the surgeon told her. She could go ahead with the mastectomy, then have the reconstruction months, or in some cases, even years, later.

"Amazing!" Hannah said as they drove home. "They can even build a nipple for it. I think you should go ahead with it now, Franny V."

But that would mean she wouldn't be able to help Faith when the baby came. And the doctor admitted it was painful. Also, Franny wanted to be able to come to the dedication of the new school the first of February, the one named for Matthew Gregory. "I'll think about it," she said.

Franny was a grown woman before she found out people actually *bought* Christmas trees. Growing up, they always cut a cedar from the small farm where her daddy raised Herefords on the outskirts of town. When he died and they sold the property, Wesley offered a standing invitation to the Fuller farm. It was a Christmas tradition, and all three of her children looked forward to it. This year, however, with Faith so close to her time, only Gib and Wuzzy made the pilgrimage with her to tramp over muddy pastures, crawl through barbed wire fences, and hurdle streams to find the perfect tree—and enough greenery for her mother to make a wreath for the door. Hannah had gradually moved back into the house she'd grown up in, but she and Wesley were coming for supper, and Franny had invited

R. W. Duggan to join them and help decorate the tree.

It was getting dark as they drove home from Wesley's farm. The town tree in the park sparkled with hundreds of tiny white lights that were mirrored in the lily pond Mr. Rittenhouse had built. And for some reason, those ridiculous reindeer on the courthouse lawn didn't look as foolish as they had the year before. Sallie's Station was getting ready for Christmas.

Later, hands burning with cedar rash and numerous scratches, they stood back to admire the feathery evergreen brush hanging from its usual place in the north window of the living room.

"Don't make dessert," R.W. had told her. "Mrs. Ledbetter's jam cake came today." Janice Ledbetter had been a patient of his for at least thirty years and had baked him as many Christmas jam cakes. Franny tried her recipe once, but it just didn't taste the same. Maybe it was the grated orange rind Janice put in her caramel icing. With the sandwich tray Franny ordered from the deli and her mother's potato salad, supper was ready when Faith and Reilly arrived with a tiny silver angel ornament for little "Esmerelda" to decorate the tree. Hannah, tired and cross from a day of waiting for appliance delivery men, brought wine, and Wesley came bearing a huge poinsettia.

"Have you made a decision about the surgery?" R.W. wanted to know as he and Franny sliced the cake in the kitchen.

"Look, this just isn't a convenient time to have my body parts hacked on," she said. "I have other things to do . . . and would you please keep your voice down? I don't want Faith to know."

He stuck a finger in a pool of icing and licked it. "Why on earth not?" R.W. took the knife from her hand and grasped her shoulders. "Franny, don't you get flippant with me. This isn't something you postpone until it's convenient. Tell me, what could possibly be more important than this?"

"I'm not entirely convinced it's necessary," she said. "Besides, I want to be able to help Faith when her baby comes."

"Good Lord, woman! Faith's baby isn't due until the middle of

February. You'll be out running around after a couple of weeks. If you're worried about reconstruction, you can always have it later."

"Do you think I'd be able to go to the dedication?" she asked. "I'd really like to be there."

He held the door as she took the cake into the dining room. "No reason why you shouldn't. Some of the old faculty's coming back for it, I hear. Imagine how they must've changed! Do you suppose we'll know them?"

Wesley, testing tree lights, looked up at them. "Will they know us?"

Hannah tied off her string of popcorn and held it at arm's length. "What a pretty little thing Miss O'Donnell was! Remember? And Miss Jacobs—she made that beat up old piano dance with . . . what was it . . . ?"

"*The Flight of the Bumblebee*," Franny said. "And she could sing too. She and some of the other teachers used to do that song the Andrews Sisters made famous, *The Boogie Woogie Bugle Boy of Company B*. We thought they were wonderful!"

"Heck, they were. Most of them," R.W. said. "But remember that time Miss Havergal accused ole Travis of writing on the front door? Tanned his hide from here to kingdom come. God, what a witch!" He steadied the ladder for Reilly who strung lights at the top of the tree. "And that poor little girl who wet the floor in the fifth grade. What was her name? Lived over on Ice House Road. I'll never forget how mean she was to her."

"Wanda. Wanda Culpepper." Franny could see her now, after all those years, in that baggy wet dress with the red flowers on it.

R.W. reached for the bowl of popcorn. "Didn't that Havergal woman kill herself soon after she left here? Poor, miserable soul! Somebody told me she was a bit too fond of little girls. Had a screw loose somewhere, no doubt about it."

Wesley, busy looping lights around his arm, didn't look up. "These are all working," he said, passing the coils of lights to Gib.

"Afraid her ghost will come back to haunt us?" Franny whispered to Wesley. She wished he would yell at her, bring it out in the open at last.

But he didn't. "Get off my back, Franny." If looks could kill, she'd be six feet under.

Her mother, ever the tactful one, chimed in about then. "I'm going to put on some coffee. Anybody else want some?"

"I'd love some, Miss Molly. Let me help." Wesley followed her into the kitchen. Probably because he didn't want to be in the same room with her, Franny thought.

R.W. inspected a loose bulb and stepped back to inspect the tree. "That's her daughter, you know, that good lookin' gal that runs around with the Curtis boy, Neely's son."

"Whose daughter?" Hannah asked.

"What's her name's—Wanda's. Wanda died, I heard, couple of years ago. Cancer, I think."

"Whoa! Back up!" Franny grabbed his arm and eyeballed him. "I can't be hearing this. Tell me you're making that up."

He twined an icicle in her hair. "Why would I do that?"

True. Why would he? This was R.W., not Travis. "I still don't believe it," she said.

"R. W. Duggan, who told you that?" Hannah asked.

He shrugged. "Shirley Dilworth said she heard it from the real estate agent who sold the woman her house."

"Shirley. That figures." Hannah rolled her eyes.

"Janine," Franny said. "The daughter's name is Janine."

Hannah nodded. "Janine. Right. Well, she couldn't have come from Wanda. Frankly, I think she's an android manufactured by the fashion industry. Sort of a life-size Barbie."

Yet there *was* something. Something about her eyes. Maybe her odd little hunch had been right after all, but she still had trouble accepting it. "She doesn't just *run around* with Walter Curtis," Franny announced. "They're getting married on Valentine's Day."

* * * * *

Lucy phoned as they were all slinging icicles at the tree. Perry Como sang *Oh, Holy Night* in the background, and Franny was warm with wine, still she had enough sense to take the call in the kitchen so Faith wouldn't hear.

"Where have you been? Don't you ever stay home? I've been trying to get you all week to find out how that biopsy turned out."

Franny took another sip of wine. The last thing she wanted to do was tell her little girl those people wanted to whack off her breast. "The second one looked okay," she said. "But they're recommending surgery for the left breast—just to be sure. We'll talk about that later. Lucy, you should see the tree," she added. "We just put on the star . . . Gib and Wuzzy are here, and they seem so happy. Maybe things will work out after all. When do you think you'll be home for Christmas?"

Her daughter sighed. "Does Faith know yet?"

"No."

"Then let me speak with Gib."

When Franny went to call Gib to the phone, she noticed Faith and Reilly apart from the others, deep in whispered conversation. Faith had hardly eaten a thing at supper, and hadn't shown much interest in decorating the tree, which wasn't like her at all.

"I'm just tired," she said, kissing her mother goodnight. "Must've eaten something at lunch that didn't agree with me. Stomach's a little upset."

Franny turned up Faith's coat collar against the cold night air and fastened the top button. (The others wouldn't meet.) "Go home and take care of Ruby Esmerelda," she said, walking them to the door. "You'll feel better in the morning." She tried to keep her voice light, but Franny didn't like the way Faith looked, and she could tell from his eyes that Reilly didn't, either.

As soon as Faith and Reilly left, Gib told her that he and Lucy had decided she would have the mastectomy the week after Christmas, and if she didn't make the appointment on Monday, he would ask *Faith* to do it. Franny didn't tell him she had already made up her mind to schedule the surgery. She didn't trust those rotten little cells, and she certainly didn't like her life being turned into a guessing game. Anybody could tell you Franny Hughes never gambled for more than fifty cents.

And Franny knew she would have to let Faith in on her plans before she heard it from somebody else. Tomorrow. She would tell her daughter tomorrow.

But Reilly called the next morning to tell them they were on their way to the hospital. Faith was in labor.

Chapter Twenty-four

February, 1944

On Valentine's Day Neely Louise Warren got candy in a pink satin box. Franny and Hannah decided she probably sent it to herself. Franny wondered if a boy would ever give her candy and doubted it. Her nose was too big. She examined it daily and was certain it was growing faster than the rest of her face. Was she being punished, like Pinocchio, for what she had done? The puppet's nose grew when he told a lie, but Franny had done worse than lie. Much worse. Soon her nose would shadow her face like a huge, bulbous tumor, and she would have to wear a black veil like Hannah's great aunt Agnes who'd been in mourning since her husband died way back in the First World War.

The Lord spake and said unto Moses, all the Gordons shall have big noses, her daddy liked to tease, but Franny didn't think it was funny anymore.

After she finished her homework, Franny switched on the radio and listened to her favorite programs: *Judy Canova, The Great Gildersleeve, and Fibber McGee and Molly.* The routine was always predictable. She knew the McGees' house at Seventy-nine Wistful Vista, knew its junk-crammed closet whose contents crashed to the floor whenever Fibber opened the door. And he always did. *No, no, McGee, don't open that door!* It brought a huge laugh every week.

They were her friends who brought laughter in those dark hours before bedtime. And for a little while Franny forgot about war and rationing and shortages and the evil man in Germany with the black, black mustache. But she couldn't forget what happened to Miss Havergal and little Dottie Crenshaw.

Miss O'Donnell didn't come to school the next day. Mrs. Hightower told them the speech teacher wasn't feeling well and they wouldn't be having expression classes. Mrs. Hightower looked like she didn't feel so good herself, Franny thought. She was pale and seemed to be getting a cold. Franny sat under the big oak at recess and made stick houses. Around the corner of the building she heard the rope slap the walk as Hannah and some of the other girls jumped, chanting, "Cinderella, dressed in yella, went to the station to meet her fella! How many kisses did he give her? One . . . two . . . three . . . four . . ."

Wesley leaned against the water fountain and watched R.W. and Travis yell and scuffle as they played capture-the-flag with other boys in the class. At the top of the steps, the teachers huddled in drab clusters whispering to one another. They seemed heavy and dull, like the skies which threatened rain.

About a half hour before they were to go home for their midday meal, Mrs. Hightower told them they would be dismissed for the day after a brief assembly. She wouldn't tell them why, only shook her head and said they would find out when they got there. Everyone was quiet as they walked in a single, straight line to the auditorium, as though they sensed, as Franny did, that something important was happening. And it wasn't good.

Franny felt Hannah's cold little hand snake into hers as they filed across the playground, gravel crunching underfoot, and for a minute they latched on to one another, interlocking fingers.

Brother Vickery, the minister from Franny's church, stood at the top of the stairs with the music teacher, Miss Jacobs. Mrs. Hightower paused when she saw him and he stepped forward, and for a few seconds, covered her hands with his, then walked with them down the aisle. Mrs. Hightower stood at the end of the row, and as her class filed into their assigned seats, gently touched each of them on the back. She had never done that before.

The gesture sent a chill through Franny that had nothing to do with the drafty room, and she guessed what they had come to hear. Her classmates stared at their teacher with strained white faces as she moved down to stand by the stage with Brother Vickery. Beside Franny, R. W. Duggan twisted the tail of his shirt. Behind her, Hannah sat forward in her chair, her hand on Franny's shoulder. Franny was glad it was there.

"I'm sure you've all realized I have some bad news for you," Mrs. Hightower began after the last seventh grader shuffled in. "I wish I could think of a kinder way to tell you, but there just isn't any." She paused. "We received word this morning that our beloved Lieutenant Gregory was killed a few days ago during the fighting on Kwajalein Island."

A great sigh went up, a collective sob. Some children cried out loud. Hannah wept on the back of Franny's chair. Franny's head felt heavy . . . heavy . . . the hurt seeped into her throat, her heart, her stomach. Initials were cut into the back of the seat in front of her: L.T.B., the carving, black with dirt and years. She ran her finger along them. They had probably been put there before she was born, before Mr. Gregory was born.

In his rugged country-uncle voice, Brother Vickery talked of courage and love and sacrifice. "A few weeks ago," he said, "Kwajalein Atoll was in the hands of the Japanese. Now it's controlled by Americans, another step in winning this war. And it's because of Lieutenant Gregory and others like him that we have won this victory, and will continue to win until this war is over." His voice broke on the last words, and he bowed his head silently as though searching for composure. "I know no more comforting passage than the Twenty-third Psalm. Before we leave today, let us all stand and repeat it together."

The words poured over the shabby auditorium, over the stage where he stood so often, the chair where he used to sit; the children he worried over, laughed with, loved—and left.

The Lord is my shepherd, I shall not want . . .

Kwajalein. A place she had never heard of and could hardly pronounce. And now Mr. Gregory had died there. He had died without ever tasting Miss Opal's good dressing again or drinking a Coca Cola. They couldn't get them over there, he'd said. He would never kiss Miss O'Donnell or sit with her in church, never walk the streets of Sallie's Station or run up the steps to the school with great long strides as he had done so many times before. He was gone, gone, gone, and Franny couldn't remember his face.

She stood by the kitchen window and stared into the rain. Her mother washed milk bottles, shook the dishrag in them with gray, sudsy water: *shug, shug, shug,* then pulled it out with a plop.

Miss O'Donnell had gone home to Savannah to be with her parents for awhile, her mother said, and would be back in a few days.

"But she won't be the same."

"No, Franny, she won't be the same, but she'll need your love and understanding, your prayers too, even more than she did before."

Franny drew back from her mama's touch. "I'm not going to pray anymore. I prayed for Lieutenant Gregory, prayed for him every night, and God didn't even listen. And I prayed for Miss Willie too. I'm not ever going to pray for anybody again!"

Her mother was right. Miss O'Donnell was not the same. When she returned the next week, her light, smooth step was gone, her bright hair, pulled carelessly back in a barrette. Their teacher looked pale and listless, her eyes dull and red-rimmed. Franny had always liked to watch Miss O'Donnell walk; she moved as if she were listening to music. And when she talked, her face and eyes were so expressive there was almost no need for words. Now she moved slowly, hesitantly, as though she had to remind herself to put one foot in front of the other. The only times she showed animation were when she read from a script, when for a short time she could pretend to be somebody else. And she still wore the diamond, a blazing reminder of what might have been, on the third finger of her left hand.

Most days after school Franny would creep into her mama's big storage closet, wrap herself in a patchwork quilt that smelled of mothballs, and sit, knees drawn up, on her grandmother Gordon's old trunk. It was the only place she could be alone.

Were they to blame for what happened to Lieutenant Gregory? They had done something horrible, something almost as bad as killing. Didn't it amount to the same thing? They had gone against God, and now He was punishing them for what they did to Dottie, who would probably always walk with a limp, and to Miss Havergal. It didn't seem fair that Lieutenant Gregory and Miss O'Donnell should have to suffer too.

"We have to do something," Franny told the others one day as they walked home from school. "Something to help Miss O'Donnell, make her feel better." After all, wasn't it because of them Miss O'Donnell was so unhappy? Franny wanted to lift the burden from the woman's frail shoulders. She would gladly bear her teacher's sadness if she could. How could she hurt more?

"I'll bet I could get my mama to make her some fudge," Travis suggested, "but you'll have to help out with the sugar. We've done used up most of our ration coupons."

"You just want to eat it yourself, you selfish pig!" Hannah told him. "Besides, I don't think Miss O'Donnell's very hungry. Mama said Annie Tate told her she just pecks at her food like a little old sparrow."

"What about roses?" Wesley offered. "We could send her roses —bright red ones in a long skinny box like you see in the movies."

It was the first time Wesley seemed interested in anything since Lieutenant Gregory died, Franny thought. He hadn't had much to say to anybody. But roses were hard to come by in Sallie's Station in the winter time, even if they could afford them, which they couldn't.

"There's this cologne she likes," Franny said. "I've seen it on her dresser. Comes in a pretty glass bottle with a diamond-shaped stopper—sort of like the kind that sits on our sideboard."

"Yeah! Smells like some of those flowers my grandmama grows," Hannah said. "She told me once it's her favorite. Reckon we can get it at Maxwell's?"

"I doubt it." Wesley stopped speaking until a bunch of third-grade girls lumbered past chasing each other on roller skates. "Probably have to get it at Rich's or Davison's, and it might be kind of expensive."

Hannah frowned. "How expensive?"

Nobody knew, but Wesley's mother planned a trip to Atlanta that Friday, and if they pooled their money, she'd be glad, she said, to see what she could do.

Franny still had the dollar her uncle Ben had sent at Christmas. She'd been saving it to spend at the trading post at Girl Scout camp next summer, but now she didn't care if she even went to camp at all. Winnie paid her a quarter to make her bed for a week, and she earned fifty cents walking the Greers' cocker, Sugar. Franny hoped they would have enough.

Wesley's mother brought the cologne from Atlanta, gift wrapped in shiny gold paper with a big shaggy bow, but they had to wait an eternal weekend to give it to Eileen O'Donnell.

Betty Joyce should be the one to present the offering, they agreed, because she was the oldest and the least likely to cry and make a scene since God had apparently forgiven her already. While the others waited, she would give the cologne to their speech teacher in her little backstage room after school on Monday.

With Hannah and Wesley, (Mrs. Hightower had kept Travis after school for talking), Franny sat on the edge of the dusty stage while Betty Joyce completed her mission. No one spoke, and she knew the others, like herself, were straining to hear what was being said. She wished Esau, sweeping under the seats in the auditorium, would be quiet or go somewhere else to clean. If only she could see Miss O'Donnell's face when she opened the package!

After what seemed like forever, Betty Joyce crept out blank-faced and empty-handed and motioned for them to follow. She didn't speak.

"Well?" Hannah demanded, outside at last. "What'd she say? Did she like it? Bet she was surprised."

Betty Joyce shrugged. "Yeah, I guess."

"You *guess?* What do you mean, you guess? She opened it, didn't she?" For somebody who made all A's, sometimes Betty Joyce acted just plain backward, Franny thought.

"What *did* she say?" Wesley asked.

"She said, 'thanks.' " Betty Joyce gathered her books in a neat stack under her chin.

Hannah frowned. "That's all? Just thanks?"

"Well . . . she said it sure was wrapped pretty," Betty Joyce told them as she crossed the street for home.

"You all go on," Franny told the others. "I think I left my English book on the stage." A lie, but she had to go back alone. She had to see Miss O'Donnell. The terrible secret inside her was like a boil coming to a head, and if she didn't spew it out to somebody, it would poison her. Miss O'Donnell would understand. She would forgive her. And then Franny might forgive herself.

She smelled the cologne as soon as she stepped backstage. It smelled like a thousand lilies in a hot room, and the sweetness made her a little dizzy.

At first Franny thought she was resting, maybe even sleeping. Eileen O'Donnell curled in the shabby old armchair with her head on her arms. Franny started not to wake her, but she hurt too much to stop now. She stepped inside and said her name. Then, before the words were out of her mouth, she knew she'd made a terrible mistake. The opened box containing the special bottle of cologne all the way from Rich's Department Store in Atlanta was in the waste basket, and from the overpowering smell, her teacher had apparently thrown it there hard enough to break the glass bottle.

Franny gasped. "Oh, Miss O'Donnell, why did you throw it away?"

Her teacher looked up, tight-lipped and pale, with such hurt in her eyes it made Franny wince. "Go away, Franny," Miss O'Donnell said in somebody else's voice. "Go home. I don't want to see you now."

Downstairs Franny could hear the plunk of Miss Jacobs' old green upright as the music teacher coached a piano student. "The Spinning Song" stopped abruptly, started again. In the lower grades Franny had come to Miss Jacobs' sunny, yellow room to bang sticks together, jangle tambourines, or—even on rare occasions—to play the coveted triangle. A million years ago. It was a safe, dependable room. She would find comfort here.

Crying, Franny ran down the wide wooden stairs, worn smooth in the middle from years of tramping feet, slid her hand along the familiar railing because her eyes blurred and she didn't trust her feet. Miss Jacobs stood in her doorway telling her piano student goodbye. Neely Louise Warren, shiny red *John Thompson* book under her arm, looked at Franny curiously. "What's the matter with you?"

"Run along now, Neely Louise. I'll see you next week." Miss Jacobs whisked Franny inside and shut the door behind them.

"Franny, what in the world has happened?"

Franny told her about the broken bottle of cologne, how she'd found it in the trash. "I don't understand," she said.

"I think I do." Gathering sheaves of music in the fading light of day, Miss Jacobs spoke quietly, briskly. The cologne had always been a gift from Matthew Gregory, she told her. It was his favorite scent, he said, because it reminded him of the woman he loved.

Softly, the music teacher closed the lid of her piano. "In fact, they used to laugh about it because he kept her so well-supplied, said he didn't want her to ever run out." She smiled. "I wouldn't be surprised if she didn't have a bottle or so in reserve."

"But she'll never wear it again," Franny said.

"No, I don't expect she will. Miss O'Donnell didn't mean to hurt you, Franny. One of these days, you'll come to understand." The two walked outside together. Miss Jacobs, looking at her watch, walked quickly, heels clicking on the cold cement steps. "Franny, you must hurry on home now. It's getting late. Do you want me to walk part of the way with you?"

"No, ma'am, I'm fine. Really." Franny waved to her as she crossed the street, then turned and headed in the other direction, past Miss Opal's sprawling house and the Victorian bungalow where Betty Joyce lived. Already lights shone from the Whitfields' sitting room windows.

Miss O'Donnell didn't even want her around, and Miss Jacobs was nice, but she didn't have time for her either. What would they say if they knew? What would they do? And Franny knew that neither of them could ever share her secret.

Because of the grocery bags the woman carried, Franny almost didn't recognize her homeroom teacher as she rounded the corner for home, and when she realized who it was, it was all she could do to keep from throwing herself upon her, burrowing into the woman's plump, comforting bosom. It was a sign as sure as she was standing there. A sign from God!

Mrs. Hightower. Of course. "I'm so glad to see you!" Franny said.

Clutching the bags awkwardly, her teacher smiled. "Well, I'm pleased to see you too, but I expect I'll be seeing you again before too long. You do plan to be in school tomorrow?"

"Oh, yes. Yes!" Franny held out her arms for one of the bags. Mrs. Hightower lived up on Crooked Oak Street and it was quite a climb. "I've got to tell you something," she said as they walked along together. "Something bad."

"Oh? And what's that?" Her teacher's voice was light.

"It's about Miss Havergal."

"What about Miss Havergal?"

"We—I as good as killed her. It's my fault she's dead."

Mrs. Hightower stopped in the middle of the sidewalk and put a hand on Franny's shoulder. "You don't know what you're saying. I don't like hearing you talk like this. How could you have had anything to do with the way Miss Havergal died? It was self-inflicted, Franny."

"But she did it because she was fired, and I *am* to blame for that. I put that whiskey there." No use bringing the others into it. She was the one who was breaking the promise.

"Dear God in heaven." Mrs. Hightower closed her eyes. Was she praying? The paper sack rustled as she hugged it to her. A potato popped to the top, teetered there. "I wish you hadn't told me this," she said.

"But I had to tell somebody! I couldn't stand it. I just feel awful! Mrs. Hightower, please tell me what to do."

Franny felt the bag of groceries being lifted from her arms.

"I can't tell you that, Franny," Mrs. Hightower said in a voice like the end of the world. "Do your parents know about this?"

"Oh, no, ma'am!"

"I think you'd better tell them."

"But I can't. I just can't."

"Then I'm afraid you'll have to deal with this yourself. I'm sorry, Franny."

Franny stood alone on the sidewalk after her teacher walked away. Somebody was cooking something with side meat and the smell of it made her feel sick. Miss Havergal was like a curse upon her causing trouble even from the grave. What would happen to her now? To all of them? Would they go to jail for what they had done? *Whatsoever a man soweth, that shall he also reap.* They were doomed. There was no escaping it.

Yet somehow Franny was sure Mrs. Hightower would never tell her secret, not even to her parents, never mention it again. But her teacher knew now what she had done and she would never, never feel the same about her.

The three blocks home seemed uphill all the way and her legs felt weak with the weight of her. She wasn't even eleven and already Franny Gordon felt old.

Chapter Twenty-five

"I hear Mr. Rittenhouse's old place is for sale," Molly Gordon said.

It was one of those wet, gusty winter days—already dark at half past four—and a fire burned low on the hearth. Franny's mother pulled her chair up close, with the purple afghan Faith had made for her spread over her lap, her feet stretched to the flames.

After a labor that lasted over forty-eight hours and nearly scared them all to death, Faith gave birth prematurely to a doll-sized baby who wouldn't even fill a shoe box. Now, after three weeks, little William Reilly Thomas was blimping out at four pounds, ten ounces in the neonatal unit in Rome, and they hoped he would soon be able to come home.

Faith, exhausted after her difficult labor, spent long days at the hospital holding, willing, and loving endurance into her tiny, purple-faced son until at last doctors began to wean him from the respirator. And when the pink came into William's face, the strength came back to his mother. Franny tied a big blue ribbon around the baby's Christmas teddy and adored her new grandson through the nursery window, counting the days, rejoicing in every gain.

Now she sat as far away from the fire as possible, fanning with a box top from a jigsaw puzzle. The completed puzzle, a thousand gray-blue pieces combined to make a picture of sailing ships, remained on the card table in the corner. It had given them something to do while they marked time over the Christmas holidays, and none of them could bear to tear it up.

Earlier, Franny had swapped her knit shirt and cardigan for a lightweight blouse, and was getting quicker than any magician at removing her bra through her shirt sleeves. Turtlenecks were out of the question. The doctor had taken away her estrogen and she was going through the change about ten years late.

"You always did like that house," her mother said, eyeing her over the tops of her glasses. "Why don't we go over there tomorrow and see what it looks like inside? I hear those last people enclosed that little side porch."

Franny did want to poke about in the little brown house again, just for curiosity's sake, but she wasn't sure that was exactly what her mother intended. "What do you mean, you want to see it? Is there something wrong with this house?"

Her mother smiled. "Don't tell me you haven't noticed. Where do you want me to start? It's too big for us for one thing. Expensive to keep up, impossible to heat." She made room for Sylvester on her lap. "And let's be practical, Franny. When I'm gone, what are you going to do with all this house?"

"I don't want to talk about that. Besides, that won't be for a long time."

"How long is long? That house has just the right amount of space and very little yard to keep up. And it's almost in the neighborhood. We wouldn't be going far."

Franny didn't know what to say. It had taken her mother sixty years to get over selling THE HOME PLACE. She took her by surprise.

"It won't stay on the market long," Molly said. "And you know the Baptists have been wanting this house for a manse for years. They'll give us a fair price for it, Franny."

"We'll have to set up an appointment," Franny said when she

finally found her voice. "I don't even know who's handling it."

"Amelia Boatwright. Isn't she the one whose son plays football for Clemson? Anyway, I spoke with her this morning. She's meeting us there tomorrow at ten."

Joey Boatwright graduated from Clemson twenty years ago. "Mama, what will Winnie say? She grew up in this house." Her sister was due in tomorrow and Franny didn't think she could handle weepy sentimentality just now.

"It's your house, Franny. You bought out Winnie's share when you moved in with me. Besides, she seemed to think it was worth looking into when I told her about it over the phone."

Winnie and her husband Ted owned a dairy farm in North Carolina, and the last of their four daughters was due to graduate from college in June. They didn't travel much. Frankly, Franny didn't think Ted would care if he never left Caldwell County, but when she told her sister about her mastectomy, Winnie was already starting to pack.

"I'll only be in the hospital a few days," Franny told her. "Hannah's here, and Faith's a lot stronger now. She and Reilly will keep an eye on Mama. Not that I wouldn't love to see you, but Ted probably needs you more."

"Hold on a second, Franny . . ." Winnie was away from the phone for a minute and Franny heard conversation in the background, then low laughter. "I told Ted I could always get another husband," Winnie said. "But I only have one sister. Besides, I can't wait to see my new grand nephew. I'm coming!"

Franny lit what was left of the fat green candle on the coffee table and inhaled the bayberry scent. It would have to last a year. If they did decide to buy the Rittenhouse cottage, next Christmas she would put hurricane lamps in those beautiful Queen Anne windows, a swag of pine over the stone hearth.

Her mother reached for a tangerine and peeled it. Franny could smell it across the room. "When's Hannah coming back?" her mother asked.

"Sometime tomorrow. She wants to be here before I go into the hospital." Because of the baby's early arrival, Franny had postponed her surgery for a week or so until both he and his mother were stronger. Reilly planned to take a few days off to help where needed, and Hannah and Winnie would take turns staying with Franny and her mother.

Hannah had gone back home to spend the holidays with Vance and their son, Martin, who had flown down from West Virginia. Franny didn't ask about her relationship with Wesley, where it was going. She didn't think Hannah, herself, knew.

Franny's present to Hannah sat, wrapped in bright Santa paper, under the Christmas tree. "I'll open it when I get back," she said. "When you open yours." She was saving Franny's gift for after the surgery. It would give her something to look forward to, Hannah said. And she looked so smug when she said it, Franny was about to explode with curiosity.

"That's like making the whole house smell like chocolate, then giving all the fudge away," Franny told her. "At least give me a hint."

Hannah smiled but wouldn't look at her. "It's something you always wanted."

"I've changed my mind about Rock Hudson. Even if he weren't gay and dead."

Hannah covered her face with both hands so Franny couldn't read her expression. "Not even close."

"Ballet lessons? I've always wanted to be graceful."

"Even God couldn't do that, Franny V.!"

She would just have to wait.

Worry over Faith and the baby had turned their Christmas upside down, but they celebrated between trips to the hospital and counted each new day as a plus. Franny was determined to concentrate on the positive, not just for the children's sake, but for her mother's and hers. Lucy and Gib and Wuzzy were there and the old house stayed drafty with all the people going in and out. Franny got so caught up in her concern for Faith and the baby, the company and the season, she put the dreaded surgery out of her mind. Almost. Her insurance would pay for most of the reconstruction, she learned, as long as she had it sometime during the next year. If they did decide on a smaller house, she could apply the profit to a "pert new boob," as Lucy called it. At least it was reassuring to know she had an alternative to stuffing her bra.

Hannah went with Franny and her mother to meet Winnie at the airport in Atlanta the day before the scheduled surgery. It was sunny after days of rain, and winter shadows purpled the streets of Sallie's Station in a water color wash. Whisk broom trees brushed the sky. Downtown was quiet, resting after the holidays, a tired lady taking her afternoon nap. The new owner had added blue shutters to the building where Franny's father had had his hardware store. They sold antiques there now, and a wreath with a gold ribbon and shiny brass horn hung on the door. It made her smile. Franny usually felt a little let down after Christmas, but now she was greedy for spring, for daffodils and lemonade. She wanted to sit on that old stone bench in the park and watch summer spread across the grass, listen to the oak trees grow.

The three of them were quiet as they drove through town, then swung left onto I-75, until Hannah, in the back seat, leaned over Franny's shoulder. "Tell me what to do," she said.

"Okay. You can tell me what's that big surprise you got me for Christmas."

"Not about that! What should I do about Vance? About Wesley?"

"Vance loves you," Franny said. She didn't mean to say it. It just kind of squirted out.

"I know. And I care for him." She plopped back against the seat. "I *do*."

233

"What about Wesley?" Franny watched Hannah's face in the mirror.

"I don't know. It's all so new with Allie, and now Wesley—like starting over. We haven't really talked about it."

Molly turned and frowned at her. *"It?"*

"Well, you know, a relationship."

"Are you seeing Wesley, Hannah? Because if you are, it isn't fair to your husband to let things go on like this." Franny's mother spoke in her lecture voice. It didn't matter to her that Hannah had grandchildren.

"Not exactly *seeing* him. There hasn't been any hanky panky, if that's what you mean." She laughed. "Not that I haven't thought about it."

"If you really want to know what I think," Franny said, "I'd put them both on hold, take some time for yourself. Just you—Hannah Whitaker. Don't make any reckless decisions." Lord, she sounded just like her mother!

"You know what? Just this once. I think you're right. In fact, that was sort of what I had in mind."

Franny glanced at Hannah to see if she was joking, but Hannah was looking out the window, watching the landscape whiz by. "Do you all remember the Burma Shave signs?" she said. "Had a punch line, always rhymed. Had to drive sort of slow to read them. I miss them."

"So do I," Molly said.

When they got home, Tommy Crowder from Tara's Garden was coming down the steps, and a basket of red tulips stood by the door. He waved at them from the walk. "We didn't have anything to do with what's in that box," he said. "Mr. Kimbrough said to deliver it with the flowers."

"What box?" Winnie said, helping her mother out of the car.

Mr. Kimbrough? What was Travis up to now? "Don't touch it,"

Franny said. "It's probably a snake." But when she picked up the flowers she found a square, tissue-wrapped package beside them. Inside was a gray flint arrowhead on a bed of cotton with a note that read: *I believe this belongs to you.*

"Now isn't that just like Travis Kimbrough?" Winnie said. "What in the world is that all about?"

"Remind me to tell you sometime," Franny said.

That night after Winnie went to her room, Franny crawled into her mother's bed, put her arms around her little old frail shoulders, and cried. She knew she made her mother cry too, but this time she just couldn't help it. You never get too old to need your mama.

Chapter Twenty-six

March, 1944

It snowed during the night on the sixteenth of March, but by afternoon there wasn't a patch of snow big enough to slide in.

On their way to check out the empty lot behind the Baptist Church, Franny and Hannah, with a Coca-Cola tray "borrowed" from the Kellys' kitchen, saw some of the teachers and Damascus Jones making a snowman in Miss Opal's front yard.

"Look at Miss O'Donnell," Hannah said. "She's just standing over there all by herself with her hands in her pockets, like she's too cold to move."

It hurt Franny to look at her teacher. Hurt deep, like something was torn inside her.

She saw Miss Cochran go over and say something to Eileen O'Donnell, then put an arm around her and sort of lead her to where the others were playing. Slowly, almost like a sleepwalker, their teacher scooped up a handful of snow and added a glob for a nose. She smiled when she did it, but Franny could tell she really didn't want to. It was the first time she'd seen her smile since Lieutenant Gregory died.

Sometimes Franny found herself thinking about Lieutenant

Gregory as if he were still coming back, and she had to remind herself that he was dead. It hurt all over again, like when she got soap in a cut. Now she would have to destroy the cottage she had built in her mind, board by board, shingle by shingle, down to the last organdy-curtained window.

There were even times Franny wished she could forget him, forget everything that had happened before: Miss Havergal and Dottie Crenshaw, Lieutenant Gregory, even Miss Willie Llewellyn. And once in a while she made a half-hearted attempt to sort things out. It was like unraveling a ball of string; if she could just find the end of it, the rest would follow. There would be a pattern to it, a strong, reliable thread. But she just couldn't grasp it.

Miss O'Donnell cried when Hannah brought her daffodils. They were late that year, and their yellow, ruffled petals made a sunny contrast to the bleak March landscape.

The fresh, clean scent of the flowers filled the stuffy little room behind the stage where the expression class sat in a circle making plans for the spring recital. Miss O'Donnell closed her eyes and held the blooms to her face for a long, long time, then laid them across her lap. She touched a fragile petal and tried to speak. Tears streamed down her face, but she didn't try to stop them. Franny looked away, frightened. Travis fumbled with his shoe lace. Hannah stared into her lap.

"It's all right," Miss O'Donnell said finally. She was smiling. "I think it's time we talked about him, don't you?"

And so they did. They talked of how they missed him and of the hole he left in their lives, of the hurt and helplessness they felt when he died.

"When will I stop hurting?" Franny wanted to know.

"I don't know, Franny," her teacher said. "I just don't know." She hugged Franny to her. "We're just going to have to take it one step at a time . . . let's start with these daffodils. Why don't you and

Hannah fill that jar with water? Then we'd better get down to business on this recital. Do you realize it's less than two months away?"

That afternoon Franny stopped by to tell Aunt Six about her part in the recital. A radio played in the kitchen where Precious sat at the table paring turnips and listening to *Young Dr. Malone.*

"Hey Precious, guess what? I'm gonna—"

"Shh!" Precious fluttered bony fingers at her. "This poor woman's fixin' to have her baby. Been having a right hard time of it too—might not pull through." She shook her head sadly. "Young Dr. Malone's trying to get in touch with her husband in the Army Air Corps."

The organ music swelled. *Will Stephanie Nottingham live to give birth to her child? Will her mother forgive her for marrying the irresponsible young flyer? Will young Dr. Malone locate the father in time? Tune in tomorrow . . .*

"Ah, well!" Precious sighed. "If it's not one thing, it's another." She switched off the radio and nibbled a turnip. "Now, what you got to tell? If it's not good, don't bother her about it." She jerked her head toward the closed parlor door. "Got troubles enough with that Honey Sue calling all the time. Wish she'd leave her poor mama alone."

Precious offered a slice of turnip on the knife blade. It tasted zippy and hot, crunched when Franny chewed it. She held out her hand for another. "Aunt Six in there?" she asked.

Precious nodded. "Playing checkers with Mr. Rittenhouse." The sliced vegetables thudded into the sauce pan. "I'll swear, I don't know what we're going to do."

"I'm going to be Amy," Franny said.

"Amy? Amy who?"

"Amy March. We're doing a scene from *Little Women* in the spring recital. That's what I came to tell Aunt Six. And Hannah's going to be Jo."

"Oh. Well, tell her then. She'll want to hear about that." Precious looked gloomily down at the peelings as if she didn't want to talk anymore. Franny didn't know who she was more worried about, Stephanie Nottingham or Aunt Six.

Mr. Rittenhouse stared silently at the checkerboard and drummed his long fingers on the table. Aunt Six had that look in her eyes, that wicked glimmer that meant she was getting ready to pounce. She cackled as she jumped two of his men. "Gotcha now, Double-A! What you gonna do about that?"

"Hmm, well now, let me see . . ." Mr. Rittenhouse stroked his chin and retaliated by capturing two of her red pieces. Franny's aunt's face fell. "Game's not over yet!" She did hate to lose.

Franny waited until they finished their game to tell her aunt about the recital.

"You'll make an excellent Amy," Mr. Rittenhouse said. "I'll look forward to seeing that production."

Aunt Six said nothing. She was still mad about losing at checkers. Franny leaned over the back of her chair. "Well, you're coming, aren't you?"

"What? Well, of course, I'm coming. Wouldn't miss it." She cleared the board for a new game. "You going to tell me when it is?"

"Sometime in May. You won't forget now, will you?"

Her aunt made an impatient noise. "You know better than that. I'm planning on it. Mr. Rittenhouse too. You don't mind if he comes along, do you?"

Albert Adolf Rittenhouse smiled at Franny with his German blue eyes. She shrugged. "Guess not. Can if he wants to."

The old man reached behind him for his cane. "I have a few things to pick up in town, so I'll be on my way and give you two a chance to visit." He nodded to Franny. "Please give my regards to your parents."

Aunt Six put a hand on his shoulder and a claw on Franny's. "No, don't go yet. Frances is just leaving." Franny felt her aunt's fingers digging into her flesh, propelling her toward the kitchen. "Besides,

Double-A, it isn't nice to leave when you're winning." She waved a hand at him. "Now you stay there. I'll be right back."

"What on earth's the matter with you? I've a mind to tell your mama!" Aunt Six hardly waited for the door to close before lighting into Franny. "Just what happened to your manners, Miss Too-Big-For-Your-Britches?" She mimicked Franny's voice. "*Can if he wants to!* What's gotten into you, talking to Mr. Rittenhouse like that?"

"How come he's over here all the time? You gonna marry him or something?"

Aunt Six clamped a hand to her forehead. "He's my friend, Frances Virginia Gordon, and yours too—or he was. Wouldn't surprise me now if he didn't care too much for your company."

"Well good," Franny said, "because I sure don't care for his!"

Her aunt just left her standing there and went back into the parlor closing the door in Franny's face. Precious rinsed a pan at the sink and scowled at her over her shoulder. "Smarty, Smarty had a party, and nobody came but Smarty!" she chanted.

On the way home Franny saw Damascus Jones walking back from town with Miss O'Donnell and Miss Cochran. He had one on either side. People sure were peculiar, Franny thought. Her own aunt was running around with a German spy, and here was Miss O'Donnell with another man, and Lieutenant Gregory dead hardly two months. It seemed like there was nobody she could talk to anymore, not even God.

That week in Sunday School her teacher, Miss Addie Grace Crenshaw, suggested they all say a sentence prayer for their men in the service. Aside from teaching Sunday School and being Dottie's patient mama, Miss Addie Grace sang in the choir, was president of the Women's Society of Christian Service, chairman of her circle, and filled those tiny glasses with grape juice whenever communion was served. Franny's mama declared she didn't know how she did it all. Aunt Six said it was because she served her husband bologna sandwiches for supper, never swept her porch, and wouldn't know a dust rag if one slapped her in the face. But Franny liked Miss Addie Grace, even though she did make them listen to little Dottie sing "The Good Ship Lollipop" whenever she got the chance.

Dottie Crenshaw was back in school now and walked with a noticeable limp, but it didn't keep her from tormenting the neighbor's cat and driving her first-grade teacher to distraction. According to Franny's mama, Martha Ashworth had confided to Miss Opal that it was near to impossible to make that young'un stay in her seat for more than five minutes.

Dottie's mama was fat and pink-cheeked and crimped her hair in tight little waves. That day her dress was purple taffeta and swished against her corset when she moved. It rustled now as she fidgeted in her chair waiting for Franny to add her part to the sentence prayer. "Go on, Franny," Miss Addie Grace urged. "We're waiting."

Franny never did like sentence prayers. She couldn't think of anything original to say, and when she did, the person sitting next to her usually said it first. Betty Joyce said that God had forgiven them for the bad things they did, but then He turned right around and killed Mr. Gregory! And she was through talking to Him anyway, through wasting her time asking for things when she knew He was just going to do as He pleased. She told Miss Addie Grace that.

Franny thought her teacher was going to tumble head-first onto the floor. She plucked at her lace collar with plump fingers. The collar had a stain on it, Franny noticed. "Why, Franny honey, God always listens. He answers all our prayers."

"Then how come Lieutenant Gregory got killed? I prayed for God to keep him safe. How come he didn't listen?"

She blinked her large blue eyes. "I don't know, Franny, but there must have been a reason our Lieutenant Gregory died. Perhaps it was God's will."

Franny went home and threw up.

Chapter Twenty-seven

"What's the matter with Wesley?" Franny asked Hannah. "One of his dogs die?" Wesley had two Irish setters, Pat and Mike, that he loved better than God, and from the look on his face, you'd have thought somebody close to him was near to death, or else he'd had a personal note from the I.R.S.

"He's been a stick in the mud about this dedication since the beginning," she said. "Thought I'd never get him over here today. I don't know why he's acting like such a wart."

They threaded through Sunday-dressed crowds toward the section of seats Travis had saved for them, tracking February slush on the gleaming new gym/auditorium floor. R.W., distinguished and handsome in his nubby tweed sports coat and the green paisley tie Franny had given him for Christmas, craned his neck to see. "Have you seen her yet, Franny? She must be somewhere up front. Wonder if she'll remember us."

But unless she had grown since they last saw her, Franny didn't think Miss O'Donnell would be easy to spot in the room full of winter-wrapped people.

"Oh good! There's Betty Joyce." Hannah waved frantically. "And Neely Louise. My God, she must've paid a fortune for that suit. What a waste!"

Walter and Janine sat holding hands beside Neely and Claude Curtis. Now and then they whispered and laughed quietly together.

Shirley made room for Franny on the seat beside her, draping her little fur jacket on the back of her chair. Shirley had brought her violets in the hospital, told her which physical therapists knew the best jokes. Franny learned all about Shirley's daughter's spastic colon, and Shirley heard a step-by-step account of little William's birth and of Gibson's struggle to grow up. "Hon, just don't expect miracles overnight," she'd advised, and Franny was beginning to see the wisdom in her words.

"Betty Joyce looks awful, doesn't she?" Shirley said in a loud whisper. "All this worry over Hubert has really taken its toll. I'm surprised she even came."

Betty Joyce had lost weight. She and Hubert married while they were both still in college and had always been especially close. A few weeks after Christmas—the day of Franny's mastectomy, in fact—Hubert suffered a severe heart attack and had to have quadruple by-pass surgery. R.W., his family doctor, didn't say so, but for a while, Franny didn't think he would've given a quarter for Hubert's chances.

"I think he's feeling much better now that he's home," Franny told her. "It's just going to be slow." She had taken a fruit basket over a few days before and found Hubert sitting in his recliner watching one of those endless pre-Super Bowl games while Betty Joyce thumbed frantically through a low fat, no cholesterol cookbook. She reminded Franny of one of those little hamsters Lucy used to have, running on a wheel that went nowhere.

Franny glanced down to see if her breast was in the right place. The first time she went out after surgery she forgot to pin the little pink pad to her bra and it ended up in the middle of her chest.

Shirley unwrapped a piece of gum, offered Franny the pack, which she politely declined. "Faith doing okay?" she asked, rolling Juicy Fruit into her mouth.

Franny nodded. "It's been like Christmas every day since little Will came home." She had never seen her Faith so happy. "Now she's making new curtains for the nursery—said the others looked too feminine."

"I can't believe they didn't want to know the sex," Shirley said. "I couldn't stand the suspense. Of course, back when we were pregnant, we didn't have a choice."

"Faith's good at waiting," Franny told her. Thank goodness the waiting was over.

Betty Joyce sat in the row in front of them, trailed by Travis and his wife Joan, who graduated a couple of years after they did, and some woman Franny didn't recognize.

They were all here together, the five of them, the wicked ones who brought about the end of the joyless Miss Havergal, and contributed as well, they suspected, to Dottie Crenshaw's mental instability. Would lightning strike? Evaporate them with an ominous sizzle like the witch in *The Wizard of Oz*?

The junior high band was tuning up when Betty Joyce turned around and tapped Franny on the knee with her program. "Tell me it's not true," she said. "You're not moving away and leaving us."

"Just a few blocks over; we can still run back and forth and borrow." Franny hadn't told her neighbor about their bid on the old Rittenhouse place because she didn't want to sling any more "you-know-what." With Hubert's health the way it was, she just didn't have the heart.

"I'd as soon believe my grandma was a flapper," Betty Joyce said, referring to her straitlaced ancestor. "Miss Molly's lived in that house since I was born."

But it never was THE HOME PLACE. Franny wondered if her mother would miss it after they left. She knew she would, it held her memories there. But if the closing went as planned, they would move the middle of March, and she didn't regret the decision. It was time for something new, not that you could call the Rittenhouse cottage new, but it had over eighty years of charm—and a new roof.

"Tell Faith I can't wait to see that precious baby," Betty Joyce said. "I caught a glimpse of your Gib and his wife over Christmas, and I'm so glad they worked things out."

Franny nodded, smiling. *So far, so good,* she thought.

"Have you seen Miss O'Donnell?" Franny asked. "I still think of her as being twenty-two and weighing about as much."

"No yet." Betty Joyce nodded toward the end of her row. "But you see that woman sitting there? That's Miss Cochran. Remember?"

Franny remembered. Linda Cochran was small and dark-haired. This woman was neither. She was what Franny's mother graciously called "pleasingly plump," and she had "dust ball" hair, like wispy strands of lint scooped from under the bed and arranged on top of her head. She must have sensed them staring at her because she looked up from studying her program to smile and wave. Her husband had died fairly young, Franny remembered, when the couple had been married only eight or ten years, and Linda and their young son went to live near her relatives in Gainesville. Since then, Franny had heard she'd married again. Now Franny smiled and waved back, remembering a certain red dress Miss Cochran used to wear—about a size six. Would Miss O'Donnell have changed as much? And for the first time Franny wondered if she should have come.

They stood for the band's rendition of the National Anthem and the alma mater, followed by seemingly endless, but enthusiastic verses of "Faith of Our Fathers," and a prayer by the Presbyterian minister. Franny smiled, remembering something Aunt Six once said. *We here in Sallie's Station know about the separation of church and state. We just don't pay any attention to it.*

The elementary school chorus sang "My Favorite Things," left over from Christmas, Franny suspected, and the principal stood to introduce guests. Franny wished Billy Ben could have been there to sing. It would have seemed right somehow, but Billy Ben Maxwell had been killed in an automobile accident during his second year of divinity school, the first of their class to die. Today his younger sister, Nannie, wearing sedate black and pearls, held forth at the piano.

Franny looked down at the old hands in her lap, at those disgusting brown spots on the backs of them, snake skin creases across the wrists. How did this happen? And when? Beside her Shirley Dilworth smacked her gum, Hannah swung her foot in time to the music. Were they really here, or did some sadistic joker trick all of them into a time machine and push the *age* button? Franny closed her eyes. When she opened them she would be back in that dusty auditorium in the old grammar school laughing at Mr. Gregory imitating Red Skelton.

The audience clapped and a woman stood on the stage. Mr. Gregory's sister, somebody whispered, but she wasn't doing an impression of a comedian, or any impression at all, she was talking about her brother and how much he had cared about their school. It was still *now*, Franny was still here, and she didn't look any younger than her classmates. She was glad.

It was hot in the gym and Franny tried to fan with her program without being obvious. The building had only been in use a few weeks, but already it smelled of mildewed sneakers, stale lunches, and sweat.

Millicent Jacobs, who had taught public school music under Mr. Gregory, said a few words, as did one of his earlier students, a local attorney. And then Miss O'Donnell was introduced, only her name wasn't O'Donnell anymore, and even without that magnificent hat she wore, Franny thought she would have known her.

The hat was emerald green, and made of soft felt with a floppy brim, like the kind movie stars used to wear. The hair beneath it, Easter bunny white, worn, Franny learned later, in a twist at the back. She might have gone up one dress size since they last saw her, but no more, and the one she now wore was knit with a full skirt and

long sleeves in some kind of swirling blue-green pattern, with a tur-
quoise scarf at her throat. Her skin still had that gentle "soap ad" texture, and when she spoke, her voice reached something deep inside
Franny and set it free.

Chapter Twenty-eight

April, 1944

In April, God had Easter, and Mrs. Haywood C. Greer III had her annual dessert bridge. Just about every lady in town was invited, and Franny's mama broke down and bought herself a new dress. It was rose colored with a peplum and would also have to do for the garden tea Cordelia Richardson would host a few weeks later.

Mrs. Greer and Mrs. Richardson were next door neighbors and every year one tried to out-do the other in entertaining. The year before, Mrs. Greer had served ice cream shaped like a lady's slipper and ordered her flower arrangements from a florist in Atlanta. Mrs. Richardson rented black uniforms with frilly white aprons for her help and hired a seven-piece orchestra that knew two songs: "Claire de Lune" and "In An English Country Garden." Franny's daddy said the hostesses had two things in common, they were richer than God, and neither of them had ever read a book other than *Robert's Rules of Order*.

But Molly Gordon looked forward to the socials, and Franny looked forward to hearing about them.

Now she hung around the kitchen while her mother, back in her faded house dress, heated up supper, humming as she worked.

"What did they have to eat this time?" Franny asked.

Her mother turned off the burner under the rice. "Charlotte russe, and cheese straws, of course, and those candy-coated almonds in such pretty colors . . . and Franny, you'll never guess what was in the punch bowl!" She shook her head and laughed. "A green frog on a water lily!"

"A real frog?"

"Well, no, it was an ice sculpture, but it looked real enough; came all the way from Chattanooga, she said." Her mama dealt out plates for the table. "And oh, the bridge prizes were lovely! I had terrible cards, but Ida Littlejohn won the prettiest hostess apron—just for having low score."

Franny couldn't imagine Mrs. Littlejohn in a hostess apron. "Who won high?" she asked, just to be polite.

"Why, Eileen O'Donnell, bless her heart. She got a pretty set of fringed napkins."

"*Miss O'Donnell* was there?" Franny looked for pickles in the Frigidaire, stood there with the door open. "What's she going to do with napkins?"

"I suppose she'll put them away for a time when . . ." Her mama frowned. "Franny, Eileen O'Donnell's still young, she's an attractive woman. I imagine she'll marry some day, or at least I hope she will."

"Sounds like she's forgotten him already." Franny slammed the refrigerator door.

The next week she saw Miss O'Donnell buying a ticket to the picture show with some of the other teachers. Damascus Jones was with them as usual. They waved, but Franny pretended she didn't see them.

Miriam Thatcher and Mr. Rittenhouse were sitting with Aunt Six on her front porch. Mr. Rittenhouse had little Tommy on his lap. They hollered at Franny as she passed and she stopped to visit so her aunt wouldn't be any madder at her than she already was. The three of them seemed awfully pleased with themselves about something, Franny thought. She wondered if Miriam Thatcher would look so happy if she knew she was sitting with a German spy—and her husband over there dropping bombs on them.

After a while Mr. Rittenhouse said he had a letter to mail, so Franny offered to do it for him. If it was a coded communication to that person he'd been talking to on the phone, she could at least find out the name and address. But he said, no thank you, the post office was on his way and he would drop it off himself. Franny could see he didn't want her to know what it was, so she went with him anyway and made up a story about how her mama was expecting a letter in the afternoon mail.

Franny got only a glimpse of the letter as Mr. Rittenhouse was licking the stamp, but it was long enough to tell her he was writing to somebody named Smith in Marietta. Everybody knew spies always took the name Smith, and she had a feeling this one was stealing plans from the Bell Bomber Plant, and that Mr. Rittenhouse was his connection—probably the head of the ring.

There wasn't much use in following Mr. Rittenhouse, Franny discovered. He never went anywhere exciting. Or maybe he was just too smart. Once she almost fell asleep behind an elephant ear plant waiting for him to come out of the Thatchers'. She gave up after that.

It was just by chance Franny happened to see him getting on the bus one day in front of Callahan's Feed and Seed Store, but it pulled away before she could look on the front to see where it was going.

On a narrow bench out front two soldiers talked softly as they waited for the next bus to camp. The smoke from their cigarettes curled upward to the stained metal awning.

Inside the store the cool, dusty floor felt soothing to Franny's bare feet after the rough pavement of the street. She had only been allowed to go barefooted for about a week and was still experiencing the newness of it. She slid an experimental toe across a grimy plank while Mr. Callahan measured squash seeds into a bag for Mrs. Kimbrough's Victory garden. The dim store smelled earthy like the stacks of grain-filled burlap in the back room and the sweat-stained overalls of its customers.

"And what can I do for you, young lady?" Mr. Callahan leaned over the counter.

"A nickel's worth of watermelon seeds, please." Maybe her daddy would let her plant them on his farm a few miles from town. She glanced out the dust-smeared window. "Just saw the bus pull out. That the one for Chattanooga?"

He rattled seeds into a bag. "No, that was going to Atlanta and all points in between. Stops in Cartersville, Emerson, Marietta, Kennesaw, and every crossroads along the way." He laughed. "I told Mr. Rittenhouse I hoped he'd brought along his supper."

"Oh, is Mr. Rittenhouse going to Atlanta?" Franny asked.

"Bought a ticket to Marietta," the storekeeper said. "Visiting a friend down there. Nice day for a trip. Hope I'm able to get about like that when I'm his age." Mr. Callahan dropped Franny's nickel into the cash drawer and grinned at her. "Don't you forget to bring me one of those melons when they come in now!" She left him standing there laughing. She didn't know why grownups think everything children do is so funny.

Franny had promised her mother she would stop by the drug store to pick up some of that special cold cream she smeared on her face at night, and as she was coming out, who should she see but Miss O'Donnell and Damascus Jones going into the jewelry store. Her teacher had her hand on his arm and they were smiling and whispering like they knew the happiest secret in the whole world.

Franny strolled by looking in the window like she was real interested in the silver bud vases they had on display. Miss O'Donnell pointed to something in one of the glass cases, and Miss Melba Thomas, the clerk, slid open the little door and lifted out something that glittered. Miss O'Donnell picked up a velvet box and passed it to Mr. Jones. Then Miss Melba put more jewelry on the showcase and the two of them examined that too. When Miss O'Donnell found the one she liked, she took it out of the box and held it to the light. Damascus Jones seemed to like it too. He studied it for a while, then smiled and said something to Miss Melba.

Even from the street, Franny could see it was a ring. A diamond engagement ring.

Franny ran from the jewelry store seeing nothing but the blurred sidewalk beneath her feet, and almost dropped the cold cream when somebody jerked her harshly away from the curb.

"Franny Gordon, watch where you're going! My God, you almost walked in front of a car!"

Franny stared woodenly as a cascade of letters fluttered to the pavement. Wesley's father released his grip on her arm and shook his head at her. "Sorry if I was a little rough, but you scared me half to death."

Franny's arm burned, but not as much as her face. "That's okay," she said, stooping to help pick up his mail. "I guess I wasn't thinking."

"I guess you weren't," Mr. Fuller said, and he stood and watched her cross the street.

Her aunt and Precious sat on the front porch shelling pecans. They both gasped when they saw her. "Good Lord, child! You look like you've just seen the preacher playin' poker with the devil!" Aunt Six eased her into a chair. "What in the world is the matter?"

"Nothing," Franny said, and cried.

Precious jumped up. "I'll go put on the kettle." Tea was their answer to everything.

"Come on now . . ." Her aunt whipped out her ever-present handkerchief. "Have a good blow and tell me what's the matter."

"Everything," Franny said, doing as she was told. "I almost got

252

run over by a car, and if it hadn't been for Wesley's daddy, I'd have been smushed flatter than a possum on the highway. Miss O'Donnell's going to marry Damascus Jones, and your friend *Adolf* Rittenhouse has gone to Marietta to steal plans from the Bell Bomber Plant."

And, of course, there was that thing she couldn't ever tell.

"Frances Virginia, if you weren't so serious I'd laugh. Where do you get all these crazy notions?"

Franny told her about seeing Miss O'Donnell in the jewelry store and how she had overheard Mr. Rittenhouse on the phone, and her aunt laughed. "Double-A has gone to Marietta, but it has nothing to do with bombers." She pulled her chair closer. "And as for Eileen O'Donnell, well, I think you're jumping to conclusions."

"But you should've seen them!" Franny blew her nose again. "I reckon she didn't ever care about Mr. Gregory at all. She's not even wearing his ring anymore."

"Now you hush that! You don't know what you're saying. Come on, let's go see if that tea's ready. Maybe we can find something to nibble on."

"I'm not hungry," Franny said. But she changed her mind when she smelled yeast rolls, split, buttered and toasted under the broiler. Franny dribbled honey on hers.

Aunt Six drank her tea fast and put the empty cup in the sink. "I guess we'd better get those pecans shelled if we're going to make that cake for your church bazaar," she reminded Precious.

"Precious," Franny whispered after her aunt had gone back outside, "do you know what Mr. Rittenhouse is up to in Marietta?"

"You leave that old man be. He ain't hurtin' nobody."

"Why won't anybody believe me? He's German, isn't he? Can't you see he's working for them?"

"You sure that car didn't hit you?" Precious asked. "You talk like you're funny in the head." She shoved the tea canister back on the shelf and slammed the cabinet door. "Ought to be ashamed of yourself," she muttered, going to join Aunt Six on the porch. Franny went home the back way.

Every day Franny looked to see if Miss O'Donnell wore the ring Damascus Jones had bought, but her teacher's finger was still bare. She didn't understand why the woman who had planned to marry their wonderful Mr. Gregory was in such a hurry to get engaged again. How could she love somebody else after *him?* And the nearer the time came for their recital, the less Franny wanted to be in it. She just didn't have the heart for it, and her lines sounded flat and shallow, like something from a first-grade reader.

"Franny, you need to get more feeling into your character," Miss O'Donnell said at rehearsal one day. They had stayed after school to go over their parts and everyone did just fine, it seemed, but her. "Amy March was a vain, selfish person; you're not getting that across." She paced the stage. "I know you can do it . . ." Miss O'Donnell shrugged. "Maybe we've been rehearsing too much, you're tired—"

"I'm just tired of this old play," Franny said. "Tired of taking expression, and of Amy March, and the recital and everything!" She ran from the stage and hid behind the curtains.

"You come right back here, Franny Gordon!" Hannah yelled. "I haven't been learning all those lines for nothing."

"Shh! I'll talk to Franny," Miss O'Donnell said. "The rest of you may go on home now. I think we've worked long enough for one day."

"Franny." Miss O'Donnell stood in the center of the stage with her arms folded and spoke softly. "You're not only letting your best friend down, but yourself as well. If you're upset with me about something, I think we should talk about it, don't you?"

Franny stroked the worn red velvet curtain they had inherited from the high school and wiped her eyes with her wrist. Her nose was running and she had nothing to blow on.

Miss O'Donnell held out a box of tissues. "Let's sit down for a few minutes. You don't have to talk if you don't want to."

Franny accepted the tissue silently and followed her to the little room behind the stage, which seemed close and shabby in spite of her teacher's attempts to brighten it. Miss O'Donnell directed her to the one faded, chintz-covered arm chair and sat on a stool at her feet. The tissue was soggy and her teacher gave her another.

"I hate seeing you so unhappy," Miss O'Donnell said. "Would you like to tell me why?"

Franny squeezed the tissue into a ball and looked at her teacher's face. Her green eyes were clouded with worry and she had chewed off all her lipstick. Miss O'Donnell stood and went to the window where dust motes swam in the sun, gave the blue-flowered curtains a twitch. Her shoulders were thin and droopy like Wanda Culpepper's. "I thought I was your friend," she said.

Franny plucked stuffing from a hole in the armchair. "I thought you loved him," she said.

Miss O'Donnell turned and looked at her, her eyes wide and sad. "I do love him," she whispered. "A part of me always will."

"Then why are you going to marry Damascus Jones?"

"What?" Her mouth twitched like she wanted to smile.

"I saw you in the jewelry store picking out the ring."

"Oh, Franny, that's supposed to be a secret!" She did laugh then. "That ring is for Linda Cochran. She and Mr. Jones are planning to marry this summer."

"*Miss Cochran!* But . . . you mean . . . I thought . . ." Franny tried to poke the stuffing back into the hole with her finger.

"I know what you thought." Her teacher grabbed a tissue and held it to her mouth so long her fingers turned white. "Mr. Jones and Miss Cochran are good friends of mine. He asked me to help him select the ring because I knew what kind she wanted." Miss O'Donnell sank onto the stool and hugged her knees. "No one is supposed to know about this, Franny! You'll have to promise not to tell. Mr. Jones is planning to surprise her on her birthday next week."

"Oh, I won't tell! I promise." Franny noticed her teacher's laughter had turned to something close to tears. Eileen O'Donnell turned her head away.

"I'm sorry. Please don't—I didn't mean to make you cry. It's just that you seemed to be having so much fun going to movies and parties and all. I thought you had forgotten him."

"I could never do that." Miss O'Donnell wiped her eyes and put a hand on the arm of Franny's chair. "Not a day goes by, Franny, that I don't think of him and feel the pain of my loss." She smiled. "That's why I try to keep busy, try to get my mind on something else. Why, just working with my students on this recital has been an escape for me. And I hoped it would help you too, because if it hadn't been for all of you, I don't know what I would have done."

"I wish it had never happened," Franny said. "I wish I could bring him back." If it hadn't been for the war, Mr. Gregory would still be there, and Miss Havergal would never have come to Sallie's Station.

"Well, you can't. He's gone, Franny. He's dead, and there's nothing we can do to change it." She took Franny by the hands and pulled her from the chair. "Do you really think he would want us to go around all scrunched up and miserable?"

Franny smiled and shook her head. "No," she said softly.

"We're alive, Franny, and if we're lucky, we have a good many years ahead of us. I think we should get on with it, don't you?"

Franny hugged her teacher around the waist. "I like Mr. Jones; he's really kind of nice, but I'm so glad you're not going to marry him!"

Chapter Twenty-nine

It was strange, Franny thought, that she didn't remember exactly what her former teacher said, but was content to sit, look, and let her words bathe her, to know that good survives.

Eileen O'Donnell had kept in touch with Miss Opal for a long time, she knew, but they lost track of her when Miss Opal died.

As soon as the ceremony was over, everyone drifted toward the reception area where sweet and salty dainties were being served along with Russian tea, and since it was a reunion of sorts, the chatter overpowered Nannie Maxwell's attempts to supply appropriate music on the piano. Franny turned at a hand on her shoulder to find Travis beside her and thanked him again for the flowers. And the arrowhead.

He stood back—at least as much as it was possible for Travis and his stomach to stand back in a crowd—and looked at her, first at one breast, then the other. "Damn it, Frances Virginia, I can't tell . . . which twin has the Toni?"

Franny laughed. Since her left side was beginning to shift, it was only too obvious to her. "Only my dressmaker knows for sure," she told him.

"But not for long," Shirley said. "When Franny gets her new boob job this summer, even her dressmaker won't be able to tell."

Franny had decided to have the TRAM flap reconstruction in August. That would give her time to get to know her new grandchild and to enjoy the Christmas present Hannah had given her. She saw Hannah now ahead of her talking with the former Linda Cochran Jones while Wesley checked out the refreshment table. Allie had invited both her parents to her home for New Year's Day, Hannah said, but they usually saw her separately. Now and then Hannah went home to spend the weekend with Vance—more frequently than before, Franny thought—although he never came there. And Hannah and Wesley had dinner together once in a while, renewing their friendship, she said.

Betty Joyce waved as she started to leave, and Franny hurried to catch up with her—almost, but not quite jostling Neely Louise.

"You're not coming to Travis's party?" Franny knew her neighbor wouldn't leave Hubert for any length of time, and she was right.

"Can't stay. I only came to see Miss O'Donnell—I mean Mrs. Whatever . . . Carrington now, isn't it? Gosh, doesn't she look great?" Betty Joyce smiled. "By the way, I saved you that travel guide to Britain; you'll find certain pages marked, but we'll talk before you go."

"Go where? Don't tell me you're actually leaving Sallie's Station, Franny." Behind them Neely Louise Curtis balanced a small plate of crackers and a teacup. Franny didn't know why Neely looked so smug. She'd never been farther than Nassau, and that was on her honeymoon. How she longed to give her a good push and slop tea down the front of that expensive white suit!

"You must be the last person in town to know," Franny told her, relishing every word. "Hannah and I are going to England in May." *England in May, England in May! Oh, happy day! England in May!* It sounded like a nursery rhyme, a favorite nursery rhyme—one she would illustrate herself.

It had been hard to pretend enthusiasm for a tin of plum pudding, purchased in London by Betty Joyce, she learned later, when Franny opened Hannah's late Christmas present in the hospital. Didn't Hannah remember that she didn't even like fruitcake?

But Hannah stood at the foot of her bed grinning foolishly. "Read the card," she demanded.

There's more where this comes from! it said, and inside she'd pasted a picture of the queen saying, *Why don't you come over and see me sometime?*

"It's good for one round trip ticket," Hannah said. "That is, if you can handle my company. I hate to travel alone."

She'd lived with them all fall, Hannah said, and it would make her happy if Franny would just shut up and accept. And so she did—with very little argument because it made her happy too. She was to be allowed to pay for her meals, but that was it. Her mother would spend the time with Winnie and her family in North Carolina, and the two old friends planned their trip for two whole weeks in May—*after* moving day for Franny, tax season for Hannah, and cold weather for the queen, who was obviously expecting them. Castles can get so drafty, they heard.

Franny turned to find Janine Hendricks standing beside her, her slender hand on Walter's arm, and when she smiled, Franny recognized that same hesitancy that had been her mother's.

"Less than a week to go now, isn't it?" Franny said, speaking of their approaching wedding. "I've always thought Valentine's Day such a romantic time to get married. What a wonderful way to begin!" And for some reason, she took Janine's hand and held it.

Franny was surprised to see tears come into her eyes. "You were Franny Gordon, weren't you?" Janine gave her fingers a squeeze. "I knew you had to be. Mom said such nice things about you. You and your friend, Hannah. You were her favorites in the whole class."

The moment of reckoning had come. Should she pretend not to know who she meant?

"You're Wanda's daughter. It's been such a long time."

"She's gone, you know. Be two years in June . . . I still miss her something awful."

While Neely dragged Walter off to meet Eileen O'Donnell, Janine told Franny how Mrs. Hightower had tutored her mother to pass her high school equivalency test. "She was so good to Mama—even left her a small bequest when she died."

Wanda used the money, Janine said, to go to cosmetology school, and Franny thought of the sallow child with lank, greasy hair.

"I'm sorry to hear about your mother," Franny said. "I wondered where she was. After Mrs. Hightower died, I don't remember seeing her around." Although, to be honest, she hadn't thought much about her at all.

"She was offered a job over in Rome," Janine said. "That's where Mom met and married my dad." She smiled. "I'm the last one, the baby. My two brothers—well, half-brothers—both live in Atlanta now."

From what Janine said about her father, who, it seemed, had made a pretty good living with a small appliance store, Wanda at last had a share of happiness. Franny was sorry she couldn't be there to show off her beautiful daughter.

But what was to stop Franny from doing it for her? She linked her arm in Janine's. "Come on," she said. "I want you to meet our Miss O'Donnell."

Franny watched Eileen Carrington's face as they wove their way toward her through the crowd. Would her old teacher remember her? And in spite of the halo of snowy hair, Franny saw her teacher's young, hurt face the day her frustrations spilled out.

She had been kind, gentle, understanding. What would she think of them all if she knew what they had done?

Chapter Thirty

May, 1944

It was getting late by the time Franny left Miss O'Donnell in front of the school and took the shortcut home. She found her mama and Mrs. Littlejohn on the front steps talking.

"Frances Gordon, where in the world have you been?" Her mother was really mad this time, she could tell by her voice and that "don't mess with me" look in her blue eyes. "Hannah's mother said she got home over an hour ago. I was just about to send Winnie to look for you. Do you realize it's almost time for supper?"

"Which reminds me, I'd better go in and scare up something to eat." Mrs. Littlejohn pulled her baggy brown sweater closer about her. "And I'm just tickled to death to hear about Six; you tell her that." She let out a long sigh. "Don't mind telling you I been worried about that one, but it looks like things will work out just fine for everybody."

"What's she talking about, Mama?" Franny asked as Mrs. Littlejohn started back across the street. "What about Aunt Six?"

"Your aunt is going to have her house remodeled. She's making it into a duplex."

"A what?"

"A duplex. That's two apartments in one building. Aunt Six will live on one side, and Miriam Thatcher and Tommy on the other." She paused to break off a dead branch from the nandina bush by the walk. "Now we won't have to worry about her staying alone, and Honey Sue will quit pestering her mother about moving to Macon."

"But Mrs. Thatcher already has a house," Franny said.

"That's Tom's mother's house, Franny, and his aunt Minnie's. It isn't the same."

"Wonder why nobody thought of it before."

"I guess none of us saw the need for it until Aunt Six got so sick," her mother said. "And we probably wouldn't have considered it then if Mr. Rittenhouse hadn't suggested it."

"Mr. Rittenhouse?" Franny trailed after her into the kitchen where she took off her shoes and kicked them into a corner. Ah! It felt good to be free.

"The whole thing was his idea." Her mama slid creamed potatoes into the oven to brown. "Used to be a contractor before he retired. Mr. Rittenhouse saw the possibilities and sent the original house plans to a friend of his in Marietta: an architect, a Mr. Smith, I believe."

Plans. Smith. Marietta. The words stung like a swarm of bees. "I've gotta see Aunt Six," Franny said, backing out the door.

"What?" Her mother stood over the stove, stirring spoon in mid-air. "Your supper will be stone cold.

". . . make a preacher lose his religion . . ." Her mother's words trailed after her. But Frances Virginia Gordon was already halfway down the hall.

Aunt Six sat on her back steps feeding Hellcat the rest of her tuna casserole from supper. "Why didn't you tell me?" Franny asked.

Her aunt finished scraping her plate. "Tell you what?"

Franny made a circle in the dirt with her toe. "About what Mr.

Rittenhouse was doing. Why didn't you say he was going to remodel your house?"

"In the first place, we didn't know if it would work out, or if I would be able to afford the necessary expenses." She tugged at the screen door. "Cranky thing sticks every spring!" Franny held it open as her aunt moved into the kitchen to rinse her plate at the sink. "And in the second place," Aunt Six went on, "it isn't any of your business what Double-A Rittenhouse does with his time."

"But if you had just *told* me! You let me go on thinking he was a spy."

Her aunt sloshed water into a dishpan. "Don't be blaming your crazy notions on me. That spy business was all your doing, Frances Virginia Gordon—nobody else's. Why, Double-A served this country in the Spanish-American War right along with your uncle Carlisle!"

"But he's German."

"Don't suppose you've ever noticed my pretty luncheon dishes, the ones with the grapes on them?" She hurled a dish towel at Franny. "Made right there in the Black Forest. That's in Germany, you know—unless they've moved it. And that little china figurine you like so much—Hummel—German as can be." She handed Franny a dripping saucepan to dry. "Mr. Rittenhouse is American of German ancestry, just like you're American of English and Scotch-Irish, and whatever else ancestry. The only difference is, his parents were born over there. He listened to stories about their childhood in Germany, and mine told me all about the War of Northern Aggression. My papa—your great granddaddy—fought in the Confederate Army, Franny. He fought *against* that flag that flies over the post office out there, the one we pledge allegiance to. But it's my flag now and I'm loyal to it. And so is Mr. Rittenhouse."

If she could, Franny would have made herself small enough to crawl into the tiniest crack in the wall. And she would never, never come out. "I guess I've hurt his feelings," she said. "I'm real sorry."

"A little late to worry about that."

"Aunt Six?" Franny ran a finger along the door panels. "Do you think Mr. Rittenhouse would come to our recital next week?"

"I don't know, Franny. Why don't you ask him?"

Franny remembered the hurt on the old man's face. "But . . . won't you ask him for me? Please?"

Her aunt stood with the kitchen light behind her, and Franny couldn't see her face. "No," she said softly. "That's something you'll have to do yourself."

Franny thought of Mr. Rittenhouse sitting with her mother in the front porch swing, his cane tapping the floor, or in the kitchen munching popcorn on a cold, rainy day, and the reality of what she had done to him turned her heart inside out. She couldn't change what happened to Miss Havergal or Dottie Crenshaw, but maybe it wasn't too late to make things right with Mr. Rittenhouse.

Her family had finished eating by the time she got home, but Franny's supper waited, covered by a red striped dish towel. Fried chicken! The wonderful smell filled the kitchen, but it would have to wait a little longer. Franny Gordon ran past it and up the stairs.

The mottled gray arrowhead gathered dust on the littered shelf above her desk. Travis would trade anything to get that arrowhead, even his last balloon. A blue one the color of an old man's eyes. Franny picked up the ancient flint triangle and stroked it with her finger.

He met her at the door, and although it was mid-afternoon and Franny's cotton dress clung to her body, the old man's shirt looked crisply ironed and smelled faintly of laundry starch.

"Franny . . . well, please come in." Mr. Rittenhouse held open the door, his blue eyes friendly as always. "And what might I do for you today?"

They sat in wicker chairs by the window where bright geraniums bloomed, the little sitting room yellow-washed in light.

"I brought you a present," Franny said, giving him a small wrapped box. Her mother had saved the paper from Winnie's birthday—green, with a pattern of violets.

"But it's not my birthday," Mr. Rittenhouse said. His hands shook a little as he unwrapped the package.

"Then let's pretend it is. And I came to invite you to our recital. I'd really like you to come."

"Well, of course I'll come. Wouldn't miss it," he said. Franny watched his face grow younger when he saw what was inside the box.

"Oh! It's lovely." He touched it, held it, letting his fingers linger. It was a simple thing, but Franny had never seen anybody take such pleasure in a gift. "Wherever did you find it?" he asked.

Franny smiled. "From a friend."

"If you don't mind doing the honors—" Mr. Rittenhouse gave her the balloon with a flourish. "My old lungs don't seem to work the way they used to."

And Frances Virginia Gordon blew up the blue balloon for her friend and tied a knot at the end.

Chapter Thirty-one

"Franny." The stranger looked at her and said her name, and Franny wasn't a plump, sixtyish woman missing part of her anatomy; she was a ten-year-old with bare feet and a heart to match.

It was Eileen O'Donnell, not Eileen Carrington, who stood there, and when the woman reached out to her, Franny saw she wore no rings other than a gold wedding band. This time when they hugged, Franny noticed, her teacher's head came to *her* shoulder.

"I've thought of you so often," Eileen Carrington said, and although she was smiling, there was an expression in her eyes Franny couldn't read. But her face lit up when she saw Janine, probably at the sheer beauty of her, Franny thought, as her teacher looked from one of them to the other. "And this must be your lovely daughter."

"As much as I'd like to claim her, I'm afraid the credit's not mine," Franny told her. "Janine's Wanda's youngest. You remember Wanda Culpepper?"

Not even a flicker of surprise crossed her face. Eileen O'Donnell had never had Wanda in her classes, but Franny was sure she knew who she was. Now she smiled at Wanda's daughter as if they'd been old friends, and listened with a sweet, familiar softness while Janine told of her mother's death.

Walter Curtis came over to claim his fiancée, and Franny

watched them stroll away hand in hand, stopping now and then to speak with well-wishers on their way out, while Neely waited at the gymnasium door looking glum as a fundamentalist at a pro-choice meeting.

Eileen O'Donnell had taught in Florida for the remainder of the war, she said, then worked for a while with a small stage company before she met and married Dan Carrington.

"And you have children?" Franny almost hesitated to ask. She still pictured cherub-like offspring looking like Matthew Gregory.

Her eyes took on that proud-mother look. "Two daughters. Mandy's a musician—plays violin with the symphony in Washington. Anne's a pediatrician. And I have three grandchildren—but don't let me get started on them!"

Franny didn't ask about the house with the picket fence.

It would have been wonderful, she thought, if they could just get through the evening without any mention of the ill-fated Miss Havergal, and for a while, Franny believed they were actually going to make it. In fact, the principal's name didn't surface until much later at the gathering at the Kimbroughs' cabin, and it was R.W. who brought up the subject.

Most of their classmates had left. ("A sack of couch potatoes ready to sprout!" Hannah said.) The ones who remained sipped coffee in front of the fire where Eileen Carrington reminisced, her lap piled with dog-eared snapshots, high school yearbooks.

Franny curled on the sofa beside her. R.W., on the floor in front of her, read aloud from faded mimeographed issues of *Echota Echoes*, their high school newspaper. Hannah, now in flannel shirt and jeans, lay on the rug watching the blaze, and Wesley sprawled in a rocking chair watching Hannah. It was nasty-wet and cold outside, and Franny was in no hurry to leave.

Shirley, whose husband, Bud, was out of town, lingered in the tiny kitchen exchanging recipes and gossip with Joan Kimbrough, and Travis had just brought in a big bowl of popcorn when R.W. held up one of the papers for Wesley to see.

"Here's the article about your appointment to West Point, Wes. Remember how you freaked out about taking the entrance exam? Heck, you must've aced it, man!"

Wesley glanced briefly at Hannah, then looked away. "Yeah—well, I was worried about the math."

R.W. nodded. "Tell me about it! I was relieved to get into med school. It's a wonder any of us could add two and two after than monster of a math teacher we had back in grammar school." He set the stack of papers aside and sat silently for a minute. "Remember the day we found out how Miss Havergal died? I felt like a jerk because I really didn't give a rip.

"I wasn't the only one, was I?"

His voice was as flat as a Texas field road as he looked past them into the fire. He didn't sound like himself at all.

Travis didn't drop the bowl, but he did tilt it so about a quart of popcorn snowed to the floor. "What makes you say a thing like that?" he said, clutching the wooden bowl to his round stomach.

"Because I want to know what happened. What really happened." R.W. looked at all of them in turn and his voice was bolder. "Look, I'm a big boy now, so please don't mess around with me. It's a little late for that. Don't you think I'm aware there was something you weren't telling? Whatever it is, for God's sake, I wish you'd let me in on it!"

Travis walked as in slow motion and set the bowl on the table. "Look, R.W., this all happened so long ago, I don't even—"

"I really don't want to talk about this." Wesley paced to the window, frowned at the slick black square. "Rain's almost stopped. I'm for home."

"Hey, let's not get melodramatic!" Travis attempted a laugh. "Lighten up, folks, the night's still young. We only have Miss O'Donnell-uh-Carrington with us for a little while. Let's don't scare her away. How about more coffee, Franny? Hannah? And there's beer and Coca-Cola in the kitchen."

"No, wait." Hannah rose to her knees and faced R.W. across the hearth rug. "You're talking about something that happened in the fifth grade, Doc. Why do you think we know something you don't?"

"Because it hangs like smog around you—all of you. I can feel it in this room." R.W. stood and walked to the mantel, braced his arms against it. "I've always felt there was something, and lately it just about smothers me. Whenever that woman's name comes up, I feel I'm up to my waist in dirty ditch water."

Eileen Carrington spoke softly. "Miss Havergal was a totally unhappy woman. Probably the most miserable person I've ever known. I've heard she had an unsettling childhood. Her mother couldn't take care of her, and she was passed from one foster home to another."

"She sure as hell spread her misery around," R.W. said. "But something made her go over the edge, and it happened right after she left here. Remember, Wesley? I'll never forget the day you told us."

"There were problems," Eileen Carrington said. "Serious problems. The school board had to let her go."

R.W. shrugged. "The drinking. I know. I remember the whispers, my parents talking . . . and later we suspected something more, just from the things that were said. I was just glad she was gone." He warmed his hands by the fire, although the room was already hot. "She was evil, you know. I always thought so. Still do. Must've had trouble finding another teaching job."

"Oh, God." Hannah crouched, covering her face. "Why are you doing this?"

"Doing what?" Shirley had come into the room and now stood beside an empty rocking chair, her hand on the back of it. "You're talking about that awful woman, aren't you? That Miss Havergal? Do you know she actually made a pass at me one time? Only I was too stupid to know what was happening. Scared the shit out of me, though. God, I was glad when she left!"

Hannah made a noise deep in her throat. "Shirley! Why didn't you say anything?"

"Too embarrassed, I guess, and too ignorant. And nothing really happened. Believe me, I never got close enough to give the old witch another chance."

Hannah shuddered in spite of her place by the fire and Wesley looked as if he might go to her, then stiffened and turned away. "Do we have to go into this?" he said.

"I'm sorry," R.W. said, "but for the life of me, I can't figure out why this woman's death affects you so. For years I avoided mentioning her name because of the reaction it caused. For God's sake, why? She was cold as a witch's tit and a drunk to boot!"

"No," Franny said. "No, she wasn't."

"Franny." Wesley looked at her under dark brows. Franny glanced away. She hadn't forgotten their promise. After Mrs. Hightower, she hadn't told a soul, but she just couldn't keep it inside any longer.

R.W. frowned. "Won't somebody enlighten me? I still haven't a clue."

"She wasn't a drunk," Franny said. "I doubt if the woman ever touched a drop." She looked at their former teacher as she spoke. "We knew the school board would fire her for drinking. It was the only way we could think of to get rid of her."

"What do you mean?" R.W. asked.

"She means we planted that liquor there," Hannah said. "We covered all the bases—the desk in her office, Miss Opal's too. Had to be sure they'd find it."

Shirley sank into the rocking chair, her face pale. "My gosh, that took guts!"

"It was the same day Dottie Crenshaw got hit by that car," Hannah said. "She saw us coming out of Miss Opal's, said she was going to tell."

"We threatened her, scared her," Franny said. "She was running away."

"But we didn't mean to hurt her. She ran right out into the street." Travis slumped on the couch, leaned back and closed his eyes. The jovial, familiar Travis was gone, and when he spoke again his voice was filled with emotion. "I feel like I've been carrying around a ten-ton rock."

"My God! Nobody knew? All these years and nobody knew?" R.W. sat in the closest chair, as if his legs couldn't support him any longer.

"We knew," Franny said.

He shook his head. "And you never told anybody else?"

"That's right, just the four of us." Franny glanced at Wesley as she spoke. Might as well leave Betty Joyce out of it. She'd washed herself Clean in the Blood years ago. And Mrs. Hightower, dead these many years, had been too appalled to speak of it."

But R.W. wasn't buying it. "Don't tell me Betty Joyce Whitfield didn't have anything to do with all this," he said. "I know all about the flowers."

"What flowers?" Franny and Hannah spoke together.

"Oh, come on! Surely you must know. Every Easter she had flowers delivered to Miss Havergal's grave. Still does, I guess."

"A wreath of garlic with a stake attached might be appropriate," Eileen Carrington said, looking rather shocked at herself for having said it.

Franny gulped back a gasp, then swallowed a giggle, but the comment didn't register with Wesley. "How'd you know this?" he asked R.W.

"Carol Delaney told me. Remember, she was the only florist in town for years before she sold out to Tara's Garden and moved to the mountains. Betty Joyce had a standing order, she said. Sent 'em to some place in Delaware, I think."

Mrs. Carrington's hand trembled as she swept aside the photographs in her lap and stood before them, reminding Franny of a tea kettle about to boil. "Dear God, I should've known you were lugging this around! And all this time. Why on earth didn't you say something?"

"I tried to," Franny said, remembering the backstage room, the sticky smell of spilled cologne. "But at the time I was afraid it would make things worse. It was just too much to heap on you on top of everything else."

Shirley leaned forward in her chair. "Look, you did us all a favor. I just wish I'd been that brave. I can see why it's been hard to live with all this time, but you were just *children,* Franny. You did what you thought was right."

"Oh, Franny." The teacher's eyes shimmered green with tears. They trickled down her cheeks and went unheeded. "I was so mired in my own misery, I just didn't think. I should've said something. I should have told you."

A band tightened inside her. "Told me what?"

"Annie, Miss Opal's cook, heard you up in Miss Havergal's room."

"You mean she knew what we did?" Hannah asked. "Why didn't she tell Miss Opal?"

"She did." The older woman looked down at Travis who sat with his head in his hands. "And Linda Cochran saw you and Wesley come out of the school office that afternoon. Of course, we didn't know until later what you'd been up to."

"You knew? You *all knew,* and you didn't say anything?" Travis Kimbrough's face was as white as paste.

"No! No, not everyone. And the few of us who did know never discussed it. We kept quiet more or less by common consent. Naturally we had no idea she would . . . do . . . what she later did."

Even now with her white Mother Goose hair and bifocals, Eileen Carrington reminded Franny of the bewildered young woman in the dusty room behind the stage. Now she sat down limply on the sofa beside her. "I must have realized you knew how she died," their teacher said. "I'm afraid I wasn't thinking too clearly at the time. How dreadful that must have been for you! When—how did you find out?"

Franny waited for Wesley to explain, but he stood apart from them silently gripping the back of a cane-bottomed chair. It reminded her of one she'd seen in the Whitfields' long ago storeroom.

Hannah spoke up. "Wesley told us—right there in Mrs. Hightower's homeroom. Remember, Wes? You were late to school that day."

"Pauline Hightower. What a strong, gentle woman she was." Absently Eileen Carrington gathered the discarded photographs, stacked them in her lap. "I suppose I should've gone to her with what I knew, but frankly, none of us wanted to set her straight. Probably because we knew she'd insist on the truth."

But as far as Franny knew, Mrs. Hightower had kept her secret. Of course by the time she'd confided in her, it was too late to help Miss Havergal. She stared into her lap and saw again her homeroom teacher's horrified expression, a grim negative in black and white that would be with her forever.

R.W. came to stand behind her. "Look, the woman had serious emotional problems. We knew that even then. Who knows what drove her to make the choice she did."

Franny jumped as Wesley sent the straight chair crashing to the floor. "God forgive me, but I hope she's burning in hell for the grief she brought!" he said. "Maybe Dottie Crenshaw would be alive right now. At least she would've had a chance for a normal life."

The others watched as the chair skidded into the far wall with an anticlimactic bump, while Wesley, his face working in anger, struggled to conquer his emotions.

"With all due respect, I don't think poor little Dottie was ever quite right," R.W. said in what Franny assumed was his soothing bedside voice. "I hope you won't burden yourself with that."

"But we don't know that do we? We'll never know if that accident made her the way she was." Wesley looked at the three of them: Travis, Hannah, Franny. "And all because of that woman."

Franny thought of Wesley's failed marriages, his problems with alcohol. Was he blaming Miss Havergal for all of this?

Hannah studied him from across the room, then sighed and shook her head. "No, we don't know. We were ten years old and we made some immature—if not downright bad decisions, but I've let it gnaw at me long enough. I don't intend to spend the rest of my life brooding about something I can't change. It's time to let go."

"Amen," Travis said, and Franny nodded, smiling.

Wesley didn't respond.

Hannah looked defeated, Franny thought, yet maybe a little relieved. She had come to Sallie's Station hoping to find in Wesley the sweet promise she'd left behind, the childhood prince she had known before guilt eroded him. But the Wesley she knew, or thought she knew, was gone. Maybe he never was.

Except for the low hissing of the fire, the room was quiet as Eileen Carrington spoke in a voice so soft Franny strained to hear. "I'm not proud of my part in this. I could've stopped it, and I didn't. Miss Havergal did have problems, problems much more serious than drinking, as Shirley pointed out, and they would have surfaced sooner or later. The woman had no business around children, but I had other reasons for keeping quiet. Selfish reasons.

"I'm sorry. Sorry for her, sorry for all of us. The war has been over for more than half a century, yet it seems to go on hurting. Hannah's right, now it's time to move on."

A log crumbled in the fireplace, sending red sparks up the chimney. Franny watched them swirl in the updraft.

Shirley studied their teacher's face. "If you could go back and change things, would you?"

"You mean knowing what I know now, would I permit Miss Havergal to be dismissed over something she didn't do?" Eileen Carrington hesitated for just a fraction of a second. "No. No, of course, I wouldn't."

The silence was so overpowering Franny could hear Travis breathing beside her. She turned and found him looking at her, and for a moment, caught a glimpse of the child he used to be. "And what about you, Miss Frances Virginia?" he asked. "What do you think you'd do?"

Franny didn't answer.

That night Franny curled on the window seat in the upstairs room she once shared with Winnie. She could almost picture the teenage Winnie, sleeping with one foot sticking out of the covers, her long hair rolled in socks for the night. At fourteen she had begun wearing lipstick to school—Tangee natural—that she put on after she left the house. Franny had seen it in her purse.

The trees, dripping from the recent rain, shivered in the cold glow of the street lamp. A solitary truck rumbled by. Huddled in the window, Franny wrapped a throw about her and looked out on her familiar street, remembering the little girl with a great big hurt who sat there so long ago.

Mr. Rittenhouse had come to her recital that night with Precious and Aunt Six, and she hadn't missed a line. Why, Mr. Rittenhouse had even said that she and Hannah were the very best ones! Franny thought so too.

A lot of people now seemed to think that sooner or later they were going to win the war. Franny hoped it would be sooner. Sallie's Station had looked the same for as long as she could remember, yet everything had changed. Miss Willie and Mr. Gregory were gone, Dottie Crenshaw would never walk normally again, and Singleton Kelly, still in Italy, wrote of rubble and destruction and nights without sleep. It wasn't an adventure anymore. He just wanted to come home.

And a woman named Havergal had shot into Franny's life like a burning cinder and left a hole where her childhood had been.